THE
SON
OF
THE
HOUSE

THE
SON
OF
THE
HOUSE

CHELUCHI
ONYEMELUKWE-ONUOBIA

DUNDURN
PRESS

Publisher and acquiring editor: Scott Fraser | Editor: Jenny McWha
Cover designer: Laura Boyle
Cover illustrator: Aaron Marin
Cover image credits: Costus spectabilis by Matilda Smith. Plate from Curtis's Botanical Magazine, 1905 Royal Tour - Nigeria: Brian Brake; photographer; January 1956; Lagos (used by permission of the Museum of New Zealand)
Printer: Marquis Book Printing Inc.

Library and Archives Canada Cataloguing in Publication

Title: The son of the house / Cheluchi Onyemelukwe-Onuobia.
Names: Onyemelukwe-Onuobia, Cheluchi, 1978- author.
Description: Originally published: Cape Town, South Africa : Penguin Books, 2019.
Identifiers: Canadiana (print) 20190239050 | Canadiana (ebook) 20190239069 | ISBN 9781459747081 (softcover) | ISBN 9781459747098 (PDF) | ISBN 9781459747104 (EPUB)
Classification: LCC PR9387.9.O59 S66 2020 | DDC 823/.92—dc23

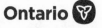

We acknowledge the support of the Canada Council for the Arts and the Ontario Arts Council for our publishing program. We also acknowledge the financial support of the Government of Ontario, through the Ontario Book Publishing Tax Credit and Ontario Creates, and the Government of Canada.

Care has been taken to trace the ownership of copyright material used in this book. The author and the publisher welcome any information enabling them to rectify any references or credits in subsequent editions.

The publisher is not responsible for websites or their content unless they are owned by the publisher.

Printed and bound in Canada.

Dundurn Press
1382 Queen Street East
Toronto, Ontario, Canada M4L 1C9
dundurn.com, @dundurnpress 🐦 f ⌾

To my parents,
Obidinma Isaiah Okoli Onyemelukwe
and
Rebecca Chiegonu Onyemelukwe,
with much love and gratitude

We must do something to pass the time, I thought. Two women in a room, hands and feet tied.

I could not see how we could escape. Both our legs and hands were still tied up in knots that I could not imagine getting free if I had another hundred years. Even if we managed to get free of the knots, there was only one door out of the small room. I heard the click of a padlock every time they came and went. The only window could not fit one of my thighs, let alone my entire body. Nor could I run to save my life; even if I was not so heavy, there was the matter of my bad knees. There would be no breakout like one saw in the movies.

We did not entertain the idea that the police might save us, guns blazing, as happened in the movies. The police themselves, people said, would sometimes tell the family of kidnapped persons to go pay the ransom so that harm would not come to their loved one. They had neither the resources nor the serious desire to pursue kidnappers. There was even speculation that the police might be complicit in some kidnappings. So our only hope, like many kidnapping victims in this country, was that our people would come up with the money.

At first, fear had overwhelmed me. I struggled with them in the car as they tried to put a blindfold over my eyes, as they tried to tie those same hands with which I tried to punch. I felt claustrophobic, my ample body squeezed into a space I could not have fit into even as a teenager in secondary school. I was going to die. With a gun dug into my back as the car sped in a direction that I could not determine, I felt certain I was going to die. Afam, my son, his wedding — what would he do?

I had now gone past that visceral and obvious fear to a quietened and more sensible state. There was nothing the ears had ever heard to make them fall off, or the eyes had seen that would make them weep blood instead of tears. Perhaps we would get out alive, like other people I had heard of. At least they had taken off our blindfolds. My friend Obiageli had told me of a man whose blindfold was left on for eleven days. Imagine, eleven days of darkness and blindness.

Once they took off our blindfolds and untied our hands, the situation became more bearable. They fed us — white bread in the morning, white bread in the afternoon, white bread at night. At home, I did not eat white bread; I only ate whole wheat bread on occasion. I needed to watch my blood sugar, the doctor had told me, because I was prediabetic, and, since my father had died of diabetes, I knew that my genes were conspiring against me and it was up to me to stop them from winning. So I complained this morning when they brought some more bread.

They asked if I thought this was a hotel.

"Mummy, if your people do not come up with the money soon," that young boy said in his deceptively soft voice, "you might stop eating at all. Where do you think the money to buy this bread is coming from?" His voice rose in anger. It was the first time he had shown any emotion. "I am sorry," I said, feeling like a spoilt child who had just been chastised. I knew better now than to add the other things on the list I had made in my head: the room was hot and sticky. People with extra flesh like me tended to sweat a lot. Without a bath, that would make me and the room smell. Could we at least have some time to bathe, clean our teeth? Could our legs be untied? Sitting in one position and lying with tied legs could not be the best thing for two women, especially one already down the old-age road. Also, it was really uncomfortable to hold in your pee, especially for a woman my age, whose insides had shifted and moved from where the Creator originally placed them. Further, it was not right that they should follow so closely when a person wanted to relieve herself. They were nearly young enough to be my grandchildren, if I had had kids at the age some of my mates did. And I kept hearing a cat mew at night and it made goose pimples stand out on my body — could they do something about that? Finally, could you please not call me Mummy? I am not your mother; you would not treat your mother this way. At least, I hoped so.

I told them, "I am hypertensive. I need my medication. Can anything be done about this?"

"Anything like what?" he asked me. It was a rhetorical question. His voice and face said that I was stepping over invisible bounds. "What you should focus on is praying that your people come through with our money." With that, he swivelled round and was gone, leaving his lackeys to run after him and lock the door on us.

I looked at Nwabulu now. Our mouths were free so we could talk, and we needed to pass the time. "So tell me more about yourself," I said, trying to encourage her. "Here we are, with time on our hands."

She looked surprised. That was not what she expected to hear in such a place, it seemed. But what else could we do? After spending the first day bemoaning our fate, the wrong decisions that had landed us there, there was really nothing much to say about our kidnapping. "We are stuck together here for only God knows how long. And as my friend Obiageli says, there is nothing like a good story to help pass the time." Nwabulu seemed reluctant still. Her stylish scarf had been torn off her head and her weave needed brushing. There was a slight bruise on her arm. Yet she remained pretty, her face serious.

"Ifechi must be worried," I said, "but I know he will be doing what he can."

"Yes," she said. "But we do not have much money. I hope they are not asking for too much money."

I hoped so too. I thought about what Afam had said about Nigeria — what brought him back from Canada, where I thought he might settle down to make a life after school. Nigeria was growing, booming, he said. Lots of opportunities, a growing middle class, emerging sectors. Not just the oil and gas people. Look at the telecommunications industry, the banking sector, the music industry. Nigerian musicians collaborating with Western ones, and making enough money to buy private jets. Internet, even in the villages. People marching on, with or without electricity, with or without good leadership. Making money, changing lives.

But there was also kidnapping, I wanted to tell him now. And it was an easy way to make money. A few people had been killed. Mostly, however, people were released after stupendous amounts of money had been extorted from their families. Kidnapping used to be like something out of the folklore that we had heard as children — that people were kidnapped and sold into slavery. Some said it was unemployment that was driving the kidnapping trade. If more young people were employed, kidnapping would

4

die a natural death. Some said it was greed. I had never been hungry enough to threaten anyone with a gun; to threaten to take away lives because mine was unbearable. I wondered what that felt like.

We had no way of knowing if our people were getting the money. Our people, I thought, hearing the boy leader's voice in my head. Who were my people? My people were Obiageli and Afam. My sisters would wring their hands but they would do nothing. My youngest brother would shrug his shoulders and carry on with whatever petty trade would support his marijuana habit. Obiageli would be terrified, beside herself with worry. But she would pull herself together and get Afam to get the money. And Afam ... he had a good head on his shoulders. Between the two of them they would manage something. I tried to imagine their fear, and I thought about the fear that I would have if Afam were kidnapped. I wished we could tell them that we were being treated well, considering.

"I am sure that they are doing what they can," I told Nwabulu now. "I am sorry I took that road," she said again.

I was almost starting to feel guilty that I had asked for that lift. My visit to Obiageli's could have waited.

"I should have gone through Otigba Junction," said Nwabulu. "This would never have happened in that busy place." She had said so over and over, but here we were; what was the use of going over what-ifs, and should-haves?

"It is not your fault," I said. "I am the one they wanted. It was just bad luck that you got caught up in it."

"They should have police on that road. It is lonely. People could be robbed there."

"Or kidnapped." I smiled.

She did not smile back. She shook her head and looked at her feet. "What is done is done," I said. A truism we had learnt at

Girls' High School Aba. And then, unable to resist, I added, "No use crying over spilt milk."

She smiled now, a tentative smile.

"So you were going to tell me how you got into the fashion business? You are really good, you know."

"It is a long story, Ma."

"Are you rushing off anywhere?" I looked around me theatrically.

She laughed. "But, Ma, I am sure your story is more interesting than mine. You have lived an interesting life, I am sure." She seemed genuinely interested. "Okay. Let us make a deal. You tell me yours and I will tell you mine."

She was a businesswoman through and through, I thought. "Okay," I agreed.

I began my story. Her emotions flitted across her face — puzzlement, agreement, even disapproval.

But, in the end, it was Nwabulu's story that ignited the fire.

PART ONE
NWABULU

CHAPTER ONE
1972

I had been a housemaid for nearly half my life when I met Urenna.

My first sojourn as a housemaid began when I was ten. That morning, before it was fully day, I went by myself on a big bus, the kind that went to Lagos. I went to live with Papa Emma and his wife. I would do little chores around the house and I would be sent to school. That was what Mama Nkemdilim told me. I was excited to go, a little apprehensive too, but I knew that anywhere would be better than living with Mama Nkemdilim after my father had died. And Lagos was the biggest city in Nigeria — everyone knew that. Mama Nkemdilim said men who had gone from our village either married Yoruba women and never came back, or they came back smelling of money and comfort.

It was no surprise that Mama Nkemdilim would send me away at the first opportunity that knocked on our door.

"Amosu," she would call me, a witch. "Why do you still hold out your hands for food?" she would ask, squeezing her face in puzzlement when I stood outside the kitchen, waiting for food.

"Is all that blood you suck from me and my children not enough? Or does it all go to your big head?" she would wail, referring to my head, which looked huge on my thin body. Other children called me Atinga, giving proper due to my bony slenderness. Mama Nkemdilim did not think that the little food we had in the house should be wasted on putting extra flesh on my bones. Extra flesh would be a drag on the speed needed to run the many errands she sent me on.

Mama Nkemdilim blamed me for all her misfortunes. And misfortunes had visited often since she came to live with us, coming down like rain in July. When she could not conceive after two years of marriage to my father, she pointed fingers at me. A dibia, she said, had told her that I was responsible for her empty womb. Bad luck, she liked to say, followed me around like the mosquito sought the ear at night; like flies followed feces. After my father died, she would point out that he had survived the war where he had served as a soldier, had withstood poverty, had held on to life after I came along and killed my mother as I forced myself out into the world. My father had weathered all this. But how, she asked, did one survive a wicked child who had killed her mother?

"You will not kill me too," she would cry, conviction ringing like a soprano alongside the alto of disgust. "Mbanu, you will not. I am not as foolish as your mother, not as soft as your father. I will kill you before you kill me," Mama Nkemdilim would insist, as if I, a mere child, were a monster with seven heads like those spirits in fairy tales.

"I did not kill my mother and father," I would say, my head turned away, waiting for her hard knuckles to rap against my almost hairless big head. A loud, painful koi.

Yet all her blows had not yet driven away the remnants of my defiance. If I could kill, the spirit in me said, Mama Nkemdilim would not be living while my father and mother lay in their almost forgotten graves, now covered by grass in front of my father's house. When she approached with the cane she hastily broke off from the onugbu plant beside the kitchen, I did not stop for her hand to go up and down my body. I ran out to the road, screaming for my dead father, even though I knew my punishment would wait until I came back to my senses and returned home. When she starved me, I woke up in the night to creep to the kitchen and help myself to some of the soup and dry fish she gave only to her children, to prevent kwashiorkor, she would proclaim.

When I turned ten, Papa Emma, a distant relative of Mama Nkemdilim's, came home to the village at Christmas. He said he needed someone to help his wife around the house. Mama Nkemdilim thought that I would be a good choice: it would get rid of me. But she also worried that it might be too much of an opportunity for me.

"Do you not think that this is too good for her?" she asked her friend, Mama Odinkemma.

I listened intently from outside the kitchen.

"Hmm," Mama Odinkemma said, "do you want her living here, sucking your blood, sucking Nkemdilim and her brother's blood every night, while blowing cool air on all of you like a rat?"

"Eh, that is true talk. Eziokwu. But what if she becomes a big person in Lagos?"

Mama Odinkemma laughed. It was a genuine laugh. And it went on for long. She could not imagine Nwabulu, the Atinga, becoming a big person anywhere. Not even in Lagos, I heard her say. For once, I did not disagree with Mama Odinkemma, Mama Nkemdilim's thick-set friend with the pointed mouth that made you wonder how food made it through to her belly. And yet she could often be counted on to be chewing something like a goat chewing cud. I silently agreed with her that it was laughable that I could become a big person by cleaning, cooking, and doing chores in a house, even if it was in Lagos, the biggest city in Nigeria. Even a ten-year-old child, who had not gone to school for two years, knew that this was like the long tales the tortoise told the other animals he had offended by his greed so that they would not throw him down from the sky.

What sealed my fate was Mama Odinkemma saying, "Mama Nkemdilim, send this child away. That child has her mother's blood. They are all witches in her mother's family. You do not want her to initiate your children into the cult, or worse still, kill them?"

After that, Mama Nkemdilim satisfied the necessary obligation of informing my uncle Nnabuzo.

I wanted to go to Lagos, climb mountains and swim seas, just to get far away from my stepmother. But I did not want to leave my uncle Nnabuzo.

My uncle did not like the idea of Mama Nkemdilim sending me all the way to Lagos. It should have been his responsibility to determine what happened to me, his brother's child, but he appeared weak before Mama Nkemdilim's verbal and emotional onslaughts. Sometimes her barbs were subtle, but more often they were blunt like the stone with which we ground pepper in the small mortar.

"Let me take Nwabulu," he said to Mama Nkemdilim. "At least we will keep our eyes on her." He rested worried eyes on my face, but his tone was gentle, as always.

"Did my husband, your brother, not say that what he would like most was for Nwabulu to go to school?" she asked. Mama Nkemdilim always knew the right thing to say.

"Yes, it is true," Nnabuzo said.

"The people with whom she will live will send her to school. Emma told me himself. I cannot send her to school," she moaned. "It is all I can do to feed myself and your brother's children."

Nnabuzo knew when he was defeated. My uncle could barely feed his own family with his palm-wine-tapping trade. His wife, Nnedi, had a baby every year. At last count, there were nine of them. Her thin frame was often to be seen with a protruding tummy as she was going about her duties. I had heard Mama Nkemdilim say that her baby-a-year habit was the result of my uncle Nnabuzo's sickening inability to keep his own penis to himself. Mama Nkemdilim reminded him as often as possible of his neglected duties to his late brother's family, always implying that, in the face of his failure to do so, she must continue to shoulder a man's burdens on her frail woman's shoulders.

On the day I left, a cold harmattan morning in January, Nnabuzo was the only one who came to say goodbye. I dressed in the dark, half listening to my half-sister, Nkemdilim, as she slept on the other side of the bed, sucking her tongue noisily as she was wont to do, the sound going *thu thu thu* rhythmically.

When I stepped out, I shivered from the cold. Nnabuzo took my hand and drew me to him. I hugged him tightly. He put a few naira notes in my hands. I curled my fingers closely to hide the money from Mama Nkemdilim, who would snatch it away if she had any idea.

"Ezechitoke will take care of you," he said, referring to the God of all the earth. "Remember your father. Remember where you come from. We do not steal. We do not lie, nor do we cheat. We are content with what we have, be it big or small. Do not shame us." I nodded solemnly. Later, I would remember hugging Nnabuzo, holding on tight, memorizing his thin frame and the tobacco-snuff smell of him, before Mama Nkemdilim pulled me away, saying that we had a long way to go to get to the bus. It was the last time I ever saw him.

Looking back at him as we left in the dark that day, the first tears of uncertainty had run down my cheeks, leaving white marks that the large-hipped woman beside me in the bus later wiped off with her fingers, moistened with spit. In the two years that had gone by since Papa's death, Uncle Nnabuzo had tried his best to play the role of father to me. It was he who told me stories of my father and my mother, stories of my birth, stories he said I must not forget because my father would want me to remember. He was the one who told me how Papa, his elder and only brother, had come to name me "Nwabulu" after my mother died while pushing me out into the world.

A child was still profitable, Nnabuzo said he told his brother, who was beside himself with grief at the death of the wife he loved deeply. Even if her mother had died pushing her out into the world, a child was still gain — the supreme prize. Why did men marry and procreate? To have children. Why did a father toil from sun-up till sundown? For children. Why did a woman marry? To bear children. Why did she stay even if her husband was lazy, or a wife-beater? For the children.

So, my father, exhausted from grief, unanticipated burial expenses, and unforeseen single fatherhood, chose the name from his brother's words, Nwabulu. And I was truly gain, my uncle told me, a benefit to the world, bearing my mother's beauty — that beauty that had made my father swim seven seas, climb seven mountains, fight off seven monsters in seven evil forests to marry her.

My father's dearest wish was that I would go to school and perhaps become a nurse or teacher. Some of the nurses he saw during the war had been sent by God, Ezechitoke himself, he told me. Teaching was good too, he said. As soon as I was old enough, he put me in the village school. Every morning, he would wake me up and we would walk to the school, one of the few houses in the village built with cement and a good roof. Every evening, he would ask what I had learnt that day. And I would recite the

ABCs and sing "A is for apple, B is for ball, C is for cat …" to him. He would nod and smile happily.

He would take me to the river to swim sometimes. It was our special thing. There, he would become the man my mother married — a light would come into his eyes, and his slightly sunken cheeks would rise into a smile. There, he would show me the spot where he first saw my mother. She had been swimming with her friends. He never failed to say that she rose up like Mammy Water, a mermaid, beautiful like no woman he had ever seen before, enebe eje olu, a woman you could admire all day, for whom you could miss going to work just to gaze at her. He always added that I looked very much like her, and that I would be just as beautiful when I grew up. In these times, it seemed to me that my mother came to the stream too and we were a family again. Until Mama Nkemdilim came along.

People would often tell my father that he needed a new wife, a woman who would be a mother to me and give him a son. One day, he listened to them and brought Mama Nkemdilim home. From that day, the peace and joy of our home moved somewhere else; peace and joy could not stay in the same room as Mama Nkemdilim's jealousy. And, after she had a son, her feet became firm on the soil of our home, and her evil began to grow.

I was eight when my father died. He had not been sick a long time, just a few weeks. He had not even seemed seriously ill: a fever and a cough. Not ill enough to die. Nnabuzo was sure that he had been poisoned by enemies of our family. Mama Nkemdilim, with the same degree of certitude, knew that I was the one who had killed him.

With his death came changes. Some things stopped immediately. Like school. Mama Nkemdilim did not see the point when she herself had not gone to school and had still been able to marry a good man. She had not gone to school and yet knew how to do all that a woman of Nwokenta could do — clean, cook, fetch firewood, make a fire, make palm oil, farm, buy, sell, and bear children.

Other changes took a little more time. Like going to swim at Amata. More than school even, it was being unable to swim in the river that reminded me that, when one's father dies, things change. Things that told me that love was not just food and shelter.

Mama Nkemdilim gave me a little food and shelter. In the morning, my broom went up and down our compound, creating neat lines on the red earth while Mama Nkemdilim's children slept. My head bore pots of water from the stream. Then I warmed last night's soup over the firewood I had fetched the day before. I went with her to the farm and we worked until she was tired or the children began to scream from the heat of the sun. I could do everything — peel egwusi, pound palm nuts for oil, fry garri. She made delicious, moist, palm-oil-reddened okpa and I sold them at Eke Nwokenta. Sometimes, when I had sold the okpa fast, I would stay and play oga with some of my friends at the market. Mama Nkemdilim did not like this, and if she found out, she sometimes made me go without food.

In the beginning, after my father died, I dreamt about him often. He came to me and took me to our river. But when the chores began to grow like storeyed buildings, one on top of the other, I would sleep as soon as my head touched my mat and stay dead to the world until Mama Nkemdilim shook me awake, calling me Amosu and asking me to come back from bloodsucking journeys. I mourned the loss of my dreams as I went about my duties, sometimes chanting my ABCs so as not to forget them.

But this was all before I went to Lagos. As I sat in the shaky bus, jingling this way then that way like an ichaka, I tried not to be too excited. Yet excitement took up residence in my heart; living in the city could not be worse than living with Mama

Nkemdilim, I thought. My belly threatened to pour its contents on my neighbours — on the woman who wiped my dried tears with her spit, and the dry-looking man who slept most of the way, his mouth wide open, dripping saliva. Even that could not blunt the edge of my excitement.

Things were not as I imagined they would be in Lagos. Papa Emma and his family lived in a flat in Apapa, and they had neighbours from all the parts of Nigeria who spoke different languages — Edo, Yoruba, Itsekiri, and pidgin. Living with them was different and yet it was the same. They did not send me to school, as Mama Nkemdilim had led me to believe they would. I worked as hard as I had when I'd lived with Mama Nkemdilim. I was cleaning, cooking, washing, and helping Mama Emma at her shop in the market. But I did not have the relief of laughing with other children at the stream, or singing to my baby sister, or playing oga in the market after selling okpa as I'd had back home. Despite the fact that we were from the same village and that Papa Emma was my stepmother's relative, Mama Emma insisted I call them Oga and Madam. To emphasize the distance between us — them at the top, me at the bottom.

The tension between Papa Emma and his wife, palpable and constant, overshadowed the home from morning to evening. In the beginning, when I first started to work there, I felt sorry for Papa Emma. He worked all day at their shop in the market and was welcomed home by Madam's thundering bellow. Like a lion, she roared at him often, spewing reminders and threats, her generous neck, arms, and buttocks jiggling. In the midst of my endless chores, I pitied the quiet, hulking man, whose lot seemed little better than mine. His shame was pitiable, shown only in a jaw clenched tight, wide eyes that looked upon the world in barely suppressed anger, and an uncomfortable quietness of being. In the compound, Adaku, the other Igbo housemaid — a rude, large-breasted girl from Anambra — called Papa Emma "ewu," a goat, because he stared mindlessly at everyone. "Maaaaaaaa," she would bleat, and I would laugh as we drew water from the well. We would stop our laughter quickly and chorus, "Good morning, sir," when he passed by, still staring. Yet, when I brought his food to the side table in the sitting room, where he often sat by himself after work while his wife sat counting her money at the dining table, he murmured, "Dalu," without looking at me. Adaku told me that the shop was Madam's, provided by her rich family.

"Why is this only nine naira?" Madam wanted to know one day in the kitchen, waving the money he had passed to her in front of him. Her voice was low, dangerous. I flinched a little where I stood before the sink, washing plates.

"Em ..." He fumbled for words to explain monies missing at the shop, his long arms trembling beside his big, tall body.

I was looking down into the dirty dishwater when a loud crack came to my ears. I glanced up. His hand held his cheek, his face turned away from his children and me. Why did he allow this, I wondered. Was he not a man?

He kept his face turned away from me, as if he did not want to acknowledge I could see his shame. That is, until months into living with them, when he began to come into my bed at night to pass that shame to me.

The day it began, the children had been playing, I had been massaging Madam's back, and Oga had just returned from work. Where had he been when she called this afternoon? Madam had demanded. The slight pause as he foraged through the day's doings for an answer had earned him an angry slap. His hand had again gone up to his cheek. And his eyes, glancing away from his wife, had this time fallen on my face. What had he seen there?

That night, Oga crept into the store where I slept amid yam tubers and bags of rice and beans. He pounced with the force of the three-storey house that had fallen in on itself down the street. He clasped my neck with one hand, fumbling with his zipper with the other, and whispered threats when I tried to shout, to struggle, to move my not-quite-eleven-year-old body from beneath him. Madam would kill me, I thought, gritting my teeth, biting down the pain. "Don't tell anyone," he ordered.

Who could I tell? The two young children? Adaku in the other flat, whose ears had never heard anything that she could keep from the rest of the world? Or perhaps the new neighbour, a young woman who taught in the primary school nearby — the one I should have been going to — who had stopped to help me carry one of the gallons of water upstairs last week? That had annoyed Madam. Why had I spoken to the neighbour, she had asked, punctuating each word with a slap. Was I too hungry *slap*, too tired *slap*, to carry a gallon? *Slap*. I dared tell no one that the night had become my enemy, just as it used to be a friend longed for amid the day's endless chores.

Hurry, I often thought as he knelt down. I lay quietly, trembling, my heart beating into my eardrums, thinking that he grunted like a he-goat, and smelt like one too. I no longer pitied him.

One night, I lay still on the mat, as usual, as Oga pulled down his trousers. My stepmother said she had sent me to Lagos to go to school to learn new things, I thought, as Oga grunted away. Was this one of those things? That thought had no sooner come than Oga yelped loudly. He rolled away, and there stood Madam, a kitchen knife in her hand, her face contorted with rage, looking not at Oga but me.

She advanced towards me and struck my shoulder, slicing into it like the neck of a Christmas chicken, red blood spurting onto my wrapper. The knife went up and down quickly, striking, slashing at my arms and hands. I shrieked and Oga moved belatedly, catching hold of Madam's hand midair. Unutterable hate shone through Madam's eyes, almost as terrifying as the slashing knife. It electrified my nerveless legs and sent me half-naked to the door.

Even as I fled down the steps of our flat, escaping certain death, my screams reverberating through dark long houses in which our neighbours slept peacefully, I knew that I would never return there. Even if I had to go back to my stepmother.

A kind neighbour, the fat madam in the flat downstairs — the one Mama Emma often called a husband-snatcher on account of the men who came at all hours to see her — opened her door to me. She drew me in and only asked questions after she had put some iodine on the gashes. I yelled out loud at the burning of the iodine, the shame of what Papa Emma had done to me, and the fieriness of Mama Emma's fury.

Fat Madam, alias Husband-Snatcher, gave me food, a bed to sleep on, and, in the morning, went upstairs to talk to Mama Emma. She did not tell me what Mama Emma said but I was sure that Mama Emma did not want me back in her house. Nor did I want to go back there.

When the gashes Mama Emma had given me had healed a bit, Madam Clara — that was my benefactor's name — made arrangements to send me back to Nwokenta on another long bus. I had not even lived a full year in Lagos.

- - - - - - - - - -

Mama Nkemdilim welcomed my return to the village with anger and curses.

"Amosu," she addressed me, in front of her friend Mama Odinkemma, "did I not say, is it not clear to anyone who is not blind or deaf that you would come to no good?" Then, turning to her friend, feigning wonder, she said, "How many people … how many people, I ask you, have been to Lagos?"

"Not me," her friend said.

"Nor me, my sister. Nor my children. How many people had anyone there — anyone who would give them a chance at success?"

"Not many. Not many at all," Mama Odinkemma obliged.

It was the answer Mama Nkemdilim was waiting for. She pounced on me, pulling my ears and dragging me around the backyard. I grunted in pain. "And here I send this goat, this sheep, this wild animal to Lagos, where the lights shine gloriously in the sky, and yet here she is, having chewed that opportunity with her dog's teeth and spat it right out." She paused for breath. "Can a child who kills her mother be expected to live at peace with the world?" she shouted at no one in particular, her veins standing out in her neck.

My story about what had happened did not fetch me anything other than, "That is what happens when you try to take another woman's husband."

"But look at her," I heard her say to her friend one day, months later, "she is as flat as my daughter, Nkemdilim, though she is all of twelve years. What can a man see in that?" Her friend assured her that some men ran that way. That was my only inkling that she might have believed my story.

I went back to life as it was before Lagos — chores, curses, hunger, shouting, sleeping, waking up, and doing the same thing all over again.

Several months passed before another job came along. This time it was a family in Enugu. Hyacinth, a man from our village, approached Mama Nkemdilim. He worked as a civil servant in Enugu and found housemaids from the village for the rich in that city. He said a family needed a good girl who would do chores and who might even be sent to school. They were prepared to give a sum of money to Mama Nkemdilim, which he told Mama Nkemdilim would be helpful to her in raising the other children.

Mama Nkemdilim was more interested in hearing about this part, this money that would touch her palms, than the possibility that I might go to school there. It would also be one mouth fewer to feed, she said to him. My uncle Nnabuzo was not there to inspect this new prospect or to say no. He had died while I was in Lagos and his family was struggling even worse than ours. This time, unlike when I left for Lagos, I went to Enugu with apprehension. I went in dread and fear. But good things happened to me there — I went to school, I learnt to read, and I fell in love with Urenna.

CHAPTER TWO

When I arrived in Enugu with Hyacinth, I had my interview in an expansive sitting room, with a red carpet into which your foot sank when you took a step. Just that room was bigger than our entire house in Nwokenta. The brown shelves held expensive-looking hardcover books with gold lettering. But, for me, the very definition of luxury lay in the dark brown velvet-covered sofas and cushions.

Hyacinth stood respectfully by the door after the owners let us in. I stood beside him, holding on tightly to the slight black polythene bag with my clothes. They exchanged greetings with Hyacinth and invited us to sit. We sat down on those soft seats and faced them. That first week, when I found myself alone, I would sit on the sofa and cross my legs as I imagined rich people did.

Hyacinth chatted with them, telling them that my step-mother was happy to let me work for them. In exchange, she only requested that I be sent to school and treated well. He spoke with some deference. This surprised me: Hyacinth was well respected in the village; he was known to do olu oyibo — he was a civil servant in Enugu township. Later, I would learn that Hyacinth was only a messenger in Daddy's office.

"Are you clean?" the man, whom I would eventually call "Sir" and "Daddy," asked me. His slender face had ears that poked out of his head and looked like they had been stuck on as an afterthought. He had a too-wide mouth, bordered by deep grooves on either side. It was his stern, piercing eyes, however, that made me anxious. They searched my face now. He would see any lie before I told it, a voice in my head said. "Did you have a shower this morning? Do you have a shower every day?"

I answered, "Yes, sir," to these questions and then was rewarded with "Here you wash your hands every time you use the toilet.

"Do you tell lies?

"Do you steal?

"Can you read?

"Can you tell time?"

The answer to these last questions was, "No, sir." Daddy shook his head at this and turned to his wife, saying, "At least she has the good sense not to lie."

She nodded approvingly. Her tall frame looked more menacing than my last madam's small but chubby build.

"We will take care of you. We do not mistreat people. You will eat exactly what we eat. In return, you must do what you are told. Laziness is a disease not allowed room in this house." With this, it looked like I had passed the interview.

I tried not to worry. I wondered where I would sleep. Daddy looked little like Oga, but that did not stop the racing of my heart as I remembered what Oga had done to me.

As they told Hyacinth that they would take care of me, I tried not to let my fear show. He thanked them and admonished me to behave well, not to take anything that did not belong to me, and to keep my eyes on my work and my schooling. He did not tell me how I could contact him if anything went wrong. In my trepidation, I did not ask.

Later, I was given a list of chores to do: some were to be done twice or more times a day, like bathing Ikenna, their young son (twice a day, morning and night); cleaning the sitting room (twice a day, before breakfast and after dinner), and the kitchen (as many times a day as I had nothing else to do). I was sent to a room towards the back of the house. I was shown my toilet, which was in the house, and told that I must keep it clean. Everything looked luxurious and tidy, not a speck of sand or the brown colour of dust to be seen anywhere.

Later still, Mummy came into my room where I had come to drop my bag of clothes and change from the clothes in which I had arrived, my church clothes.

"Here," she said, holding out a small blue polythene bag. I took it in my hands. It had something inside that wasn't quite soft, but it was not hard either. I wanted to ask what it was but I was too shy.

"Have you had your period?" She began the sentence in Igbo, which I could understand perfectly and which was the language I spoke and thought in. But she said "period" in English, and this confused me: "I fubago period gi?" My confusion probably showed itself because she immediately tried to explain: "The blood that comes at the end of the month."

I was relieved that I knew what she spoke about. I had just begun my period three months before I'd arrived in Enugu. The day it started, I was on my way to the market with some of Mama Nkemdilim's okpa on my head. I had felt pain in my belly all morning but I did not want to complain so that Mama Nkemdilim would not shout at me. But the pain kept growing and gnawing in my belly, especially the lower part. As I walked, I felt something running down my thighs. Curious, I looked down but saw nothing. I walked until I got to the market. It was there that Mama Okechukwu saw what was happening to me. Mama Okechukwu was my rival in the okpa business. She was often irritated that I managed to sell all of Mama Nkemdilim's okpa while she waited for customers to look her way. She must have seen the red spot on my faded wrapper, because she immediately took off one of her own wrappers and wrapped it around me. She insisted that I go home at once. I told her that Mama Nkemdilim would kill me if I came home with no okpa sold. She said that Mama Nkemdilim would understand. When she saw that I would not budge — so great was my fear of my stepmother's wrath — she said she would accompany me home. She packed up her unsold okpa and we walked home together.

When we got there, she drew Mama Nkemdilim aside and spoke to her, pointing at me and gesturing at her own buttocks. Mama Nkemdilim was not pleased to see me with the okpa unsold. But, to my surprise, she did not accuse Mama Okechukwu of meddling.

"You know the tradition," I heard Mama Okechukwu say to my stepmother as she was leaving, "kill a chicken and welcome her into womanhood." Then she smiled at me, said jisike, and left.

Mama Nkemdilim told me to put the okpa away. She went into the room and brought some pieces of cloth. She explained to me that I needed to put this in my underwear and, when it was soaked through, wash it and use another. She said that I would get the blood every month, for three, maybe four days. She also said that I was no longer allowed to go near a man, otherwise I would get pregnant right away and the shame would kill my father in his grave all over again. She said that she had no cock to kill to welcome anyone to womanhood. It was all she could do to take care of all of us with no help from anywhere, the earth or the sky.

I knew about the blood that came every month, I assured my new employer. She nodded with something that looked like relief and said, "This is what you will use. Do not use my tissue paper. The last maid I had used up a month's supply of tissue each time. This," she said, gesturing at what I had in my hand, "is what you will use. It is called a sanitary pad."

"Yes, Ma," I said.

"When you've used it, you tie it up in a polythene bag and throw it in the dustbin. Do you understand?"

"Yes, Ma."

"Make sure you do not try to flush it down the toilet, do you hear?"

"Yes, Ma."

"You throw it in the garbage."

"Yes, Ma."

When she left, I opened it and touched it. It was so white and so soft. Maybe this new town, this new home would be all right. Maybe Enugu would treat me well.

--- --- --- --- --- --- ---

I need not have worried about Daddy. He barely threw me a glance when I saw him. After I had lived with them a few weeks, I found it almost laughable — that frisson of fear that had shaken my heart on the first day. It was clear that I would never be clean enough for Daddy.

Daddy insisted that I go to school. It was not merely kindness. He said he did not want me to act like a goat in the house. I would be around their young son, Ikenna, and he did not want me infecting him with dullness. Plus, I needed to know basic things such as how to tell time, read a list if I needed to be sent to the market, and read signposts if I was sent on an errand outside.

So, at twelve years old, I started primary one at St Mary's Primary School. I went to school in the afternoon, after Mummy came back from work in the secretariat. Mummy was a civil servant and often complained that moving up the ladder from administrative officer was like pushing a rock up the Miliken Hill. Her boss sent her on errands that his secretary or messenger should run, refusing to recognize her seniority. She often talked about going back to get a different degree, as if she was making a threat. Daddy ignored her complaints, and I acted the way I was supposed to — listen silently.

Living with Daddy and Mummy was hard work. Not because the chores were too many, though they were almost as many as Mama Nkemdilim had given me to do. It was because Daddy suffered from an obsession with perfection that kept me on my toes, unable to relax. I had to do everything twice, I was warned. Sweep, sweep again. Dust, dust again. Flush, flush again. Wash, wash again. We lived on a dusty street, with roads that had seen some tarring once but had now been abandoned, letting dust pile up on pictures, side tables, wall dividers, every minute of the day.

I had to scrub the veranda every morning, dust the book-shelves in the sitting room and library, and sweep the entire house, three or four times bigger than our house in the village or even the house I lived in in Lagos. And I had to do it twice, morning and night, making sure that I had left nothing behind. I had to scrub the three toilets with Harpic, three times each, Mummy empha-sized, and then take a tissue paper and wipe just below the wide mouth of the toilet. I had to wash my hands four times after I was done with the toilets, which were the last chores. When I was done, I could not touch anything in the house for at least thirty minutes to be sure that the disinfectant with which I washed my hands had done its work.

Unlike where I had worked in Lagos, our neighbourhood in Independence Layout was clean, a neighbourhood of top civil servants and businessmen, Catholic priests and bishops, some of them European. The houses looked different, but they all had rows and hedges of flowers. Hibiscus, morning glory, and neatly cut rows of Ixora were the most popular. Our neighbour at number 9 had pink flowers overflowing her fence; Daddy thought she needed to trim them. When I have my own house, I will have flowers everywhere, inside and out, I told myself. All the houses had outside lights at night, long fluorescent tubes. Mama Nkemdilim would say that the city was a place where light bulbs shone in the sky. All families had a housemaid. Except number 21: the husband there insisted that he could not live with one. Strangely, I heard, he helped his wife with the cooking, bathed the kids and took them to school. Many families also had a driver. We did not; Daddy preferred to drive himself — he could not stand the unwashed odour of drivers in such a small space, he told his wife.

My village ways were constantly being smoothed out of me, as with a dull knife that was rubbed against another to sharpen it. For example, drinking glasses had to be clean and dry. The first time I served Daddy water, I rinsed the glass to make sure it was clean, just like I had done in Lagos, then took the glass and a bottle of cold water to him on a tray. He stared at me coldly as I stood before him with the tray in my hands. "Why have you brought me a filthy glass to drink from?" he asked at last. "Get out of here."

I walked back into the kitchen, my legs trembling so much I thought they would give out on me.

Later, I heard him telling Mummy that it was hard to be married to a woman who could not even take a little time to teach a housemaid how to do things in the house. When she came into the kitchen, she shouted at me.

"Did you not learn a single thing at all in your stupid village? Did they not say you have done this work before?"

I was puzzled. What had I done wrong?

"Has no one, no one at all, taught you that you do not serve anybody, anybody at all, water in a wet glass? That even if you serve God Himself water in a wet glass, you cannot serve my husband water in a wet glass?"

Frozen by her anger, I did not reply; I was not required to.

Thus, I learnt to wash glasses, make sure I laid them out on a tray to dry, and, no matter what, have at least two dry glasses ready for whenever Daddy needed water. I began to understand that the temperature inside the house rose gradually as the day wore on, approaching evening, and only dipped when Daddy left for work the next day. When he entered the house, the first thing Daddy did before he answered his wife's greetings was point out that he had seen a broomstick, a speck of dust, or a strand of hair on the veranda, or that the flowers were dying. Then he would proceed to complain about dinner: too salty; too spicy; too bland; not enough salt; too much meat, which meant his money was being recklessly spent; too little meat, which meant that he was being fed like a pauper.

He nitpicked until he made his wife scream like a child who had been tickled too long. I often thought that living inside his skin must be so prickly that he had to reach out and make others uncomfortable too. He would lash out at his wife, though hardly ever at me. But I was the end point of all that itchiness, because no sooner would their shouting match end than his wife would take it all out on me.

Mummy was not a mean woman, not in the active, bitter-leaf way of my stepmother. I ate all I needed. She left me to my own

devices when there was no work to be done. I learnt to understand her body clock — she was happiest when Daddy left for
work and right after she returned from her own work between
three and four. Between five and six, she became anxious, finicky,
panicky. Coming in from school, I ran around making sure all
was well with every part of the house — no dust, no cobweb, no
spider in sight, food perfect, and the house not smelling of said
food. By ten past seven, she could be her most cruel or her most
pleased, depending on her husband's mood. She was really only
cruel when her husband pushed her buttons. Which was often.
Just like when Ikenna switched on the light on the wall and then
ran to his bed and switched off the light with the rope switch and
ran back and did the same thing over and over. On, off, on, off.

I did my chores as well as I could not only because I was
required to, but out of pity for Mummy, because her husband
looked for dust underneath the bookshelves, and specks of hair
on their combs, and scraps of food between her teeth. And then
he would turn on her once he found something.

Still, Mummy tried hard to please her husband. Sometimes
she would come into the kitchen and cry quietly after a particularly bitter argument.

"I am sorry, Ma," I said, the first time this happened.

She lifted up her head and stared at me with so much con-
tempt that I knew I had stepped out of line. Afterwards, I would
keep quiet and avert my eyes, just like other housemaids who
saw husbands beat their wives or bring home women while their
wives were away at work.

I could have told her that her husband loved a clean house
more than he would ever love any woman but it was not my place.
I often thought that worry would age her faster than anything
else, worry at not being good enough or at least as good as her
husband expected her to be. She would shout back at him, but he

had perfected the art of needling far better than she ever would. When she turned on me, I knew she only needed an outlet for her frustration. I was willing to be that vent. They sent me to school, they fed me well, Mummy spoke kindly to me when her husband was not pricking her with pins, and Ikenna was a delightful child.

Ikenna was five when I came to live with them, and, in caring for him, my experience with my half-sister and half-brother came in handy. I was the one he called for when he had nightmares. Mummy would come running to my room at the back of the house. I was also the only one who could feed him when he was feverish with malaria. His exhausted mother would hand him over gladly and then proceed to hover over me. Perhaps she did not want to seem useless.

I potty trained Ikenna. Years after, I would think that it may have been the reason why Daddy kept me on: for the singular act of potty training his child. It was well known up and down the street: Daddy's penchant for sacking the help — a seemingly uncontrollable habit of getting six, some said ten, housemaids each year, finding them incapable of meeting his impossible standards, and then proceeding to send them home, sometimes after only a day. It was rumoured that he once sent one home within hours: she was fat, she sweated too much, and she smelt.

When I arrived, Ikenna had refused all efforts to potty train him. At the age of five he preferred the convenience of his underwear over any toilet, no matter where that toilet was or how clean it was. Once, when his father noticed that Ikenna needed to relieve himself, he sent the boy to his room. There, Ikenna stood by the toilet and quietly pooped on himself. Later, I came upon Daddy cleaning the toilet in his son's room. He looked up at me and then went on washing the toilet I had washed that morning, the brush going vigorously, punishingly, against the white bowl. I looked away, my heart trembling. I had cleaned it myself that morning,

I wanted to say. But Mummy said that Daddy wanted to be sure that Ikenna was not avoiding the toilet because it was dirty.

Nothing else had worked — not flogging with the cane, not treats, not threats. Even his teachers had given up, requiring his parents to put a diaper on him, an act which many parents of children of that age would have considered evidence that their child was abnormal, or that they had failed in the school of parenting. That is, until I came, and we began to exchange fairy tales for every pee that found its way into the toilet bowl.

When his father was in one of his perfectionist moods and began to look for ants under flowerpots, Ikenna would come to me in the kitchen, where I would tell him fairy tales — of the goat and the tortoise, of the squirrel whose wise mother stored food in heaven in preparation for a famine, and his favourite, in which the tortoise found a way to eat a large pot of spicy peppers without stopping once by cunningly getting his hosts to allow him to sing while eating. When I discovered how much Ikenna loved my stories, I began to insist that he relieve himself in order to get a story. Where treats, floggings with the cane, and cajoling had not worked, our story-for-pee exchange did.

His parents were grateful. And Daddy let me stay.

Ikenna seemed the only whole person in that house, not letting the tension between his parents bother him. He often said what was on his mind, in the way that only children could.

"How come you are only one class ahead of me when you are so much older?" he asked me once.

I explained that I had had interruptions in my studies and why. "But why would your stepmother not send you to school?"

We had no money, I explained.

"Why do you not have money?"

His questions were endless. He asked them with an open heart, with no preconceptions, just curiosity. Why was my world different from his, was all he wanted to know. I could not give him really good answers when I did not know myself.

He was a precocious, smart child who was reading before he turned four. It was to keep up with his constant reading, and to read the books he placed in my hands every spare minute, that I became a more fluent reader myself. He went to a good school, a better school than mine, and often came home with books that he made me read to him when his mother got tired of his pestering.

My reading improved, exponentially it seemed, and I came top of my class at my school every term. Being an afternoon school, my class was full of houseboys and housemaids, many of them going to primary school late in life, like me. Even so, Mummy was impressed by my report card and my consistency. She suggested to Daddy that I should be sent to the commercial school close by to continue my studies.

Daddy, I think, was less impressed by my report card than my ability to withhold tears as I cleaned the sitting room as many times as he wanted me to on any given day. He agreed.

I was happy. I was not going to be a nurse or a teacher like my father had wished, but I was sure he would be happy that I would be going to school, and perhaps become a typist, even a secretary, as I heard Mummy tell her husband. My path was becoming clear.

I was content with my lot, my potential. Nobody in the household died, as Mama Nkemdilim had predicted when I left for Enugu. I cleaned and scrubbed and mopped and dusted and potty trained, and all seemed to go well. Except that Mummy had been unable to give birth to another child, and had gone from hospital to hospital with no result. Daddy blamed his wife. I thought that if he would stop his nitpicking even for two months, she might stand a better chance. Even I knew that stress was no helper to fertility.

- - - - - - - - - - - -

Chidinma was my friend from down the street, at number 16. She was a housemaid too. We walked to school together — me, tall, lanky, with hardly any spare flesh on me; she, chubby, small and round. At school, we did everything together — we sat in class in adjoining chairs, gossiped together during break, inseparable as the two blades of a pair of scissors joined by a screw. She was about my age, but carried herself with greater self-assurance. She had been in the neighbourhood longer and, because of that, thought she knew more than me. I let her think so — it was easier that way.

"Please come to the back," I pleaded with Chidinma. She was fiddling with the knobs on the big television in the sitting room, trying to get it on.

"Did you not say Daddy was travelling?" she asked, paying no heed to my plea. She watched television in their house and often wondered why I was not allowed to do the same. Nobody had said I could not, but I knew better than to try. My fingerprints on the big dials of the TV might make Daddy go a little crazy.

I managed to draw Chidinma to the kitchen. "Give me a dry glass," Chidinma ordered in the best male tone she could muster. We both laughed.

Daddy was travelling overseas. Mummy had said he had gone to London. She smiled as she said this, a strange glitter in her eyes. And for the past two days Mummy had been happier than in all of the four years I had lived in their house. She asked me more questions about Mama Nkemdilim and Nwokenta than she had since my first interview. I had smelt freedom in the air as I did my chores, almost stopping to sniff it to make sure it was there.

When Chidinma had had a drink of water in a dry cup, we ate some of the yam and vegetables I had made the previous night, digging in with our fingers and polishing the plate. Then, at my insistence, we got to work on our homework for school. I sat on the kitchen floor, pulling up a small stool for a table. Chidinma sat silently by, not working, not hindering. Just quiet. She was waiting for me to finish so that she could copy it in her workbook. Her writing was like the dance of a hen as it scattered the ground in search of food.

The homework was multiplication. Ten times, eleven times, twelve times. I thought we could chant it and maybe that would help.

I started with the ten times table; it was the easiest. "Ten times one, ten; ten times two, twenty; ten times three, thirty." Chidinma got stuck at eleven and refused to try further.

Chidinma's head was blocked — that was the way she described it. "Like a cement block coming down, every time I try to understand this book thing," she laughed, unabashed. Academic knowledge could not find a smooth path into her head. I could learn from the books that Ikenna brought home, but Chidinma could not learn. It was no use, she would say, when I tried to explain things to her as simply as I could: her mind was a slab of cement. "My head," she would say, "is too full of common sense, ako na uche, to take in book knowledge." She did not bemoan her lack of academic ability or envy my endowments. She looked forward to finishing school and going to learn the tailoring trade. "Hmm, I don't know how you will be a tailor if you cannot measure o. Ehn, or how you will calculate your money," I said to her, trying to goad her into trying.

I should have left well enough alone. Chidinma did not care. She laughed, a hearty generous laugh that came from deep within her gut, dimples sinking into both sides of her cheeks.

"Don't worry," she said. "Don't worry, you will calculate my money for me and I will pay."

"No," I told her, standing up for emphasis, "I will be a secretary in a big office, and wear ready-made. You will see."

"Ah, secretary? Okay, after you have won Miss Nigeria. Black beauty. You will walk around half-naked in that thing they wear," she said, referring to the one-piece swimsuit. She stood up to demonstrate, walking like she was on high heels. Her chubby frame with buttocks stuck out comically was the funniest thing to watch.

Unlike my friend, I had retained my slenderness, not out of hunger, for I was fed well, if often worked to the bone. I was going to be tall like both my father and mother.

When I was done laughing, I said, "Do you know that Urenna heard you call me that once? Now he too calls me 'black beauty.'"

"Eeehn," she said, her tone noticeably cooler.

"Yes," I plunged on, heedlessly, seeking every possible chance to speak about her bosses' son. Chidinma thought my crush on Urenna — the only son of his father, a university student and two years older than me — was foolish. She could not see him as I saw him, I mused. To her, he was a chore; to me, he was the world.

"And do you answer when he calls you that?" Her eyes were now on the books that we had abandoned on the floor.

"Ee nu," I said, emphasizing my yes in answer to her question and poking her arm a little, trying to get back to the lighthearted mood of a few moments before. But it was gone and not planning on returning. "It is getting late," she said, gathering her books. "The children will soon be back. Let me go and get lunch ready for them." The children were Ugomma and Njide, Urenna's younger sisters.

I walked with her to the gate and said goodbye. She smiled at me but the easiness was gone; it was a forced smile. "Come and get me when you are ready for school," she said, as she walked away.

I often finished my chores and got ready for our afternoon school before she did. Then I would go down the street to her house to wait for her before heading out for school. She had to fix lunch for the children then wait for their lesson teacher before heading out to school. Ikenna, my ward, stayed on at the house of his headmistress until his mother picked him up in the evening, leaving my afternoons freer than Chidinma's.

I watched her back as she walked back to number 16, buttocks swinging a little, and I thought that it would be sad if I were to lose my friendship with her. It was, after all, our friendship that had led me to Urenna.

CHAPTER THREE

I met Urenna in the month of September. I had started primary six. I was sixteen, on the way to seventeen.

That evening, I checked in to see Chidinma. She had not come to school that day and I thought I would stop by their house on my way back. I hoped that Mummy would not be irate if I was a few minutes late, but I was ready to risk it. It was not like Chidinma to miss school even if she understood little of what the teacher taught. She loved to play oga at break time and tease all the boys in class. Unlike me, she was not shy. She was friends with almost everyone.

Urenna answered the bell at the gate. Chidinma had spoken of him and I had seen him in the photographs his parents placed prominently in their sitting room. He had been in boarding school, and now he was a student at university and came home infrequently. A compact, fair-skinned, not very tall boy with eyes that seemed to caress you when he placed them on you. He wore an afro and a blue shirt, with slim long sleeves, the buttons too far down from the neck, the type that the man who sang that song "Zombie" wore. His name was Fela Kuti and Daddy did not like him, but his music sounded good. Mummy had bought the record but only played it on the turntable when Daddy was not around because Daddy said he was a "rebel" and a "radical." And whatever a rebel or a radical was, Daddy did not like it.

Urenna's voice was deep yet soft when he said, "Kedu?" to my tentative "Good afternoon." My mind registered his politeness and his deep voice. I saw him incline his head to me in questioning. I shook myself from the pleasant assault on my senses and reminded myself why I was there. "I am looking for Chidinma. We go to school together." I wanted to see if she was all right, I was hoping to explain, but my tongue suddenly lost its ability to move in obedience to my thoughts.

"Chidinma has not been feeling well. But I can give her a message. Who do I say is looking for her?" He looked at me quizzically.

I wanted to tell him that he did not know me but that I knew him — Chidinma mentioned him in our conversations. I wanted to say that I had never seen him before but I felt like my insides had known him since I was born.

My tongue was smarter than my beating heart. It simply said my name.

"Nwabulu," he repeated, as if to be sure he could say it right. "She is not very well," he repeated. "But I will tell her you came."

That night as I lay on my bed at home, I thought about our meeting again. I liked the sound of my name on his tongue. I wondered at my silliness and shook myself a little; fantasies and daydreams were journeys that led nowhere. Still, I envied Chidinma, who got to see him often.

Two days later, Chidinma was at school. The malaria, she said, was the worst she had ever had, the fever was like the heat in the

Sahara Desert that Mr Ibe, our social studies teacher had taught us about. Although my friend liked to be dramatic and exaggerate, she had lost a lot of weight in only four days and looked almost as lean as me. While I was feeling her head and neck with my hands, she added in a low voice that Urenna had told her to say hello to me. He had remembered me, I thought wonderingly. Something must have shown on my face, for Chidinma looked at me with a question on hers. Then she laughed. She teased me about my interest in her employers' son.

"Lekwanu love o," she laughed, hitting the top of my blue-pinafored shoulders.

At first, I pretended not to know what she was talking about. Then I laughed. We both knew that it was a cul-de-sac, like the street on which our school stood, our teacher once explained.

Things would have gone on as they always did — do chores, go to school, gossip, sleep, wake up, do it all over — if I had not run into Urenna at the market a couple of months later. I had gone to Abakpa to buy some food for Mummy. I was struggling with the squawking chicken who was flapping its wings as if it knew that its parts were going to decorate a fragrant pot of tomato stew that evening. It was not the best position in which to meet a boy that one liked.

Someone tapped me on the shoulder. I thought it might be a trader trying to sell something else to me. I prepared the sharp end of my tongue. Could they not see that this hen was trying to make its escape from my grip?

I looked back and it was Urenna. *Urenna!* my mind screamed. "Are you going home?" he asked.

I looked on like a fool, my mind emptied of words for a moment. "Would you like a ride?" he said, peering into my face when I did not say anything.

I found my voice. "Yes."

My mind was struggling to organize its contents, otherwise, I asked myself later that night, how could I have said yes? How could I have said yes without thinking that Mummy might see me in his car and ask if she had not given me money for the bus?

I got into the car.

"I came to pick up some gallons of oil for my mother," he said.

"Okay," I said. I could think of nothing else to say.

"I saw the chicken trying to run away from you, so I thought I should offer you a ride before it got away." He smiled. I could not tell if he was teasing me.

What else we spoke about I could not remember. So many things were happening to my senses all at once. I was not often in a nice car. Sometimes I went to church with Daddy, Mummy, and Ikenna, but that was not very often, as they were Anglicans and I was Catholic. More often I went to the market on foot or by bus, hardly ever in an almost brand-new Volvo.

The nearness of him, the musky smell of something that he had put on his skin crowded out reason and memory. I must have answered his questions automatically. But I must have said something that made an impression, I thought later. He began to send me notes in sealed brown envelopes with Chidinma. Books also. I must have said something about liking books.

The notes said nothing too serious. At first. I told Chidinma, but she wanted to see, so I showed her. The first read:

> How are you? I hope school was good today. It was
> nice meeting you at the market. Urenna

That was it. Short. Not really saying anything much. His writing sloped in one direction, as if the wind were trying hard to blow the words to the ground. Yet it made me almost delirious with joy.

I always wrote back in my careful cursive with the letters joining each other at the right places — my *a*'s reaching out to my *m*'s with a hand of friendship. I slipped my own note back in the envelope in which he sent his. My first note said:

> *I am fine. I hope you are fine too. School was fine.*
> *Thank you.*

"What are you thanking him for?" Chidinma asked. She was irritable about being an emissary. She said that I was being foolish. I agreed, but I was happy being foolish.

"Wait until Mummy finds one of those notes, then you will see what will happen," she warned. I took her warning seriously and hid the notes under my mattress. Another note said:

> *I miss you. Can we meet again? Affectionately,*
> *Urenna*

"What does 'affectionately' mean?" Chidinma asked, struggling to read the word. She did not look impressed. I thought it meant something like "like." I told her this, and she curled her mouth in a sneer. The next day, when everyone had left the house, I looked up the word "affectionately" in the dictionary, one of the hardcover books in the sitting room. I walked on clouds after that. But only my friend Chidinma noticed. And she did not think it was a good thing.

"What does he want to meet you for?" she asked.

I did not listen to her suspicion. I was busy formulating ideas about how I could get away.

At first, we would meet for very brief periods after school. The first time this happened, my tongue felt stuck to the roof of my mouth and I could only answer his questions about school, about my teachers. But he did not ask about the people I worked for, Daddy and Mummy, and I did not say much about them.

He would meet me outside the school in the evening after our classes. It was awkward, me walking with him, Chidinma walking on the other side of the road. Both of them acting like they did not sleep and wake up in the same house.

"What does he talk to you about?" Chidinma would ask.

"Nothing much," I would reply. "He asks about school and teachers and the subjects we are taking."

"You know that others," she said, referring to our fellow students, "will soon take notice. Hmm, take the monkey's hands away from the soup before it comes to look like that of a human," she quoted an Igbo proverb. With her nostrils flared in disgust, she asked if I had looked at my face in the mirror lately. As if I did anything else. I wanted to see what he saw when he looked at me. Suddenly, I was unsure of my beauty, the beauty that my mother had bequeathed to me. I saw only my head, which my slim body was growing into, and my breasts, smaller than they should be at sixteen, smaller than Chidinma's. I wondered if I looked like a boy.

But Urenna must not have thought so because, one day, he sent me a note suggesting that we meet in a more private place. I went about my activities with my heart beating, my lips and hands trembling in anticipation.

That day, I left school early. We met at an unfinished building, whose owner had died the previous year, just after he had begun serious work on the house. It was rumoured that he belonged to a cult, which had given him wealth on the condition that he would die as soon as the building was complete. Even though my stepmother called me amosu, a witch, I was afraid of ghosts, of witchcraft, of fetishes of any stripe or colour. But with Urenna, none of that mattered. It was the perfect meeting place because fear drove people away from the building. And it was not far from our street, so I could get home quickly.

That first day, he spread a sheet on a dusty windowsill, and asked me to sit. He stood in front of me and smiled at me. In shyness, I turned my face down. He lifted it up with a finger under my chin.

"At last," he said, "it is just me and you."

"Yes," was all I could whisper.

He kissed me, his tongue gently parting my unresisting lips. His mouth tasted of cigarettes. I had never been kissed before. I was not sure what to do, and I let him show me.

We did not go far on that day. He pulled away from me and began to ask about my work.

"Do you like it in Mrs Obidiegwu's house?"

"It is all right," I said, smiling and looking away. I was a house-maid. He was the son of the house. He would not really know what it was like to work in a place and live and sleep there but still know that it was not home. He would not know, and I could not put it into words. Chidinma said he was spoiled and left his clothes all over the floor in his room. He did not seem spoiled to me. He seemed very mature. But there was really no way he could know what it felt like to serve in a home.

"And do you go back to your village sometimes?" he asked.

This was not a comfortable subject for me — Mama Nkemdilim and the rest of my family. I had not gone to the village in the four years I'd lived with Daddy and Mummy. This was my choice, since they said I could go home at Easter, though never at Christmas. I chose to stay and they seemed pleased. I heard Daddy once say to Mummy: "It is better she does not go. They often forget every good thing they learn in the township after only a few days in the village."

"No," I said, hoping Urenna would not pursue it.

He did not. Instead, he spoke about university and how he was happy being away from his parents' scrutiny, though he was also happy to be home for some holiday and to spend time with me. He kissed me a little more, pressing himself against me. As his hands began to seek my blouse, I became frightened. I remembered Papa Emma in Lagos, his big body falling on top of me, doing painful things to me. I pushed at Urenna's chest a little. He stopped. He seemed puzzled. I prayed he would not be angry with me. But he did not seem to be. He smiled at me.

"Don't worry," he said. "We will have more time."

I wanted to explain that it was not him. It was me. No, it was not me. It was Papa Emma in Lagos. I was getting confused. I shook my head and said, "I have to go."

"Wow, right away? We barely spent any time together. Okay. Don't worry. We will see each other again soon. Maybe in two days?"

I nodded. Anything he wanted. He told me to leave first and he would come later. I glided through the air, giddy with excitement until I stood in front of our gate at number 9. Then I came down to earth, rehearsed my lies, and went in.

Flirting with fire, that was what I was doing. Chidinma warned me. She reminded me about the warnings of our madams. When Mummy gave me my regular sanitary towels, she would say, almost in an aggressive way, "This is Enugu. Men here say sweeter things than sugar. If you open your legs for any man and come back here with a big belly, I will put pepper between those legs and pack you home like fish in a carton.

"I have never had a girl become pregnant in my house, do you hear?" she would assert, her hands pulling on both her ears for emphasis, her version of birth control. I lay on my mattress at night and prayed to the Virgin Mary that I would not get into trouble, but I knew that I had no power to say no to Urenna, and that I did not want that power.

- - - - - - - - - - -

It took two weeks before I succumbed. And when I did, it did not quench my infatuation. Instead, it grew like wildfire in the harmattan season.

"You will be all right," he said, after he had made me lie on the floor. It was uncomfortable, but I hardly felt it. Urenna was gentle. He was persuasive.

"You will be all right," he repeated as he took off my underwear. "You will be all right. I promise I won't come inside you," he said, as he plunged himself into my moist yet unprepared insides.

And I was all right. I was better than all right. Chidinma complained that I was giddy. Mummy grumbled that I was becoming lax. Daddy said that Mummy needed to keep an eye on me, as my cleaning skills were no longer what they used to be.

In those short, furtive meetings, I basked in Urenna's beauty. In my village, only women were described as beautiful in the way that I thought of Urenna, women with round, smooth cheeks and curvy figures that could keep a man from going to work, enenebe eje olu. But this was how my eyes saw Urenna, as beautiful, with his slender smallness, his assiduously groomed and oiled afro. His nose stood straight, not like my round one, which had made only a half-hearted attempt to rise up and then fallen back to the floor of my face. His eyes were dense and enticing, his lips generous and perfectly shaped, as if their maker spent hours drawing the perfect outline for them. When they nibbled my ears, I forgot all my sorrows, all the outstanding chores — indeed anything besides the nameless pleasure they offered. He was short, shorter than me. I was a tall girl. Yet he seemed confident of his place in the world. And this comforted me.

In that dark, uncompleted building, we talked about everything. I told him about my mother and father and their love. He spoke about the burden of being an only son and his father's outsized expectations of him. I told him about my stepmother and her cruelty. He told me about his desire to paint, to be an artist, and how he was forced by his father to study law at the university. I told him about my plans to be a typist or a secretary in the civil service, how my father had wanted me to be a nurse or a teacher.

Sometimes, his face went blank when I told him stories about the village, about my wild dreams, dreams that I did not know *how* or even *if* they would come true, dreams like having a big house here in Independence Layout and a family like his.

We made no long-term plans for our lives together. We did not need to. Today, this very minute, was enough for us. When he drew me into his arms, I went from being just a housemaid to a girl experiencing a man's love.

At first, I was scared. It was wrong, I said. But he reassured me. He was being careful, he said. Nothing would happen, he told me, because he was careful to pull out in time. The spilling of his seed outside, sometimes on my lap, made me love him even more. I felt my heart expand with love, I told Chidinma, growing so large I could hardly keep it within my chest. She worried about my silliness and melodrama, and asked where I had left my head. Still, she wanted to hear every detail. I told her what I could tell, but kept some for myself to savour at night after my chores.

After the holidays, Urenna went back to the university. Luckily, it was in Enugu, so he came home often. If his parents wondered at this or spoke to him about it, he did not say. Sometimes, he came straight from the university midday to our house. Sometimes, we would go to their house if he was sure that no one except Chidinma was home. We took risks. There were times I was sure we would be caught. Once, I had come into the kitchen to get some water, when I heard his mother's voice. She had come home unexpectedly. She was walking from the sitting room to the kitchen. I darted behind the electric cooker and crouched there, my heart beating fast. She must have heard my heart running like Mama Nkemdilim's female goat when chased by the male, I thought — frantic, anxious, loud. But she merely opened the fridge, took something out, and left.

Another time, Urenna was at our house when Mummy had come home from work with a headache. I was frantically sending him away, but not before Mummy came to the gate to see who it was. He made up a story about his mother thinking of setting up a meeting of all the women on the street and wanting to find out who might be interested.

"That arrogant woman, carrying around her big buttocks as if shit does not come out of it," said Mummy, when he left. "She should have come here herself, but no, Madam High and Mighty is too busy to bother," she hissed, while I hoped that my heart would quiet its dance of fright.

I wished I had Urenna's freedom to come and go as I pleased. But my excuses for leaving the house had begun to make Mummy irritable and suspicious. Sometimes I skipped classes and left school earlier than closing time. Chidinma covered for me as much as she could to the class teacher, but it put a strain on her and on our relationship. I suspected that there was a little jealousy mixed in too, especially now that it seemed I was getting away with the impossible.

In the evenings, Ikenna would read stories from books to me, while I told him folk tales I had heard in the village. "And they lived happily ever after," he would say of Sleeping Beauty and the prince. My own stories had realistic endings: the tortoise got his due — a cracked shell and a sealed throat — for trying to deceive the other animals and eat all the food meant for them; the beautiful girl who spurned all the good men seeking her hand ended up marrying a spirit with seven heads. But in Ikenna's story, Cinderella, an orphan with a cruel stepmother, dared to go to the party and was rewarded with marrying the prince.

I could not tell how my story, of the housemaid and the heir to number 16 Trinity Avenue, Independence Layout, Enugu, would end, but with hope in my heart I tried not to think too far ahead.

CHAPTER FOUR

The morning came to Enugu bright and sunny and cheerful. Except in our household. I was watering the Ixoras when Daddy came storming out of the house, briefcase in hand. He walked briskly, his angry words punctuated with spit sprayed into the air. If anybody else had sprayed spit like that, Daddy would have run to find some disinfectant. I ducked my head, hoping this would prevent him from seeing me and issuing one of his impossible commands. But luck was not my friend this morning.

"Nwabulu," Mummy shouted, "come here, osiso," indicating that I was to hurry. I imagined that even the neighbours who lived at the end of the street could hear her.

I dropped the water hose and ran in before Daddy — who was now looking at me, no doubt thinking up hidden dusty windows, non-existent weeds at the back of the yard, imaginary rubbish in the gutters in front of the house — could say a word. But he ignored me, and went to the car. When I heard the car door slam, I turned around and ran to open the gate.

"Why is this not working?" Mummy stood in the middle of the kitchen holding up the top of a blender. She was sweating profusely, even though the morning had not yet met the full wrath of the sun. The wind was drying out everything in its path but Mummy's face.

"I don't know, Ma," I said quietly.

"What do you mean, you don't know?" she shrieked. Anger did not look good on Mummy. The veins in her fair face stood out, her new braids looked like snakes crawling slowly in different directions, and her lips, painted with the bright red lipstick reserved for work and church, seemed out of place, as if screwed on by force. She looked a little like the witch Ikenna had been reading to me about from his storybook the night before. It could be — and this was not the first time the thought had occurred to me — that this was the reason why her husband could not control his cursing when they quarrelled. But, when she was happy, she was a pretty woman, elegant in her svelte tallness, inclined to be at peace with the world, including me. Until her husband came home.

"When I used it the other day, it was working, Ma." What kind of trouble was looking for me this morning? Was it not time that Madam went to work?

"Stop turning your head this way and that like tolotolo," she shouted at me as I peered behind her, trying to see if I had left the bucket of water with which I had been mopping the floor.

I did not take offence at being called a turkey so early in the morning. Nor did I say that she already knew that the blender had stopped working because she had tried to grind some tomatoes in it the day before. She was merely searching for relief from her quarrel with her husband.

"Why did you not clean up the room this morning?" she asked.

This was not unusual. When she was agitated, Mummy would jump from one complaint to the other like Atuocha, the schizophrenic at Abakpa market.

I patiently explained that I did. "He said it did not look clean."

He said? What was new? I wanted to ask her. But my father had not raised me to be stupid, so I was mute.

"Go and scrub it again and don't let me catch you being lazy in this house."

Any laziness I had ever cultivated in my idyllic childhood before my father died had long since been swept, scrubbed, dusted, and cooked out of me. So had any backchatting or sassiness, except when I was gossiping with my fellow housemaids.

I was looking forward to some of that gossip as soon as Mummy left the house. Chidinma would come, and together we would chat about the wicked madams on the street who made their housemaids do chores from sun-up to sundown with no breaks, while they, the madams, slept all day. Like Mrs Udeh, who would order her housemaid, Ebele, to pick up and hand her things that were right by her feet. Or the madams who would not send their maids to school or to learn a trade like they had promised the maids' parents. Like Mama Odinaka, who kept her housemaid at home doing chores all day after promising the housemaid's parents that she would be apprenticed to a tailor. We would talk about fat Mama Nkolika, whose specialty — besides eating — was employing young gardeners and gatemen who did service that went beyond the remit her husband had assigned them. But we would also marvel over Papa Obinna, who lived in the last house on the street, number 22, the one with the Gmelina trees, who checked the homework of their houseboy, Ogechukwu, every day. Then we would switch to the maids who beat the children of their madams without mercy, and somehow got the children not to talk; the maids who wore their madams' clothes when their madams were out and were never found out; and Theresa, who served Madam Beer Parlour, and who managed to shut down her madam's business by selling all the cartons of beer in the woman's store. There was so much to exclaim and clap hands over in excitement. But mostly, I looked forward to talking about Urenna.

A smile came to my face automatically, as it always did, when I thought about him.

"Why are you smiling?" Mummy shouted.

I'd brought that one on myself.

"You think I am a joke, eh?" She smacked me on the head before I could step back. Even I agreed that there was no reasonable explanation for my smile.

"I have told you this before and I will say it once more — if you are tired of living here, of getting good food and education, you pack your things and go back to your mother. You will not destroy all the things in my house. None of these things walked in here on their feet; they were bought with money obtained with sweat. Before you leave for school this afternoon, make sure you scrub this house and wash the toilets. I did not bring you to the township to laze about and make me poor."

And with that, she stomped off to her room, presumably to get her car keys and drive off in a huff. I sighed and hoped that her red Volkswagen would start this morning, otherwise pushing the car and begging passersby to help us would be added to my list of chores.

I stood in the kitchen waiting for my day to begin. Waiting to meet Urenna.

- - - - - - - - - - - -

Later, Chidinma came to stand beside me at school. She listened to me talk, but did not laugh at me as she was wont to do when I spoke about Urenna. Instead, she bent to scratch her legs. She had not put any oil on them and the harmattan made the scratches turn nearly white on her dark, dry skin. She did not have a message from Urenna. There was something else on her mind beyond our budding, foolish romance.

She was silent for a while — a very unlikely behaviour. Usually her mouth would be working overtime trying to give me all the gossip, the word on the street, and what Urenna's parents were discussing in their bedroom while she was cleaning their toilets. Her round face was solemn, and her eyes were worried. Was she about to be dismissed? I would not have thought so. She took really good care of the children and they were very fond of her. There was something motherly, nurturing, comforting, about Chidinma. She had been with Daddy and Mummy for a long time, six, seven years — a lifetime in housemaid years. She had told me that they would have loved to send her to secondary school, but Chidinma had no head for books. Like me, at seventeen she was too old for elementary six. Unlike me, who had had several interruptions in my school years, she had already repeated many classes and would often joke that she had only managed to get to the last year in elementary school because the teachers had grown tired of seeing her face. When we finished, she would go and learn the sewing trade, while I study shorthand and typing, hoping for that job with the government. I told her often that she would make my clothes for free when she became a tailor. She laughed, but I knew she would do it for me, as I would do anything for her.

I knew Chidinma's ambitions were more realistic than mine. She was the fourth child in her family; there were seven of them. Her brother, the first child, her sister, another brother, and Chidinma had all been sent out by their parents to work as help in homes from the time they were ten. Chidinma often told me in those days how she and her elder siblings were working hard to make sure that they could be "settled." That way, the younger children would not have to work as help. Her sister, Uzoma, had succeeded. She was the first to be settled. She had lived with her madam in Enugu for eight years. During that time, there had been no complaints. She did not steal; she was respectful; she did her work well; she did not complain about the Christmas holidays when she could not see her parents. And she had been rewarded at the end of it with a year of sewing apprenticeship and then a sewing machine. She had started her shop, and, in no time, she married.

Even if she was dismissed, Chidinma had somewhere to go, a place to start from. I had no one.

"What is the matter?" I asked at last, when I could no longer contain myself.

"Someone touched Ugomma." It was an outburst; it had been sitting on the edge of her tongue and it came tumbling out with no adornment or explanation.

"How do you mean?" I asked, sensing immediately what this was about, but a little confused as to how it could be. "Who?" I continued when she was silent. "Was it Okechukwu?" Okechukwu was the new houseboy whom Urenna's parents got to do the cleaning, sweep the compound, trim the flowers, and those sorts of chores, so that Chidinma could focus on taking care of Njide and Ugomma. Unlike Chidinma, he came and went and did not live in the house. Why would he touch Ugomma?

"No, Mr Nzom, the lesson teacher." Mr Nzom had been hired to give the children private lessons at home.

"Ehn?" I screamed. "What exactly did he do?"

She stared at me for a second. "You know, like this." She made a gesture with her finger. "She said he also asked her to touch him."

"What? Has he gone mad? When was this? Did she tell Mummy?"

She looked around to make sure no one had heard me. We were standing at the end of the corridor; the other students did not seem to be paying any attention to us.

"No, she has not told her mother. She only told me. She said it has happened twice. I was at school on those occasions. She feels that she has done something wrong."

"Nonsense," I said. "It is the idiot, the goat, the onukwu, who does not know how good he has it; it is he that deserves to be stripped naked and walked through the streets like they do to thieves in my village."

I thought of the lanky, hungry-looking Mr Nzom, whom I had seen on a couple of occasions in Chidinma's house. Once, I had taken the risk of going to Urenna's room; we had come out together, and there sat Mr Nzom, perhaps waiting to teach the children. He said hello to Urenna and smiled at me. There was speculation in his hungry, Uriah Heep–like smile. Creepy, I remembered thinking.

I thought now of him telling that little girl of seven — or was it six? — to touch him, and something came up in my throat.

"What will you do?" I asked my friend.

"I don't know how to tell Mummy Urenna," Chidinma said.

"What do you mean? Will you let him continue this?" I fumed. How did these rich people raise children who could not tell them anything? "What mouth would I employ in the service of passing across that information?"

I knew her — she could be shy and timid when you did not expect her to be. Like when a teacher called on her to answer a question in her class, her brash all-knowingness would disappear like a rat that met the house owner.

"But you cannot let it continue."

She nodded, but did not volunteer when or how she might tell Mummy. Mummy was a good employer, but she was a busy woman who had a top position in a bank. She had little time for her family. She could be brusque and short. Sometimes, to hear Chidinma tell it, the only thing she wanted was an efficient household — place kept clean, soup stored in freezer, her husband's clothes washed and ironed, and children in bed by eight o'clock. So long as things were taken care of, she left the running of the house and the nurturing of her children to Chidinma. Now, Chidinma felt responsible for this situation too.

Chidinma leant against the wall, once white but now brown with dust and the dirt of schoolgirls' and schoolboys' fingers. Her face was worried. I thought for a while. This affected me in a way I could not explain: I thought of Papa Emma fondling me and all my sense of justice came rushing from my toes up through my body into my heart. It caused an almost painful, choking sensation there.

"Tell Urenna," I said. "Tell him and he will take care of it." I said this with full assurance — once Urenna knew, he would take care of it.

"But you can tell him," Chidinma whined. "Tell him, inugo? This thing is too bad to speak about."

I did not spend time weighing why Chidinma would not tell Urenna. "I know what to do," I told her. "Leave it to me. I will tell him."

She nodded, eager to have someone else take care of this smelly situation.

"He gave me this to give to you." She passed me a piece of paper. Now that she had put her load on my head, she felt free, it seemed, to talk about my dalliance with her employers' son. She had ceased telling me that it was dangerous, and foolish, and unlikely to go anywhere good. She had stopped talking about how he was only using me, and asking if I had not seen the girls from university who came to visit him. She had stopped telling me that Urenna's mother would report me to Mummy once she found out, and that she was bound to, and that Mummy would send me home after giving me a thorough lashing with the cane. She had now put away her fear of Urenna's mother sending her home for being complicit in what should not be: a relationship between a housemaid and the only son of a rich family. Four months of subterfuge, hundreds of love notes, and weeks of secret meetings later, she had resigned herself to my stupid but exciting love affair with Urenna.

I opened the folded paper. It was another love note, asking me to meet him at our usual place. How many times had I thanked God that I could read well — well enough to read his flowery notes — and at the same time regretted the fate that placed me in primary school, many rungs of the ladder below Urenna, who was in his first year of university? In this one, he said he missed me. I had not seen him in a whole week; I missed him too. Although Chidinma had once said that the sons of rich men never marry housemaids.

After Chidinma told me about Mr Nzom, I could not wait to see Urenna. That evening, as I prepared to sneak out to meet him, Mummy was watching Zik on the television, and gesticulating at him. "Leave these people o, they will disgrace you, Zik — you are on a much higher level than they are," she was saying loudly as if they, the political candidate and the party people, could hear. Zik, the first president of Nigeria, must know what he was doing, I thought, and it would be nice for an Igbo man to be president. Maybe then water would run in my village and we would not need to go to the stream for it but have taps flowing inside the house the way they did in Lagos.

I thought that I could go out and be back quickly while the program had Mummy singing and making commentaries on politicians, their lives, and wives. For once, neither of us was worrying about Daddy and which part of the house might not be perfect. He had travelled to Lagos on business. So Mummy might spend longer than usual watching the television, which gave me time to sneak out. I asked for money to buy tinned tomatoes. She obliged.

When Urenna and I met at our spot, we embraced each other — he, boldly, like I belonged to him. I had to tell him what Chidinma had told me that day at school. It was not the stuff that romantic evenings were made of, but it had weighed heavily on me all afternoon.

"Mr Nzom has been touching your little sister," I blurted out as soon as I left his arms.

"What?"

"Yes, Ugomma told Chidinma," I said and waited.

"He has been fondling a little girl when he should be teaching her English and maths? What nonsense! Mummy must hear this. The man has to be dismissed and reported to the police!"

Were those kinds of things ever reported to the police, I wondered. Did children ever get justice for such awfulness? Maybe the children of the rich did. At least Ugomma had Urenna. I thought of Lagos: Papa Emma, going up and down on top of me in painful thrusts; Madam's knife going up and down; me, screaming into the night. The memories came back as fresh and strong as morning palm wine.

I saw Urenna looking at the scars on my hand. He knew what I was thinking because I had told him the story, the first person I had told since my stepmother's angry incredulity all those years ago.

"Yes, please tell your mother. Tell her to find a female teacher for them. Tell her to tell Chidinma to stay in the room when they are being taught. Tell her to let the girls know that they can tell her anything, that it is not Ugomma's fault," I said urgently.

Urenna's face was dark; anger made it look red, thunderous. Yet he stroked my hands, up and down, up and down, as he digested the news and pondered what to do. He was gentle.

"I will," he said, responding to the force of my words. He drew me into his arms and we stood there in silence, our meeting coloured by the situation. When we sat together we were brooding instead of engaging lightly and happily in love talk. He did not reach for my underwear in the dark; our mutual disgust over Mr Nzom contaminated the atmosphere.

It was not long before I had to go. I had rushed out on the excuse that I had to buy tinned tomatoes for jollof rice that evening. We took leave of each other regretfully.

- - - - - - - - - - - -

I did not hear anything for a week. Chidinma had no news for me and no notes from Urenna. Mr Nzom, she told me, had not shown up on Tuesday, but had been there on Wednesday, and then had not come for the rest of the week. Urenna had gone back to school on Thursday. I was by turns anxious and exasperated. Anxious, because I wanted to know what had happened and if Mr Nzom was going to face any punishment. Exasperated, because Urenna should have known better than to keep me waiting for news.

Mr Nzom had not come to work, Chidinma told me the next week. It was safe to think then that he had been dismissed. But what had happened?

Meanwhile, it was almost time for our First School Leaving Certificate Examination. I stayed up late at night after doing my chores, studying for the exam and wondering how Urenna was doing. I resisted the temptation to look at the novels Urenna had given me — two Agatha Christies and *Things Fall Apart* — because I had promised him I would study. When I studied for English and maths, I took care not to peek at the answers at the back of the practice book Daddy had bought me, until I had attempted the questions. I revised the social studies questions. Who is the Head of State of the Federal Republic of Nigeria? *His Excellency, Major General Olusegun Obasanjo,* I wrote. Who is the Governor of Anambra State? *A colourless man,* I wanted to write — that was what Daddy called him. I did not know if colourless meant that he did not have a colour or if it meant something else. He was clearly not colourless. He was dark skinned, as the picture of him at the teachers' office showed, almost as dark as me. There was nothing in the questions about the new political parties that I overheard Daddy and his friends discussing. Nor was there anything there about the new constitution that my teacher, Mr Azari, kept talking about with so much enthusiasm. Nobody in the class understood or really cared why it mattered that there was a new constitution and that we soon would be seeing the end of military rule and the beginning of democracy. It would certainly not change the amount of food one was allowed to eat or the number of chores that had to be done. At night, I fell asleep reciting the names of the states, their governors, and the local governments in my state — Anambra State, Lagos State, Oyo State, Bauchi, Kano, Kaduna — and woke up to my chores and to wondering when I would see Urenna and what had happened with Mr Nzom.

One evening, about two weeks later, as we walked to school, Chidinma passed me a note from Urenna. We were to meet at the usual place.

I was eager and anxious to hear what had happened. Urenna told me he had spoken to his mother. Naturally, he said, she was angry and disgusted. She waited to talk to Mr Nzom when he came to teach the next day and confronted him. Mr Nzom did not deny it. He apologized, Urenna said. But Urenna, who was there for the confrontation, said he was angry that Mr Nzom would be let go after his apology, with nothing more by way of punishment, not even a threat to report him to the police.

So, Urenna followed him outside and told Mr Nzom that they would report him to the headteacher at the school where he taught.

Mr Nzom had been frightened; Urenna could see it on his face.

And then, Urenna said, Mr Nzom had sneered at him. "Well, I guess we would have to report you too to the madams of the house girls you sleep with."

At that moment, hearing his words, fear rose from my heart and went down my body. People knew about me and Urenna; the thought rang through my head like a bell in a bad dream. People knew.

It was a short meeting that evening, even shorter than usual. Urenna was tense. We did not discuss when next we might see each other. There was too much else on our minds.

For days, I waited for Mummy to call me in for interrogation. But nothing happened. Life went on as usual. Except that I did not see or hear a word from Urenna for weeks.

"Maybe he has forgotten me," I said to Chidinma. I mopped my brows. The heat of the day seemed too much punishment for all that I had to endure.

"Would that not be best?" she retorted. "Eh, I am asking you, would that not be better? Is it not time for you to come back to your senses? Where is this thing with Urenna going to get you? Maybe in a pot of hot, sticky okra soup? Or maybe in Mama Nkemdilim's wicked grip when his parents or Daddy and Mummy find out?"

I knew she was not trying to be mean. But her words felt too harsh to me. It was true that the possibility of returning to my stepmother in disgrace was enough to put the fear of hellfire in me. But what I wanted to know more than anything else was whether Urenna had been with other housemaids.

"I do not think so," Chidinma said when I asked her. "And you know I have lived there for a long time."

I felt comforted, my jealousy and suspicion quelled. Yet my heart ached like the toothache I had had years ago in the village before the tooth fell out — the pain by turns sharp and over-whelming, then dull and heavy in the middle of my chest.

"I know you will not like to hear this. Truth can be as painful as a thorn," she said, sounding wiser than her years. "But you and Urenna must stop this thing." As she spoke it was as though she was pulling out a shard of broken bottle from my heel — painful but necessary.

I wept for hours in the middle of the night, sobbing quietly so that no one would hear. Perhaps it was best, as Chidinma had said. Perhaps it was best, I repeated to myself. But it was too late. And I had no way to know this at the time.

CHAPTER FIVE

Daddy called me into the sitting room one Saturday evening. Panic came but went quickly; it was a Saturday and I had cleaned and mopped, scrubbed and dusted. I even got Ikenna to take a nap, an increasingly difficult task. He was now playing ncho, a game I had taught him, while I prepared supper.

"How was your exam?" Daddy wanted to know. He was drinking water from the dry glass I had given him only moments before. Mummy was sitting beside him. She smiled at me. They looked peaceful together in that moment.

"It was fine, sir," I said, wondering what was wrong.

"You think you will pass?"

"Yes, sir."

We, Chidinma and I, were waiting for the results of our First School Leaving Certificate Exams. I was confident I would pass; Chidinma was sure she would fail. Pass or fail, the release of the results would mean taking the next step into our future.

"That is good. We will send you to the commercial school on Dhamija Avenue. We have told Mr Hyacinth to tell your mother."

"Thank you very much, sir." Although that had always been my hope, nothing definite had been said before now.

"We like your work here. Keep working hard, do you hear?"

"Yes, sir."

Daddy seemed content, unusually expansive. It was no surprise that Mummy was happy too. I allowed their benevolence to envelop me. I felt relief, even though the results of the exams were yet to be released. Now I knew what I was doing for sure. In 1978, I would be learning typing and shorthand, getting ready to be a secretary.

Chidinma would be happy for me. I would tell her when we walked to church tomorrow.

There was only one more thing that I waited for. Urenna. Waiting for him to say yes or no. To go forwards or back. An uncertainty had settled into our relationship after Mr Nzom's revelation. His words seemed to have poured cold water over Urenna's love for me, I thought sometimes, chilling its fervour like hot spicy pepper soup that had been diluted with too much water. He made little effort to see me, certainly not as often as he had done in the past. When we did see each other, he was in no hurry to touch me. True conversation — that rubbing of hearts that had so delighted me and made me happier than the rubbing of bodies — had moved house. When I tried to probe, Urenna said that I worried too much. He said that I was no longer in school and that meeting as we had been doing was dangerous; that he was concerned not to get me in trouble. This was why he no longer dropped in at midday. He stopped bringing me books and did not talk about how well he thought I would do at school.

There was an unfamiliar dishonesty in him. I think it was this, more than anything, that I disliked — this obstinate refusal to acknowledge that something was wrong, this determination to speak less than truth. And yet, I pined for him, longed for those notes that came so rarely these days. Chidinma had told me that lately a girl from university had been paying him regular visits. Jealousy threatened to eat me, swallow me whole. Was this what kept him away, his eyes averted from me?

Perhaps I should have been more concerned with my body, with the changes that forced themselves on my consciousness as vigorously as I tried to push them away. I had no symptoms, just a knowingness that something was different. I had never kept track of my periods, but I knew that I had missed at least one. I knew that I was in trouble.

I kept this knowledge inside of me as much as I could. It would become real as soon as I said it out loud. And I did not want it to become real, for then fearful things would happen. I kept it inside, stuffed like clothes in a too-small bag, until I no longer could. One day, when Chidinma came over to the house, I took her to my room and told her.

"Chidinma, I think I am pregnant." My eyes welled up with tears.

She was stunned. I saw shock and disbelief and anger and myriad other emotions come upon her face.

"Mbanu, no, are you sure?"

Now that I had said it, I was even surer of it. She held me while I cried. "I knew this was trouble; I knew this was dangerous," she said, looking ready to cry too. "I thought you said he was being careful."

"Yes," I said simply. I could not bear to remember. I just cried, and Chidinma cried with me.

"You will tell Urenna, won't you?" she said finally.

Neither of us had any faith in what would happen when I told him, but there was nothing else to do. I wrote a note and gave it to Chidinma. For the first time, I was the one requesting a meeting. I even suggested a day and time. Perhaps this surprised him, for he did not reply with silence or empty notes saying he was very busy, as he had to my other notes in which I'd asked how he was and given him snippets of news. He sent a note with my friend. It said that he would see me on the day planned.

That day, he hugged me and immediately began to caress me. Even though my heart was not in it — I had far too much on my mind — I obliged him. Afterwards, we lay on the floor, on top of the newspapers he had brought for the hard cement. His eyes were closed and his breathing even, but I knew he was not sleeping. I blurted it out. The news came out differently from the speech I had rehearsed so many times to myself.

"I am pregnant."

His eyes flew open, and I could read shock in them before they turned opaque. A lustre left his face and never came back after that.

"Are you sure?" He sounded frightened. And this made me more afraid.

I thought over his question. That was what I had asked myself too at first. He had always ejaculated outside me. Always, without exception. He had told me he did this to protect me from this very situation, in my mind at least until we got married.

"Yes, I think so," I said, a little timidly. His voice was cold, distant, as if he were far away and not on the same hard, uncomfortable floor as me. "I have not had a period for two months."

"Hmm," was his reply. By this time, he was sitting up, looking away from where I was still lying, half-naked and awkward.

The conversation was not going as it had gone in my imagination.

"Don't worry, I will take you to a doctor." His eyes stared at me, but I could tell he was not really looking at me; he was thinking.

"A doctor?" I asked. I almost heaved a sigh of relief; he was taking me to a doctor to make sure I and the baby would be all right.

"No, no, no," he said, a little harassed, almost angrily. "No, not a doctor. Em, I know this woman who some of my friends have used. She will give you something to drink that will remove it quickly and no one will know." He tapped his fingers on his lap now as if in thought. "Yes, no one will know."

A current like an electric shock ran through me. Did he say he would take me to a woman to remove the baby? Our baby?

"But ..." I began, sitting up.

"But what?" he asked, frowning.

"Am I not keeping the baby?"

"Do you want to keep the baby?" he asked. Now he was putting on his clothes as if in a hurry, looking everywhere but at me.

"Yes," I said, wondering if I could relax now. Perhaps he was testing me. He must know that was wrong, so utterly wrong. And it was our baby, the baby we had made together. I knew it would be difficult; Mummy and Daddy would send me away. Urenna's parents would not be happy, but there must be something we could do.

"You cannot keep the baby. What will you tell Mrs Obidiegwu?" he said quietly and patiently, as if lecturing a three-year-old who was demanding a sharp knife for a toy.

Confused, I stared at him.

"What will you tell your stepmother?" His face now wore a sneer. He did not wait for an answer. "Get dressed," he told me brusquely.

"I will talk to someone this evening, and I will find out about that woman. You must remove that thing as quickly as possible."

After my meeting with Urenna, I repented from my stupidity. Of course, I would have to remove the baby. Urenna was still a student; he had no money. Besides, his parents would never allow him, their only son, to marry a housemaid. I told Chidinma, but she had no solution for me. She said I had to be careful. We agreed that it was best that I did as Urenna said. If I insisted on keeping the baby, Mummy and Daddy would find out. They would send me home. I had nothing to give a baby. And I could not imagine the shame Mama Nkemdilim would pour on me.

I cried myself to sleep each night. It felt to me that death itself could not be as hard as the life I was forced to endure, knowing what I had to do.

I waited for Urenna.

But Urenna never did send me to anyone. Instead, after a week, he sent me a note. It said that he was travelling and would not be back for a little while and that he hoped I would take care of "that thing."

Ikenna saw me crying in my room. He asked, "Are you all right? Did Daddy make you cry?"

That made me cry harder. But I made him promise not to tell his mother that I was crying. I wanted to keep my secret just a little longer. I had been foolish. This knowledge did not galvanize me to action; instead, it made me numb. Numb with the knowledge that soon I would be found out and that I had no recourse. Not even with Chidinma did I discuss it, though she was clearly worried for me. The title song of NPP, one of those new political parties, rang in my head — "Ebe ka anyi ga-ebinye aka, ebe esere mmadu, ebe esere mmadu ebe esere mmadu." That jingle played on the radio and in my head incessantly. Vying for the position of governor or president seemed so much easier than dealing with the position I had found myself in.

"Are you putting on weight?" Mummy asked me one day. If I was not so afraid I would have muttered, like I did when

Chidinma asked me the same question, that hunger gnawed at me as never before, and that I walked through the kitchen several times a day looking for leftovers, anything at all to eat.

I did not have the bouts of nausea and endless vomiting that Mama Nkemdilim had had with her children. My slender figure had hidden its secret well. But I knew that my breasts were bigger, that there was a small curve to my belly that had not been there before, and that, even though I still got my monthly ration of sanitary towels from Mummy, my monthly visits had ended months ago — I was not even sure when. I still could not be called fat, but it was obvious to the discerning eye that I was bigger than I used to be. My clothes clung to me, announcing the changes my body was undergoing.

"No, Ma," I responded. I saw her eyes narrow at me. I knew that trouble was waiting for me.

It was almost another month before anything else was said. This time, it was Daddy. He stood watching me as I cleaned the sitting room. His staring made me uncomfortable, not only because I worried, as I had in the past, about whether his perfectionist gaze was picking out my ineptitude but because I now had something to hide. He must have said something to his wife, for Mummy came out a few minutes later and summoned me to the dining room.

"Are you all right?" was how she began.

"Yes, Ma." I had a pounding headache. But that did not count. I knew what she was asking.

"Are you sure?" she insisted.

"Yes, Ma."

Then she came to the point. "When was the last time you saw it?"

I knew what "it" was, but I did not speak. I remembered the first day I'd come to the house — how she had come to my room with the sanitary pads in a blue packet and how I had not known what they were but was happy that I knew what the "blood at the end of the month" was.

I could not speak. Instead, I let my eyes roam to an old black-and-white picture of Daddy's parents, which took pride of place in the centre of the wall, next to where Mummy was standing. They sat side by side, Daddy's parents, staring at the photographer, the woman smiling a little, the man serious. They were dressed in the inimitable makeup of youth, and in old-style clothes — the man in a suit that looked a little too big on him, the woman in a dress and hair braided with black thread. I must have seen this picture thousands of times, dusting, cleaning, serving guests, appearing to answer a query before Mummy, sitting on the soft red couch, pretending to watch TV as I sipped water from a glass when my employers were away. My eyes must have fallen on these people from another time so often that I ceased to see them. But today I desperately stared at their image, etched in time.

"Have you gone deaf?" she shouted when I did not respond.

"Last month," I lied.

"Last month?" she asked with disbelief in her face, her tone.

"Yes, Ma." It was an untruth. After a fashion. I truly was not sure what the truth was, how long those periods had gone missing.

"Stand up straight. Let go of the chair," she commanded.

I released the chair that I had been leaning on, partly because I was tired — I got tired so easily these days — and partly because I hoped to hide how tight-fitting my clothes had become. I sucked in my stomach, scared, unable to pray.

Mummy stared at me with wide-open eyes. I saw when the truth came into them, like a blind woman seeing for the first time.

"Ewu Chi m o!" she exclaimed. "Nwabulu! Nwabulu, are you pregnant?"

I looked down at my feet. I had not prepared for this question, this moment. I had no plan for handling it.

"No, Ma." It came out wooden, sounding like the lie that it was. She came to me, walking quickly past the two chairs by the side of the table, chairs that remained empty when Mummy and Daddy ate together as a family because no other child had come since Ikenna. I did not know her intent until she pulled up my dress with a sharp movement.

The small round curve was obvious, even though I had kept my belly sucked in. It spoke the truth my mouth had denied.

"Hey!" she shouted. "Chineke! Who did this, eh? Who got you pregnant? Is this how you reward me for all the training you have received here?"

Tears fell from my eyes unbidden and made their way down my face. Ikenna came out of his room and, perceiving that all was not well, ran and put his arms about me. "Mummy," he asked, "is Nwabulu all right?"

She did not wait for me to answer. Instead, she said, "Ikenna, go to your room," pointing in that direction. He made to argue but the look on her face sent him scampering away. Then she burst out, "Emeka, Emeka, come."

Daddy came. He simply stared at me when his wife told him. I had never seen him control himself like that before. His cold, silent gaze whipped me more than his wife's hysterical anger.

"Who got you pregnant?" he asked.

"Urenna," I said. Afterwards, I would think that it was the fear of the cold fury in his eyes, his rigid, controlled body, that made me tell. I had not planned to.

"Who is Urenna?"

I explained.

"What?" Mummy shouted. "That boy?" I could see her recalling seeing him at the gate those two times.

They made me put on my slippers, and Mummy and I walked to Urenna's house at number 16. Mummy did not complain about the dustiness as she often did. Instead, she railed at me and told me that I had thrown my life away; after all they had done for me, all the opportunities they were giving me to better myself and be useful to my family, here I was carrying a big belly about …

At the black gate, fear overtook me and I almost ran back home. Mummy pressed the bell and waited. I prayed Urenna would not be home.

Chidinma came to the gate.

"Good morning, Ma," she said. I saw that she was trying not to look at me.

"Is your madam home?" Mummy asked.

"Yes, Ma."

We walked into the house. Chidinma led the way.

We stood inside the sitting room, waiting for Mrs Aniagolu. I had been here before many times, sat on the brown leather and watched the big three-legged television with Chidinma. Yet, in my fear, it felt different, strange.

"Good morning." Urenna's mother breezed in with the smell of some perfume. I felt my belly heave in protest. "How are you?" She smiled at her visitor. Her eyes touched on me but slid away. She had seen me before, coming to the gate to get Chidinma for school, but that was all.

"I hope all is well. Please sit."

Mummy sat. I kept standing. No one invited me to sit.

"What do I get you?" I could see that she was curious. She and Mummy were only neighbours, not friends. They did not visit each other. Mummy said that Mrs Aniagolu felt too big because of her career and because her husband ran a brewery. Chidinma said that Urenna's mother thought that Mummy was not friendly.

"Nothing, thank you. It is still a little early. I came to discuss a problem."

"A problem?" A frown came on Urenna's mother's face.

"Yes, you see, we have had this girl with us," Mummy said, gesturing at me, "for over four years. Never a problem before now. But we have just discovered that she is pregnant."

"Hmm," Urenna's mother murmured, still frowning.

"Em," Mummy began and hesitated, "she says your son is responsible. I am not sure what to think, so I thought I should come here and talk to you."

"That is impossible." Mrs Aniagolu's face had taken on a pinched look. "My son is in the university where he meets lots of nice girls. I am not sure why your girl," her eyes raked me in derision, "wants to pin her trouble on him."

"Hmm," was all Mummy said for a moment.

"Urenna is not home," his mother announced. A whole lake of relief poured over me. I could not bear to see him in these circumstances. "I will speak with him when he returns." A tone of finality and a closed look on her face told us that the discussion was over. For now.

Mummy had just got to her feet when the door opened and Urenna came in. He was wearing running clothes and he was sweating. He looked as handsome to me as he was the day I saw him in the Fela shirt and afro.

"Good morning, Mum," he greeted his mother. "Good morning, Ma," he said to Mummy. His face was closed to me, serious.

"Good morning," Mummy said.

Mummy stood up, but waited. She was not going home empty-handed. Urenna's mother looked at her.

"Do you know this girl?" His mother gestured at me.

"Hmm," he said, considering. "She looks familiar." *Me, familiar*, my insides screamed, thinking of the uncompleted building and the hard, uncomfortable floor. "Oh, I see. I remember now." How smooth he sounded, how confident. "I think she has come here for Chidinma."

Was Chidinma going to get in trouble? I wondered.

"She claims she is pregnant and you are responsible," said Urenna's mother. Hers was a tone of complete disbelief.

"What?" Laughter escaped him. "The housemaid? Mum! I can't believe you would ask me that." He looked like he had never seen me before. "Something is wrong. Is she crazy, the housemaid? Do you know me?" he asked me angrily.

In the face of his vehement denial, my tongue refused to move. He was not Urenna. Not the boy who brought me books, who said my name was beautiful. This was a demon in running clothes, his good looks obliterated by anger and hate and lies.

"Could you tell them what you told us?" Mummy said.

I stood there, unmoving, silent, numb with fear and disgust. They were all against me, even Mummy.

After a minute or two, Urenna's mother said, "These girls can be mischievous. I suggest you take her home and question her some more. It is likely that another houseboy has done this." She was dismissing us from her home, all effort at friendliness gone.

After we came back from Urenna's — having left behind his denials, his determination to look everywhere, even at the raging anger of Mummy, everywhere in the world but at me — I sat in my bathroom, the housemaid bathroom at the back of our house, and wept aloud. Mummy had told me that she would not keep me in the house and that I would go back to my stepmother the very next day. I had expected nothing different. But still, my heart felt broken into many pieces.

I heard Ikenna come and hover around outside, heard him say my name, but I did not answer. He waited a little and left. I wept and wept. Tears flowed until I thought blood would come.

Later, I went to the kitchen to get something to feed my belly, which asked for food incessantly now. As I was about to leave, I heard Mummy speaking with Daddy in the sitting room.

"Here I am, trying everything to give Ikenna a brother or a sister. And yet Nwabulu opens her legs once, and she is carrying around a belly. And that boy is denying it. I know he did it."

"It is his word against hers. I will not enter into a wrangle with my neighbours over a girl who lacks common sense." His voice conveyed finality, like he had already closed the door on me. Like I was already with Mama Nkemdilim in Nwokenta and he was interviewing another girl and asking, "Do you shower every day, do you wash your hands when you use the toilet?"

"Idiot," his wife agreed. "And here we were, thinking of her future." I heard her irritation, but I thought that she sounded the way she did when Ikenna hurt himself or asked when he would have a brother. Sad.

With tears coming down, I rushed to my room. I could not stand to hear more.

Later that night, as I packed my things in preparation for going back to the village, I tried to suppress the bitterness that rose in my mouth, the fear that made my heart beat fast and filled my belly with dread, the regret of throwing away an education, a future. I could not even say goodbye to Chidinma, though our eyes had met as Mummy and I left their house. There had been tears in them, though I did not, could not, acknowledge them at the time.

I wiped my eyes now of the tears that poured from them unrelentingly. I put my clothes and the small collection of books in my bag. I did not stop to read the titles of the books. I knew them by heart — *Things Fall Apart*, a simplified version of *Oliver Twist*, another of *Gulliver's Travels*, and Agatha Christie's *Sleeping Murder*.

My packing done, fear felt free to engulf me. Mama Nkemdilim would certainly kill me and my baby. I stopped short at the thought. Baby. I had not thought too deeply about the growing baby in my swelling belly before now. But now that it was out in the open, it crystallized itself into something almost solid. How would I raise a baby? In Mama Nkemdilim's house?

A small sound came at the door. It was Ikenna, my young friend, the one who had taught me to read. He hugged me tightly, tears running down his face. I hugged him back, holding him close as long as I could, until his mother called for him.

He had brought me a book, a present to remember him by: a book of fairy tales.

CHAPTER SIX

Mr Hyacinth came to the house to get me the next day.

"We are very disappointed. We thought we would send her to Commercial School," Daddy told him.

"It is too bad," Mr Hyacinth agreed.

"Let her tell you whose baby it is and how she tried to blame it on the son of our neighbour," Mummy said, with remarkable restraint.

As I walked with Mr Hyacinth, Ikenna ran out and held me. "Nwabulu, please don't go." Tears blinded me as I held him. Mummy came out and took him by the hand and led him back to the house. His wails followed me, yet I could not bear to look back.

I cried all the way to New Market, the dusty place from where we took a bus to the village. A small, dark man who made himself big or small as the occasion demanded, Mr Hyacinth showed little emotion as we boarded the small bus back to Nwokenta.

"Your stepmother will not be happy," was all he said. The very definition of understatement.

When we got to the village, Mama Nkemdilim wailed for all the neighbours to hear. She told him that this had not been her expectation when she agreed to his proposal to send me off to live with Daddy and his wife. She reminded him that he had said they were good people, yet they had dumped me on her in this condition without ceremony and without as much as a backward glance, after five long years.

Who did this to me, she wanted to know. Could he not be made to marry me? Mr Hyacinth was conciliatory. He did not look at me, but I heard the blame in his voice when he said he had never had this sort of situation before, and that he would enquire and let her know what he found. He came back the following weekend and said he had spoken to Daddy and to Urenna's parents. He said that Urenna denied responsibility in vehement terms. These were rich people, he warned Mama Nkemdilim. As he saw it, there was nothing that we could do. His parents said they believed him. We did not have money and could not talk to the police or sue them in court. Even if we could, there was no way to prove that I had spoken the truth. It was best to let the matter lie and live with things as they were.

And so I returned to the red dusty earth of the village. Almost all the roofs were now corrugated, replacing the thatch of the huts I had left behind. People who still lived in mud houses put a modern roof on top of the mud, like the wide, colourful hats Mummy and her friends wore to All Saints Church. Still, Nwokenta was not Enugu; the gulf of development lay wide between them.

My protruding belly, which seemed to have shot out overnight as if it had been waiting for me to be found out, was a personal affront to Mama Nkemdilim. She called me names and let me know that I had done the unforgivable: I chased after men. That was why I was bundled back from Lagos. Now I had gone and given myself a big belly and been bundled back from

Enugu. Where else, she wanted to know from her friend Mama Odinkemma, could I be sent where I would stay put? The moon?

She said she knew that I would come to no good. But she had hoped — how she had desperately hoped, she told anyone who would listen — that I would prove her wrong. Yet here I was, having disgraced myself, cheated myself out of a bright future — had those people not sent me to school? — and humiliated her in the eyes of the world. Here I was, an extra mouth to feed, about to produce yet another creature whose hand would remain perpetually out in the mode of "please give me, give me." She was almost gleeful with having been proved right, and she lost no opportunity to drive it home to me and to anyone who had ears on their head.

I did not blame her. After living in Daddy's spotless home with a toilet that flushed, with the possibility of living there longer while I went to school, after dreaming that I would get a job as a secretary and live in my own home in the city, there was nothing that Mama Nkemdilim said that could rival how much I tortured myself with guilt. I had not just thrown my future away; I had lost Urenna. Had I ever had him? In my mind, I saw him the way he had been that last day, perhaps the way he had always been, how I might have seen him, had I not been blinded by love.

Nothing would blot that memory from my mind, I knew. Not time, not forgiveness. Nothing would erase the way he had denied me before his parents, his eyes averted as if I were beneath his attention. Standing before his parents, who called me a liar and whose defence of their son I could not fault, and my employers, whose anger I could not assail, in that moment, I recalled how he had touched me the first time, had laid me down gently on the rough floor in the dark. I remembered how he had taken up my skirt and told me that he would be gentle and how I had watched him fumble with his fly, how frightened and full of love I was. He would not hurt me, he had said over and over. I believed him and gave myself to him. Completely. It did not hurt as much as I feared that first time — as much as Oga Emma's roughness had — but it did not bring great pleasure; it was over very quickly. But, that time and other times that followed, I had been desperate in my desire to please him. And this caused me shame now, because I remembered his averted gaze and his staunch refusal to throw the briefest of glances at my face that day.

"The housemaid?" he had said, pouring scorn that I never would have thought existed inside him into that word. "I did *nothing* with the housemaid."

The housemaid. He had forgotten my name. Nwabulu. The name he had said was beautiful.

Sometimes, the thought came to me that he had been trying simply to save face before his parents, before Daddy and Mummy. He was after all still dependent on his parents. He was an only son from whom much was expected, certainly more than a dalliance with a housemaid. Perhaps he had been hurt by my exposing him in so embarrassing a manner, with Mummy brandishing angry words and looks. But what about me? Did he think about me and what I was suffering — what I would suffer — in this situation?

— — — — — — — — — — — —

I had done the worst thing an unmarried girl in Nwokenta could do — I had opened my legs to a man and announced it boldly and foolishly with a pregnant belly. Ime nkpuke! I had declared to the world that something essential was lacking in my upbringing and that I lacked chastity. I now would be unable to marry a young man from a good family, for what right-thinking family would want such a girl? What family would let in a girl who had no bloodstained sheets to show after the wedding?

I would bring a bastard in the world who would be laughed at by his peers. If it was a boy, he would have no automatic inheritance of land. He would have to depend on the charity of his grandfather or uncles to get a small piece of land on which to build his own house. Better that it was a girl, for she could marry and hope that someday people forgot how she came into the world. But even that depended on which bold suitor could convince his family that she — the daughter of a wanton, unworthy woman — would not turn out the same as her mother, for these things, as the people of Nwokenta would say, tended to run in the blood.

The best opportunity for a woman such as I had become was to marry an old man as his second or third wife. This might be a man who had no sons and who was hoping that what I had in my belly was a boy. It might be a widower whose wife had died and who had young children who needed a mother. Or it might be an old man, who simply wanted young blood that would be difficult to get otherwise, and who was not averse to taking the baby as an extra. That way, a child would have a name and some protection from the ignominy of being a bastard. A woman in my situation did not refuse such an offer. Indeed, her family would accept thankfully and with relief on her behalf before the words were even completely out of the old man's mouth. It was like selling rotting tomatoes as the evening approaches in the market; one quickly and without much haggling accepts the bid of one of the few remaining, straggling buyers, perhaps one who has waited in the wings, biding his time, waiting for the day's market to end.

I had sold my beauty for "afu na kobo," Mama Nkemdilim reminded me, the cheapest amount possible. It was the first time she acknowledged my beauty. Now, she told me, I had to pray to the Virgin Mary that such an opportunity arose, though she could not think readily of an old man currently seeking a young woman in my situation.

This was not just Mama Nkemdilim's spitefulness. Not only would it give my son or daughter some covering, such a marriage would reduce the burden on her to provide me and the child with a home as she was obliged to do, with all that that entailed. She worked very hard on the farm to raise a few crops to harvest for sale in the market. She had only a small number of goats that she could sell when things were tight, as they often were. She, unlike many women in Nwokenta, rejected offers of marriage from my father's family. She did not want to be covered with their protection as custom permitted. Privately, she said she did not want to be smothered by anyone. She valued her independence, and wanted to keep her late husband's lands, which would revert automatically to any man who gave her his "covering," at least until Nnanna, her young son, grew up. My father's cousins were angry at her show of independence, so irritated that they washed their hands of her and left her to fend for herself and her children. And now, here was I, she complained, to add an enormous load to the already neck-breaking load on her head.

She made me work as hard as I could. I went back to my chores of old and acquired some new ones: getting water from the stream, fetching food for the goats, doing work on the farm, cleaning the house, and peeling egwusi until my fingers became by turns painful and numb. She told me to pray that a man would want me, a man who befitted my status as a common prostitute just returned from Enugu.

I did not pray for an old man as Mama Nkemdilim told me to. I simply lived, moving from one day to the next, numbly accepting what each day brought, with no thought of the future, and no joy at the thought of the coming baby. I did not pray for it to be a boy or girl; I did not think of its sex at all. I only knew that it would be here one day, a solid reminder of my shame.

Perhaps if I had known what was to come, I would have spent some time praying.

I did not pray for a man to come. But towards the end of my pregnancy, when my feet were so swollen that I could not imagine they would ever return to what they used to be, when I was so bloated that moving around had become in itself a chore, a proposition came to Mama Nkemdilim. I did not think she would accept; how could anyone take such an offer seriously?

This proposition came because a young man from our village had died in an accident. His name was Nathan. He was a truck driver, one of those who drove big trucks of food from the north down to the south and back again. It was a blow to our village, which had lost many young men during the war nearly ten years before and was only just recovering. Many speculations went round about who might have killed him. It was said that he had quarrelled with the owner of the truck and had died right after leaving the man's home en route to Kano. He had slept with his oga's wife, someone said. Others speculated that friends of his who were envious of his success had poisoned his drink the night before. The true explanation, the elders agreed when the first rumours died down, was that he may have had a little too much to drink: young men never really understood the value of life — that they were more important to others, to their families, than they were to themselves.

He was an only child, the only son of his parents. Mama Nkemdilim said that to say he was dear to his mother's heart was to say that sugar was sweet. Everyone knew it. The woman was also a widow; she had lost her husband during the war. The death of her son devastated her. For weeks it seemed that the entire village reverberated with the sound of her weeping and wailing, a heartbreaking sound. Women, including Mama Nkemdilim, came and went from her compound, bringing her food and company. After a while, the sound of her wailing became irritating, then worrying, when it went on ceaselessly day after day. She sang, she wailed, she wept. She refused to be comforted. Even during the akwa, the mourning rites for the dead, her wailing filled the air, making the mourners who came from all the corners of the village for the four days shift their feet uncomfortably and mutter and whisper among themselves. Some said she had lost her mind, that grief had robbed her forever of her senses.

About six weeks later it stopped and I thought no more of it, but one day she came to our house. It was a hot afternoon and I was home alone. I had taken off my blouse and had only a wrapper around my frame, which seemed enormous to me. I sat outside, fanning myself with Mama Nkemdilim's akupe, praying for a breeze to miss its route and stop by our house to relieve me from the unrelenting sun and its companion, humidity.

Mama Nathan had been a woman with flesh to spare, and I was surprised to see how grief had eaten away most of it, leaving her almost as thin as I had been before I became pregnant. Her looks, the talk of the town in her youthful days, had faded, and an expression of bitterness was now etched, permanently it seemed, into her face. Age had dug grooves into the sides of her cheeks and her mouth curled downwards — disdain at life and death, I imagined. Her hair, which she had not bothered to tie with a scarf, had grown out since her son had died and was now more grey than black. But her eyes glowed with a fierceness that made me uncomfortable, a brightness that seemed to speak of madness. She stared at my belly.

"Good afternoon, Ma." I greeted her.

She looked up at my face and answered. "Afternoon, nwa m. Can I come in?"

I led her to the backyard, where we often received visitors. She sat down on a low stool and looked at the small pile of egwusi I had been peeling since that morning.

"Mama Nkemdilim is away at the market. She will be back this evening."

She made no response to that; instead she asked, "Did you peel all of that egwusi?" Her hands gestured to the small mound. I said yes. She nodded. A nod of satisfaction, it seemed. "You are almost due," she said. I said I was. There seemed no awkwardness, at least on her part, about my pregnancy. The entire village knew what I had done.

She sat quietly for a while, her hands supporting her chin, simply staring at me. This made me uncomfortable. Perhaps the people who said that grief had driven her mad were right. Did she plan to stay until Mama Nkemdilim returned in the late evening?

After some time she stood up and said, "I am going. Tell Mama Nkemdilim I came by."

"I shall tell her," I began to say, but she was already leaving, striding purposefully away.

That evening, when I told Mama Nkemdilim that Mama Nathan had come by but that she did not say what she wanted, Mama Nkemdilim shook her head and said, "Poor woman." She carried on breaking apart the dry fish with which she wanted to make soup. And so the incident was forgotten.

Until the next week. This time, Mama Nathan came in the deep evening when she knew Mama Nkemdilim would be home. She was wearing a yellow blouse and a brown wrapper, not the black china cotton she wore the first time she came. It made her look different, lighter, less gloomy. Was she out of mourning, I wondered idly.

She sat with us behind the house where we cooked each evening, waiting for the night to come and bring with it supper and sleep. Nnanna, my half-brother, was kicking an old Bournvita can that Mama Nkemdilim had thrown out — the bottom had fallen out in protest after years of use. I was pounding ogbono for soup. The baby moved, as if it wondered why my body shook with each thud. My sister, Nkemdilim, was rolling the stone in the little mortar, trying to turn the red pepper into a smooth paste, while Mama Nkemdilim was plucking ugu leaves for the soup. It seemed like a normal evening, with everyone doing their work, but Mama Nathan would soon change the atmosphere with her words.

"Di nwe uno," she hailed Nnanna, master of the house. "Dalu o." He looked up briefly from the mechanics of turning a tin can into a football but went back to it.

Mama Nkemdilim nodded her head vigorously; it seemed right to her that Mama Nathan chose to refer to her son as the master of the house.

"Dalu o," she continued her thanks. This time, they were directed to Mama Nkemdilim. "You have done well, Mama Nkemdilim," she began. Never one to turn away praise, Mama Nkemdilim smiled. Mama Nathan continued, "It is not every woman who can do what you are doing: widowed at a time when other women are still enjoying the embrace of a man, his protection, and his hard work. I, too, was widowed like you. When my husband lived, he beat me until my people threatened to beat him up. Yet, when he died, I knew that life was more difficult for a widow than a woman, even a woman who had a married a man who beat her." She paused.

We said nothing. We waited. I wondered how she could speak well of a man who beat her, even if he was dead.

"Mba, not every woman can raise children like you have alone, without the help of a man. And, even now, in these trying times," she stopped and looked at me, "you have not abandoned your duty even though Ekwensu had brought you trials to bear."

I was the trial the devil had brought to Mama Nkemdilim. I bent my head and pounded a little more, and felt the baby heave lazily from one corner of my belly to the other, looking for a more comfortable position.

"Hmm," Mama Nkemdilim sighed, dramatically. "It is only God" — she pointed to heaven — "only God Himself who knows what I am going through. It is only by His strength that I have survived the scorn of my fellow women."

I sat down to rest, fanning myself, acting as they were doing, as though I were not there.

Mama Nathan began to talk about her son. "Life," she moaned, "life is the most difficult thing. If God were to ask people whether or not they wanted to come to earth, and told us what we would encounter, and asked us to choose whether or not to come, that would be better than throwing us here and letting us swim the rivers of life whether or not we had learnt to swim.

"Do you know that only the weekend before the accident, Nathan, my son, brought back the gwongworo, the truck that he drove, and asked me to get in. He drove me around the village, making jokes and laughing with me. You know he liked to laugh ..." Here, the woman turned pensive and her voice shook, but no tears came. Her voice was still tremulous, but strong when she stood up and told Mama Nkemdilim to come with her. She led her away from where we sat, to the path that went to the pit toilet. I wondered what they had to discuss in secret.

When she came back, Mama Nkemdilim was alone. She looked over at me speculatively from time to time as I sat peeling off egwusi shells. I was too exhausted to wonder what was on her mind and longed only for sleep. But I could tell from the way she glanced at me that I was the subject of her thoughts.

One day, soon after Mama Nathan's second visit, I put my hand in my bag to get a small mirror that I had picked out of the garbage can when I lived with Daddy and Mummy. I had paid no attention to my appearance since I had come back to the village two months before. I knew that my body felt heavy, that sitting up or lying down, or getting up from either position, was painful and full of effort. Without looking into a mirror, I had seen that my legs were swollen and that the veins had risen out of the cavern in my hands where they must have hidden all these years. My once-flat belly was now big and round as if it had a small ite ona pot in it. But, in that small mirror, I could see that my face was swollen and round too, that it looked weary and without hope, and that my youth was barely there.

I laughed aloud at the thought of an old man wanting me in this state.

I put back the mirror and, as I did so, my hand felt something else. It was the familiar form of a book — the book of fairy tales that Ikenna had given me the night before I left Enugu. I took it out, and the tears that I had steadfastly held back these two and a half months gushed out with abandon. I wept because I missed that young boy; I cried for all that I had lost. I wept because I had no hope for the future.

This was when I began reading again, going over the stories that Ikenna and I had read together. It was not easy to steal time to do so, but I read one of the twenty-four stories whenever I could.

One afternoon, I was reading it under the orange tree behind the house when Mama Nkemdilim came back unexpectedly. I scrambled to get up when I saw her shadow fall in front of me. It was no mean feat in my condition. She waited for me without helping me, but thankfully she said nothing about my wasting time when there was egwusi to peel and ogbono to pound.

"Good afternoon, Ma," I said.

"Good afternoon," she responded. Then: "You must be the most fortunate girl in the world to get another chance after what you have done."

Some spirit poured cold water on my heart and I heard the sound of defeat in my head. Someone had asked for my hand. I was to be the wife of an old man. Which old man, I wondered.

"You remember Mama Nathan," she said. I nodded, not sure what this had to do with anything.

"Eh," she began, uncharacteristically picking her words. "She wants you to be part of her family."

I was puzzled. Was there an old man in that family? I did not know.

Mama Nkemdilim looked past me when she said, "She wants to marry you for her son, Nathan."

I could feel my forehead furrowing the way it did when I was confused. Like when I saw Mummy make salad in the first week of my stay with them. Were they going to eat that, I wondered. Green, red, and orange leaves, and other things? Without first boiling them? I smiled as I remembered that now; I had really been a "bush girl."

"I knew you would see the good sense in this proposition," Mama Nkemdilim said, seeing the smile spread on my face. "I told her that you were an intelligent girl despite this terrible mistake you made. You should really thank me for opening the door for this opportunity to come to you."

I was in a bad dream. What was she saying? That she thought I had agreed to marry a dead man? Marry Nathan or marry his mother? None of this made sense to me. "I cannot marry a dead man, Ma," I managed to say at last. "Nobody marries someone who is dead."

"Listen," she said patiently, a trait that was alien to the woman I had come to know, "you are a child. You do not know our customs. You do not know that, by custom, a mother or father can get a wife for a deceased son, especially when that son died prematurely, like Nathan, and therefore did not plant a seed in his family. It is particularly the case when it is an only son. The family name, the family line, needs to continue, you see. There are some who do it too when there is no son at all in the family. They can persuade a daughter to remain within the family and thus not marry, in order to bear children that would bear the father's name. Or a good daughter might opt to do so to save the family line and win the eternal gratitude of her father. Or the family can marry a wife who would then produce a son to continue the family name."

That was all good and well, this lesson in customs and those to whom it applied, I thought, but it had nothing to do with me.

"I will mention this to the umunna and I know they will be agreeable. Indeed, they will be happy. Your child will have a name, lands even; if he is a boy, he will be a full member of Nwokenta." She smiled at me. "Even if it is not a boy this time, you can have a boy later on."

Have another child? By whom? I looked into her face and wondered what I had done to this woman to deserve all the hatred she had shown me — and now this. Her cunning smile could not hide the truth — that she wanted me out of this house, which had been built by my father and mother.

"I will not marry Nathan or his mother or his family," I said firmly. There must be no room for doubt. I had been docile, doing her bidding like an onukwu, but this was going too far.

She stared at me. Then, with a sudden movement, she grabbed my book of fairy tales and threw it into the mud, as far from where we stood as she could.

"Do not think that because you acquired some polish in Enugu, do not think that because you can read, you have ceased to be as foolish as a goat," she shouted. "If you think that I will feed you and feed the bastard you are pushing around like a wheelbarrow, then you are even more stupid than a goat."

"I will not marry Nathan or his mother," I repeated.

Mama Nkemdilim stepped back, as if to avoid the foolish disease that now inhabited my head in case it was catching. "We will see about that," she spat as she walked away.

Strangely, I was not afraid. The proposal was completely outside the bounds of reason. I would not marry a dead man.

CHAPTER SEVEN

For a while, it seemed that all was forgotten. I was not getting much bigger, but I felt heavier and slower. As Nwobodo and Onoh vied for the governorship of our state in 1978, I thought how nice it would have been to serve drinks in Daddy's sitting room and overhear his friends discuss the merits of each candidate over whisky and wine. They would talk, at the tops of their voices, about which candidate would best serve the Igbo cause, and who had hidden during the Biafran War and was now coming to reap votes they did not sow. I could see Daddy occasionally requesting a new glass when he felt, as I often thought then, that his friend's saliva had somehow escaped from his mouth into Daddy's glass.

Then three men from our umunna, our family clan, arrived at the house one morning. Two of them had the anklets and red caps that indicated they were titled men, ndi ozo. The last time I recalled such a visit was soon after my uncle Nnabuzo died, and after my return from Lagos, when they had come to persuade Mama Nkemdilim to pick a husband — a protector, they had said — from a man in the umunna. When she told them she intended to raise her son to take his father's place, they had left her to her fate, to raising us by herself, since she needed no man. In private, she had called them vultures — they found the taste of human flesh more delicious than beef, she had said. They could not wait to grab lands that did not belong to them. They went to church, she sneered, some of them at least, but continued to engage in cruel pagan practices.

They summoned Mama Nkemdilim, who received them and served them kola nuts. From the spot where I sat washing my clothes at the back, I heard only the rhythmic rise and fall of their voices.

It was not long before Mama Nkemdilim came out and said that I was wanted in the sitting room. I wiped my hands, heaved myself up, and went with her, wondering what this was about. I could read nothing in Mama Nkemdilim's face, and I knew better than to ask. But she did not seem as unhappy with the delegation as she had been the last time. "Ndewo nu," I greeted them and sat facing them on one side of the room.

I knew these man from the umunna were the custodians of the family honour by custom. They were the ones receiving prospective suitors and their families, providing lists of items that must be presented to the family in exchange for giving out its daughters in marriage. They settled disputes and provided, or at least ought to provide, support to a family member who found himself or herself in trouble, even outside the village. But the coming of Christianity had diluted many things, I remembered my father saying when I was a child, and the concept of family and community unity, the idea of one for all and all for one, more than anything else. I was not sure at the time what he meant, but since the death of my father and uncle I had witnessed how little help the men from the umunna had given us. When they did show up, it was to eat, to issue commands about which choice parts of the goats that were killed at the burial were to be given to the umunna. Now they had arrived this morning, but for what?

Mama Nkemdilim stood on their side of the room. I was facing judgment, it seemed. But for what? By now my pregnancy had been common knowledge. They had no business with me unless I was getting married. My mind paused at the thought. Marriage?

Ichie Okeke spoke first. A tall, spare, fair-skinned man, he was known for his love of women. At last count, he had four wives and many children, some old enough to have their own children, others young enough to suck milk from their mothers' breasts. He went to church but did not take the Communion. He was of the firm view that one religion should not come in where another existed and say that it would not share living space. So he worshipped his ancestors and the gods that he said had provided for our village from the era before time, and he also went to church and made sure each of his many children was baptized.

"Ehen, nne," he said, responding to my greeting. "Kedu?"

"O di nma," I said. I was not really well, but the answer to "how are you" everywhere is "fine."

He cleared his throat. "We, my brothers and I, have heard about your condition."

And you show up after three months, I wondered silently.

He continued. "Hmm. We have been at a loss, yes, we have wondered how a properly raised daughter of ours would put herself in a condition of this sort."

"Eziokwu, ikwulu ife mele eme, it is just as you have said, you have spoken well," one of the men, Ichie Anyabuzo, said.

"Your mother," Ichie Okeke continued, "has done well." Mama Nkemdilim beamed. "But she has younger children; she cannot continue to suffer. We have all wondered what we could do. But our chi does not sleep. No indeed." He paused. I waited. "As we wondered what to do, a solution arrived. Ezechitoke himself brought the solution. Someone wants to marry you."

My heart began to beat fast at his words, the implications of the message driven home by his measured tone and unhurried pace. He glared at me as he spoke, gesticulating with his arms on which the spare flesh was beginning to sag. His fingernails were black, I saw, and I wondered when he had last washed his hands.

"I know your mother has spoken to you. So this will not surprise you." He peered into my face and, seeing the dismay there, continued. "Perhaps," he said after a little pause, his brows furrowing, "this was not a proposal you would have considered in other circumstances. But, as the Igbo people would say, afuro ka-eme, eme ka afu. It is the best offer, indeed the only offer, you are likely to get in your condition. It is necessary that your child have a name. This would spare him or her much embarrassment in the future.

"You are a child, and probably did not know these things," he said. The two other men nodded vigorously at this. He paused again. "Your mother," he said, "has done her best. You cannot expect her to carry even more on her already-worn shoulders."

The three men and Mama Nkemdilim looked at me intently, trying to determine if I was a fool who would reject the wisdom of the people who had gone before, or whether I would right my steps from now onward. When I said nothing, Ichie Okeke continued.

"In your best interests, ehn so that it will be well with you, we have accepted the proposal," he said. "We have told Okoye's family to come and commence the marriage rites during the coming weekend. I am sure, yes, I know it, Mama Nathan will see that you want for nothing. They will treat you well. We are here; we will make sure of that. We have no fears. We know you will be well taken care of and your baby will have a name." By this time, Mama Nkemdilim's smile was as wide as the River Niger.

"I will not marry Nathan or his mother or his family," I said quietly when I found my voice. I knew it was a foolish thing to insult the men of the umunna, but they had to know that what they proposed was impossible.

"You will," said Ichie Anyabuzo. He was a palm-wine tapper, known to be strict but fair-minded. "You have no choice. This child needs a home and if someone has come forward to provide that home, you shall marry into that family."

"Yes," said Ichie Okeke. All four of them were nodding their heads like lizards: up, down, up, down.

At this, I broke into tears. Quicksand was threatening to swallow me. Where was my uncle when I needed him? Where was my father? A bulldozer had shoved me to the ground even before I stood up to fight, and rolled right over me.

The three men looked away at the sight of my tears. Ichie Anyabuzo looked down; Ichie Okeke swatted an imaginary fly off his legs. I looked at each of them. I waited. The third man, who had not spoken yet, cleared his throat.

His name was Papa Ugonna, the one who had stuck by his childless wife for years while the whole village marvelled at his stoic acceptance and eventually began to gossip about the possibility that his manhood was useless. Ugonna, their child, was born many years after the marriage. Perhaps he had something to say that would change the minds of the others, I hoped.

"Do not cry," he said kindly, his eyes sincere. "It is for the best."

It was said that if you did not want Mama Ugonna to hear a thing, you did not say it to Papa Ugonna. I wondered if he had told his wife that his mission that morning was to compel me to marry a dead man.

-- -- -- -- -- -- --

After they left, Mama Nkemdilim walked around the house singing, joyous, like a prisoner about to be made free. Made free by my own captivity, I thought bitterly. That night, I resolved to run away. I was unsure where I would go, especially with a baby about to be born. But I was certain that I could not, and would not, marry a dead man.

In the end, I had nowhere to run to. This was no fairy tale; there was no rescue at the end of the story. In the morning, I went to the church, the only place I thought might offer some reprieve. I met the catechist, a man from our village, and he said that Father had gone on holiday abroad to England and would not be back for a month. That would be too late, I explained to him. It was a barbaric custom, he said, but he could do nothing. He could not take me in, nor could he order Mama Nkemdilim, a member of the congregation, to cease the joyous preparations she was making for handing me over to the dead man's family that weekend.

As I left the catechist that day, I left behind my faith in the Church, in the Virgin, in God. I went back to the house emptied of all hope in the goodness of humans and God, and resigned myself to fate.

That Saturday, I was numb throughout the proceedings. I barely knew what was happening. When it was time for the groom to speak, a man from their family rose and said that he was only there as a representative of Nathan. He knew that Nathan would have wanted to be there himself, to bring home his beautiful bride himself. At this he glanced at my swollen self, dressed in clothes that Mama Nkemdilim had made hurriedly that week. They all sounded mad to me, but when the time came, I went with them, my numb legs moving stiffly forwards as if they had a mind of their own.

CHAPTER EIGHT

I went to live with Mama Nathan in her house, a two-bedroom place surrounded by orange and mango trees and fenced with dried palm fronds. Nathan had roofed the house with aluminum sheets just before he died. The windows had been newly put in, in preparation, Mama Nathan said, to receive "our new wife." I had no emotion left to hate her, to curse at my fate. I sought refuge in numbness as I often did when faced with an overpowering challenge.

She did all she could to make me comfortable. I did not need to lift a finger, except to swallow the smooth balls of pounded yam she made. She cooked a fresh soup every day — spicy ora with snails one day, steamy and pungent onugbu with goat meat the next. I did not sweep, cook, fetch water from the stream, or feed her goats. My only job, she said, was to eat, take short walks around the house and bring down this baby in my belly safely. I was relieved not to have to do all the chores that Mama Nkemdilim had made me do, but eating was hard these days. I got full quickly and heartburn followed immediately after every meal. Mama Nathan said this meant that the baby was a boy. She was confident that it was a boy, but also said that she would accept even a girl. Whatever God chose to give her, she would accept.

If I could have summoned the physical strength, the emotional energy to do so, I would have laughed at her continued belief in this God who had taken her son at so young an age; this God who could not soften the heart of his servant the catechist to take me in when I desperately needed help; this God who would now gift her with a child that only the most wicked of customs had made possible.

I could not wait for the baby to arrive. There was no excitement in this waiting, the kind of eagerness that I sensed in Mama Nathan. I had no name picked out for it. I was not curious about its sex, though I thought that it might be nice for Mama Nathan if it turned out to be a boy. Yet, towards the end, I longed for its arrival; the discomfort was interminable. Even sleep was now almost impossible, from finding a less painful way to lower myself onto the soft bed Mama Nathan had made for me, to turning from one side to the next, to getting up many times to relieve myself in the small potty Mama Nathan put in the corridor at night so that we would not have to use the latrine outside.

One day, when I had lived with Mama Nathan for three weeks, the baby decided to relieve me of the agony of my existence and make its entrance into the world. But it chose the most painful way possible to do this. The pains began as soon as we woke up that morning. Mama Nathan was a midwife; she had delivered many babies in the village, using the old ways. When I first came to live with her, she told me often not to worry, not to be afraid; the pain I would experience was only the body trying to push the baby out. This made me smile; I was not worried about the pain, I gave no thought to it at all. That would have meant thinking about the baby and all that lay afterwards.

But that morning the pain grabbed hold of my thoughts and held them captive. There was no numbness; all my nerves were alive as they had never been before, and they tormented me. Mama Nathan made me walk round and round the compound. Two other women came to assist her. They chatted amiably while I endured the sort of pain that surely no other human had borne on earth. They listened to my moans and complimented me. I was doing well, they said. To each other they would admit that first babies often took their time. They asked Mama Nathan if she had given me nchi meat, to which she responded a vehement no. She knew better than that — how could she want me in labour for hours unending, she asked. They told me not to scream, otherwise I would scream each time I had a baby. I would never do this again, I cried emphatically. They laughed, but not in mockery. All women think that, Mama Nathan said, until they saw the reward of their pain, and then the joy was boundless and they forgot the pain; it was like the pain had never been. I ignored them: I knew in my heart that this was the last time I would do this.

When it was time, they took me into the room, where they proceeded by turns to cajole and persuade, to plead and command me to push out the baby. When I thought that pain was all that existed in the world, something plopped out from between my legs. The pain let go of my body. The next instant, I heard the cry of a baby, and despite my exhaustion, I stretched out my hands for it. They put the baby boy on top of my chest. I touched him carefully, and tried to sit up to see him better.

He was the most beautiful thing I had ever seen, this wrinkled, sticky, squealing, bloody baby. I loved him from that moment. Love flooded and swallowed the numbness, the bitterness, the negativity. I came alive. I had a purpose in life again — to love this baby.

-- -- -- -- -- -- --

I could not imagine anything more perfect than the peaceful baby who had grown inside me. He slept through the night almost from the first week, a miracle, Mama Nathan told me. He was quiet, rarely cried, and in the first weeks often gave those involuntary smiles that made my heart leap with joy, never mind that they were so short you could not tell if he was teasing or you had imagined them.

From the first day, Mama Nathan and I vied for who could love the baby more, who should name him, change him, pick him up when he cried. I was his mother, but Mama Nathan preferred to forget this. She wanted to call him Nathan, after her son. I could not agree to that — to name him after a man who had no part in his making. We eventually settled on Ezinwa: good, beautiful, perfect child.

Because he slept through the night, Mama Nathan wanted him to sleep in her room, in her bed with her. I said no, but she often crept in to try to take him. I found that I had lost all the diplomacy, all the docility that I had learnt through years of being unloved, through harsh and indifferent treatment, through my years of tending the children of others even when I was still a child myself. I became like one of Mama Nkemdilim's cats after it had just given birth — protective, fiercely so. I would not let Mama Nathan sleep with my child. I wanted to feed my child myself, pick him up myself when he cried, change his nappy when he made that liquid yellow yet strangely sweet-smelling mess. I wanted to sing him to sleep. I did not want to share him with anyone, even less with Mama Nathan.

We argued about everything. She wanted him baptized; I did not. The God who had stood by while my mother died birthing me, and had taken my father, and then refused to provide me with an escape route when I needed one, did not deserve our belief or devotion. But I gave in, and had Ezinwa baptized in the church, with the catechist standing by and smiling and bowing obsequiously to Father, who had now come back from his holiday.

Mama Nathan wanted me to feed the baby pap as early as three weeks. But I refused. I remembered Mummy saying that it was really best for babies to have milk for four months before anything else was introduced. I was adamant; I won that battle. Mama Nathan and I both kept our ears open for when he cried, and we both made a mad dash to the room to get him. When I got to him first, she would hover over me, waiting for him to finish nursing at my breast so she could snatch him, burp him, and begin singing nonsensical songs to him. Sometimes I caught her calling him "Nathan."

Soon, the kindness that she had shown me in those last weeks of pregnancy disappeared. She had brought me into the family for my baby, and my refusal to let her be his primary guardian did not suit her. She began to send me on errands outside the house, including fetching water from the stream. I went, but with Ezinwa strapped to my back most of the time.

Mama Nathan complained to her friends that I was a bad mother, spoiling the child by holding him too often. He would never learn to walk; I held him so much. This was the son of the house, she said, but I was already teaching him that breath came and went from his lungs only so long as he held on to my wrapper. She grumbled that I spent too much time reading him books that he could not possibly understand, and which, in any event, could not make him a man.

She grumbled unceasingly. She expressed displeasure at my cooking, annoyance at how sluggishly or quickly I carried out my duties, and irritation at my forays out of the house with Ezinwa. When her grumbling failed to make me cry, she stopped talking to me altogether.

As time passed, my life with Mama Nathan became even more uncomfortable. Chores began to bear children and even grandchildren. Mama Nathan was my mother-in-law, Mama Nkemdilim warned me one day, and she was doing me a favour by feeding me and giving me a roof over my head. The child was hers; Ezinwa belonged to the people who had paid good money as my bride price, the people who had given him a name. I rejected this idea vehemently. But I also knew that I had nowhere to turn.

Until the day she pushed me out.

That evening, I returned late from the market, where I went to buy food for us. I had taken Ezinwa, now a winsome though small four-month-old boy, strapping him on my back. Several of the women had crowded around me, staring admiringly at him, as often happened when I went to the market. They exclaimed at how handsome he was. He chuckled when someone sneezed; to me, his chuckle was the sweetest sound on earth, and the women seemed to agree. They laughed, relishing his enjoyment. Someone begged to hold him, and I indulged her. Nothing made me happier than people admiring my son. He was the reason I was now accepted in the village, I thought sometimes, carefully ignoring the fact of my marriage into Mama Nathan's family.

When I entered the house, Mama Nathan was livid. Her outsized anger was not unusual these days, so I ignored it. I put Ezinwa down — he had been on my back all day. She grabbed him and headed out to the neighbours'.

It was a couple of hours before she came home. She returned empty-handed, declaring that she no longer wanted me in her home. At first, I thought her leaving Ezinwa at a neighbour while we argue must be a new form of punishment, a bringing-in-line for her wayward daughter-in-law — or was it wife? I was never sure which. I quickly assured myself that it was a tactic she would not use again, for I would glue my son to my body if necessary.

But first I had to find out with which neighbour she had left him. She ignored my calm then annoyed demands for Ezinwa, who must by now be getting hungry. My breasts were filling up, engorging on the milk that I still fed him even though I had started him on solids. But when I stomped out to our neighbours' homes, Ezinwa was in none of them.

I began to panic. I went back and demanded my son.

Ezinwa was not my son, she said, but Nathan's. Though her voice was calm, she sounded like she had gone mad. Perhaps she had. Losing my son, as she had hers, would make me mad. Now I understood.

I had enough. I began to scream and stamp my feet; red dust rose like a cloud of confusion. I called out to the neighbours, shouting their names: Mama Josephine, Enenebe, Papa Michael. They all came out of their houses, too quickly it seemed to me in retrospect, bringing their eyes to join their eavesdropping ears to feast upon the unfolding drama. Some asked Mama Nathan where the boy was. In response, Mama Nathan said that I was a witch who in her dreams had threatened to kill her several times. She accused me of stealing from her, and wailed that I was a luxury she could no longer afford; she could not stand to live with me one day longer. I was a witch, she repeated; at last she announced that she had taken the boy to somewhere safe until things were resolved.

I could not understand what she was saying or fathom what was happening. Neither could the neighbours. I might be a witch, Mama Josephine tried to intervene, but that did not mean she could hide a baby from his mother.

It was growing dark, yet Mama Nathan made no move to fetch Ezinwa. By now, my tension had given way to tears. One woman, Mama Chukwuma, held me and consoled me. Some pleaded with Mama Nathan; others shouted abuse at her. She was adamant: I would not sleep in her house that night. She stormed inside and brought out some of my things, already packed in a bag. Clearly, this was not a spur-of-the-moment decision; it had been in the making, growing like a baby in the womb.

In the meantime, the head of the family, Ichie Ucheagu, had been sent for. When the situation was explained to him, he ordered Mama Nathan to bring the baby. She did not budge. I was a witch who ate human flesh and who planned to eat her child.

Leaving the resolution of the problem in the hands of Ichie Ucheagu, the neighbours started to return to their homes when their children began crying and asking for food. Mama Nathan continued to insist that I would not sleep in her house that night. Mama Chukwuma advised that it was best I went home. I had thought this *was* home, my mind protested. Having nowhere else to go, I went to Mama Nkemdilim's, where I stayed awake all night, wailing at the thought that my little boy had not eaten.

The next day, a meeting was called by our umunna and held at the home of Ichie Ucheagu. For once, I could not tell what Mama Nkemdilim thought. But she was not unkind to me. She stayed with me while we waited to hear from the umunna. After two hours, I was summoned. I went, hopeful yet afraid. Mama Nkemdilim came with me.

At the meeting, Mama Nathan was present, but not Ezinwa, which brought tears to my eyes. Ichie Ucheagu asked me to sit and began to speak in the gentle tones one would use for a child who had malaria. Mama Nathan had said that we were not living well together. I began to protest, but he raised his hand and bade me be quiet. Mama Nathan did not want to live with me any longer. This was not a problem, I assured him; my son and I would return to my father's house.

There was silence.

Mama Nathan put her head down and stared at the floor as the men looked at me, and I could see pity in some of their eyes.

It would not be possible for Ezinwa to go with me, Ichie Ucheagu said. As things were, Mama Nathan and her family had demanded that the bride price be paid back. I would no longer be married to Nathan. The child was theirs now, because they had married me. In our culture, he explained patiently like one would to a young child, a child belonged to the father, not the mother. Ezinwa belonged to his father's family. He was sure that Mama Nathan would let me see Ezinwa when I visited her house, Ichie Ucheagu tried to soothe me. After all, I was his mother, he said.

But Mama Nathan said no. She was calm in her vehemence. I was not a good mother. I smothered the boy, I refused to feed him solids. The difference in the child's growth was clear for all to see.

Ichie Ucheagu tried to reason with her, saying that the boy was too young to be taken from his natural mother. At this, Mama Nathan threw herself on the floor and wept loudly and bitterly. The elders asked us to leave the room. When they called us back in, they had reached a temporary decision: Ezinwa would stay with Mama Nathan and I could go see him as often as I wished. They would meet again after two weeks to review the situation.

I let out a pained wail. It was clear that my umunna would not help me in the end. Mama Nkemdilim came and held me. I wept with abandon, not caring that they watched me.

Later, my story would elicit some pity, but no intervention from any quarters. Everyone agreed that, as much as English law had come with the colonial masters, and Christianity had come with the missionaries, these institutions did not interfere with certain accepted and ancient traditions. In the minds of the men and women of Nwokenta, as in all of Igbo land, there was no disputing that a child belonged to the father. It did not matter how that came about, whether the woman had committed adultery or not; so long as her bride price had been paid, the child was her husband's. It did not matter that her husband was violent and she had run away from constant beatings. Her family might come to take their daughter home, but even they knew that the children belonged to her husband. If her family was exceedingly influential and forward-looking and took the children too, everyone reminded them still that the children were the man's and that, one day, they would return to their father.

The day after the meeting, I went to see my son. I reached for him and he smiled and gurgled. What I feared most was that he would recoil from me as he had begun to do with strangers. I clung to him and would not let go when the time came to leave. Mama Nathan had to pry him from my arms, with her friends watching.

That night my heart bled and my eyes seeped tears. On my second visit, I tried to take Ezinwa away. He was sleeping in my arms, when I stood up and ran. But Mama Nathan and a woman from their clan, whom she had engaged perhaps specifically for this purpose, caught up with me and wrestled him from my grip. That was the last time I saw my son. When I arrived the following morning, I was told that Mama Nathan had gone away to Enugu to visit a friend. He never came home.

CHAPTER NINE

I lived life with an ache in my heart. I knew too that I would die with and perhaps because of that ache. It grew and expanded until I thought my insides would burst. I could speak to no one of this ache because Mama Nkemdilim forbade all talk with the statement that "it was God's will, uche Chukwu." Perhaps, she said, I would be fortunate to marry someone else when all was forgotten. I did not remind her that I had not married at all.

Each breath of air that I drew without my son was punishment, each awakening from sleep a reminder that the rest of my life waited without Ezinwa. My inclination was to lie in bed and do nothing, but that was impossible in Mama Nkemdilim's house. As I went about the chores that had sat and waited for me to return from my sojourn with Mama Nathan, the ache pulled at me, wanting to make me lie in death at the bottom of the stream or in the middle of our farmland.

One morning, I awoke and knew like I had not known before that my son was not coming back. Mama Nathan had not returned. Her people showed no signs of unease at her disappearance. My people carried on as though my son had never existed.

I could not see hope. It had hidden itself from me, but I became determined to seek it out wherever it was. I had to leave the village.

When Mama Nkemdilim and her children had gone to the market, leaving me with a pile of clothes to wash, empty pots of water to fill, and supper to prepare, I packed the few clothes I had and my books of fairy tales. In my bra I had some money that I had stolen from Mama Nkemdilim's cache the previous day. I did not have a thought-out plan. I only knew that I could not stay — that if I had run away somewhere when I was pregnant, I would still have my son in my arms. I planned to go back to Enugu. Not to see Urenna. I knew now that he was weak, that he was still a boy and he could not help me. But perhaps Chidinma would. She had relatives in Enugu. They might be willing to take me in. I set out that morning. The lightness of my bag of clothes reminded me that I had little in the world, that I had lost what was most precious to me, and that my life was as light now as a bag of worn-out clothes. The sun was scorching. My heart beat loudly in my ears but I walked resolutely, prepared to run if anyone tried to stop me. I need not have worried; it was a short walk to the main road and no one appeared. They had all gone to the market, to the stream, to the farm, or wherever it was that their hungry stomachs had dictated they should go. I waited for what seemed like a long time before the bus came. In that time, I willed myself not to think for fear that I would lose my resolve. I only knew that I would kick, scream, and punch, should anyone question me or stand in the way of my escape.

When the bus to Enugu came, I jumped in. As we passed the trees, the familiar houses and their tin roofs, the red sand of my village, my heart continued its loud thumping. My fingers held my bag so tightly, I thought it might be impossible to unglue them when we got to Enugu. But Enugu, that township of electric lights that many people in Nwokenta sought escape to, had never seemed so far away.

The bus moved slowly, with a clanging sound at the back and a passenger stopping it every other minute. I tried not to think about all the things that could go wrong in Enugu. No one there owed me a roof over my head. No one owed me food. The only thing I was relying on was my friendship with Chidinma, herself a housemaid depending on others to give her food, a place to sleep, and some education.

It was afternoon when we got to the market at Ogbete. It was the final stop and the few passengers who were left alighted. I got off, breathing in the powerful, familiar scene — food smells, the smell of bodies, the sounds of people buying and selling, the odours of merchandise, and the red dust of Enugu. I stood for a moment in the sun and savoured my relief.

It was not long-lived. A woman walked past me and stood before me, her child strapped to her back. She put a hand behind her, underneath the little boy's buttocks, for extra support. It was a gesture that was intimately familiar. I had done the same many times after Ezinwa turned three months. The pain seared me, sizzling like onions thrown into a pan of hot oil. I breathed in and out, in and out.

Then a sudden desire seized me: to see the face of the little boy. As I stepped forwards to look into his face, his mother began walking away with quick, short steps. I walked after her. I had to see his face. A young woman, about my age, with a tray of groundnuts on her head, came between us. "Buy groundnuts," she shouted, obscuring my view of the woman and child. I wanted to hit her. Instead, I sidestepped her just in time to see the woman heaving herself and the little boy onto a bus. "Agbani

Road," the conductor shouted. As the bus moved away, I still had not seen the child's face. And now I never would. What if it had been Ezinwa?

It took a while before I got myself together. This was not why I had come to Enugu. I did not know where Mama Nathan had taken my son — Enugu, Onitsha, or Kafanchan. But being rational did nothing to ease my pain. I tried to calm down and focused on my plan. It was sketchy at best, but it would have to do.

I began the long trek to Independence Layout. As I neared the place, I prayed that I would not see Urenna, my former employers, or anyone else. I kept my face down as I passed through familiar routes and places. Things had not changed much and this surprised me. My life had undergone so many changes in the past year, I expected that to be reflected in the area I had lived in once.

It was almost five when I got to my destination. I was tired; sweat poured out of me. I stood by the big tree where my friend and I had chatted many times. Peering from a distance, I searched for her. Would she be there? Or at Mrs Okonkwo, the seamstress's house? Did Urenna's parents send her to sewing lessons like she had hoped? Or had she perhaps been dismissed? If she was not at Mrs Okonkwo's house, could I enter our street? Would anyone else come to her gate if I knocked?

While I stood wondering what to do, I saw her small, chubby figure. Two other girls came out of the house with her. She had a small bag, which she clutched under her armpit while she shut Mrs Okonkwo's gate behind her. I could have cried with relief. I called out to her. She looked about, but did not see me immediately. Then her eyes widened, first with surprise, then with fear. She stepped away from her friends and came towards me. Even though I could see the anxiety in her eyes, she hugged me. It was a close and tight embrace. I soaked it in; it had been so long since I felt any affection.

She told me what had happened on the street in the past year. Urenna's parents were upset with Chidinma. "They said I brought you into their house," she told me. Urenna was still at university. I wanted to ask how he was doing, but stopped myself. I did not want her to think I was still pining for him. For me, life had moved on since he had been the sun who brought the day each morning. I had longed to know how Ikenna was doing. Was there another help living with them? I asked now. Was she good to Ikenna? Yes, they had another help. It must be the tenth one since I had left; they changed help almost each month. She did not know how Ikenna was doing; she and the new help were not friends.

After I had left, Chidinma continued, most madams on the street became even stricter. She had to get home before six, she told me. She liked sewing school. I saw her eyes brighten, but then, perhaps remembering my own thwarted ambitions, she looked down at her feet. I longed to reassure her. There was no envy, only self-pity that my destiny had not been as kind as hers.

"You look well," I told her.

She did, her skin brown and smooth, oiled by good food and youth. She did not return the compliment. I knew that I looked worse than I had when I'd lived with Mummy and her family. Sorrow, chores, and too little food had left their marks on my face and figure. "Black beauty" I was no longer.

I willed myself not to cry when she asked about the baby. "The baby died," I said.

This was what I would tell everyone, I had resolved. It was easier than the true story. I could not tell her about my son's beauty, that he had begun to smile when he was ripped away from me. I could not tell her about the love that took you out of yourself, that was larger than you, and yet did not threaten you but gave you more joy sometimes than you could bear. I could not tell her that I had borne the death of joy and knew it to be the worst thing that could happen to a human being.

Tears came to her eyes. "Are you okay?"

"I am," I answered, with as much reassurance as I could muster.

There was a pause as she felt around for something to say. "Was the child a boy or a girl?" she asked timidly, as if she did not want to stir the waters too deeply.

She was quiet for a few moments when I told her I had had a boy, and I wondered if she was trying to imagine what he had looked like.

"But what are you doing here?" Chidinma asked, getting to the question that stood between us. "Did you get another job nearby?"

"No," I answered, but this was my opening, and I knew I had to pick the right words to make my request. "Mama Nkemdilim …" I started. "It is hard for me to live with her, very hard."

Chidinma nodded. She knew this from before.

"Chidinma," I continued, "I have nowhere to stay." Please, I begged her, asking if I could go stay at her sister's, the one who was settled with a sewing machine when she had finished serving her madam as a house help.

"Adannem?" she frowned.

"Yes, Sister Uzoamaka. May I go and stay with her until I get another job?"

Chidinma stared at me. Was she wondering why Nwabulu, the smart housemaid who had wanted to be a secretary and work in the ministry, was asking her for help?

She sighed. "Adannem just had a baby. I don't know if her husband would be willing to take you in. Their flat in Abakpa is small."

Discouragement brought tears to my eyes, but Chidinma hugged me and held me close.

"I cannot go back to Nwokenta, to Mama Nkemdilim," I sobbed. If I could not go to Chidinma's sister, I was lost. I knew no one else in Enugu.

"You can go to my sister's house," Chidinma said after I had calmed down a little, "she may even help you get another job as a housemaid. I will give you her address." She tore out a page of her book and wrote down the address, then hugged me again.

She had to go, she told me. I could feel the hurry and the worry in her hug. I thanked her.

I would go and see what Chidinma's sister would say. I would go on my knees and beg, I resolved. I would do anything — anything that would let me stay in Enugu.

Chidinma waved to me one last time, then hurried away. Back to the street on which we both had once lived.

As I stepped into the evening about to turn night, I prayed to God — the one who had let my child be stolen, the one I did not believe in any more — that Chidinma's sister, Uzoamaka, a woman I had only heard about but never met, would help me.

PART TWO
JULIE

CHAPTER TEN

He touched the gold necklace between my breasts, lifting it slightly with his long fingers, weighing the pendant. His touch was familiar, possessive.

He nodded in approval. "Oriaku," he hailed. "Consumer of my wealth." He laughed at me, his satisfaction with me and with life beaming out of his too-wide mouth. I pushed my irritation down into my belly and found an answering smile.

"Orimili," I gave him his title. And in calling him that, a river without end, a river of wealth, I felt the irritation dissipate. There were parts of Eugene I could quarrel with, but his generosity of spirit, often reflected in various gifts, was not one of them.

A little after, we went to the door, he with regret, I with relief. No one saw me look out furtively as I let Eugene out of my flat into the sticky night. He wanted me to come downstairs with him; I would not. It was enough that my neighbours already talked — what single woman entertained a man in her house at night, a man who arrived ostentatiously in a brand-new Peugeot 404, as if by right?

I returned to the sofa from which we had arisen only moments before, picking up the little black bag on the Formica-covered side table. Jewellery. A gold teapot pendant on a long chain. It was beautiful. More striking, I thought, with its intricate detailing than the long pendant of an index finger that Eugene had just admired on me. I had coveted Obiageli's for a while now. It was I who had pointed out the jeweller on Asata Road to Eugene. And he had followed through with this beautiful set that I now would add to my growing gold collection. But I was curiously unsatisfied. I had not even experienced that brief thrill, that short-lived high that came with material acquisition, particularly when you had not paid for it. I had smiled my thanks to him, putting my free hand on his hand, stroking his arm between elbow and hand, conveying my appreciation with fingers and eyes. My empty heart mocked me silently — it knew well that what I had in my right hand paled in comparison to what I truly wanted. Perhaps I had gone about this the wrong way, I chided myself now. I had given away too much too soon.

I got up and went into my bedroom. There was no escaping Eugene's heavy cologne. I stood in front of my mirror. It was not full length, yet I could see my full figure, big breasts, and arms that should have been slimmer, especially since I did not yet have any children. My chest rose in a sigh and then came down in defeat. I took off the index-finger pendant necklace and put on the teapot one, studying it against my skin, my fleshy neck, the long chain hanging between my breasts. I had hoped to feel some respite. It did not come. The nagging feeling stayed. Needing distraction from the heaviness that came over me, I searched for my bag, and brought out my book, beginning to prepare my lesson notes. Work was what I needed now.

I scribbled, yet my mind wandered. "Do not put up to your nose to smell what you do not intend to eat," my mother often said when I was younger and able to attract suitors like bees to honey. But what about what you wanted to eat? What if you had put it up to your nose? Smelt it? Taken bites off it? And still it belonged to someone else?

Giving up on my pretense of working, I stood up and went to the kitchen, which I surveyed with critical eyes. It was too small, I thought, not for the first time. Yet it was too big for one person, my mother said the first time she visited. Did she sound critical, or was I just too sensitive? I knew she did not approve of me, a single woman, living by myself. "I am not a child," I reminded her.

"You are somebody's child until you become somebody's wife," she retorted. Would it not scare men away, she worried. A single woman on her own, living alone. I followed her train of thought and added silently to myself: a single woman, living alone, making money, independent, frightening to men, fat. Yet these thoughts did not shake my resolve to live alone. A year of living with a fellow teacher, whose untidiness and gossipy ways had made me miserable, had cured me of any illusions. I had even gone ahead and bought a car a few months earlier with the car loan for teachers. They — my little apartment and car — gave me some measure of calmness with which to deal with the world.

I dished some ora soup and meat into a bowl and went into the sitting room to eat. The first spoonful helped. The spicy pungency of the hot red pepper and ogili in cocoyam thickener and the distinctive taste of ora leaves hit my taste buds. It made the world all right. But only for a few moments. My thoughts wandered from my mother to my father. Ada eji eje mba, my father had often called me. I would go far, he said, when I brought home exercise books full of good marks, with words like "excellent" and "very good" praising me. So I set about going far. I came first in many of my classes. From primary school, I moved to the prestigious Girls' High School Aba on a government scholarship, after coming first in the entrance examinations. I smiled appropriately and lowered my head in humility when people said that I was a brilliant girl, the first in our village to go to university.

But my mother worried about my marriage prospects.

"Who will want to marry a woman who has gone to university?" she had asked my father.

"You are stuck in the days of your mother," my father would reply, waving his hand as if to chase an irritating mosquito from the ear. He would look down at his crisp, white, charcoal-ironed shirt and his khaki shorts with their iron-sharp lines, and nod in the satisfaction of knowing that he understood what he spoke about better than his audience.

My mother was perhaps stuck in days past. The domestic chores that she thought I should stay back from boarding school to do were all done by women. Yet, in the days of my grandmother, women were powerful, my mother had told me. While each woman was required to obey her husband, when women came together in their umuada group, the hearts of men trembled. When they tied their wrappers on their waists, bare breasts hanging down, and confronted an issue, no man dared to challenge them. The collective force of the umuada quelled every machination of the men that was not favoured by the women.

My mother would furrow her fair brow, wishing that she could go back to those days, because these days women still had to do all the chores but had much less power. Less power to stop a husband from ruining the marriage chances of his daughter.

"It is the 1960s," my father had reminded her, brandishing his superiority not only as a man but as the one who was educated. "Nurses and teachers are in high demand everywhere as wives. Plus, did you not raise her to know her place no matter what level of education she attains? I don't know about you, but

I know that I have done my best. Not so?" he would turn around to ask me.

"It is so, Papa," I would respond meekly.

My mother, never one to speak back to her husband, would sweep to the back of the house to continue with the chores that would not do themselves while a girl spent her days going from one school to another in the name of education.

A woman must know her place. A woman must also, like a man, have integrity. Integrity, my father had said, was the most important thing a person could have. Not to lie, not to deceive, because that was the hallmark, the defining characteristic of Satan. Not to covet or take what belonged to another, to strive always to do good. And he had brought each one of us up with these values, he would say, with no small amount of pride. He had lived that way, too. I wondered what score he would give me if he were to see me today.

I sat still, adopting the quiet-time pose that we had been taught years ago in secondary school. I would prefer not to engage in deception. My father often said that liars were always found out. But nothing in Eugene's bearing today — not in the careless way he swallowed his messily moulded balls of garri, in the way the meat went down his throat, nor in the sticking out of his Adam's apple — said that he was thinking seriously about buying the cow now that he had tasted its milk.

I shivered a little. The night was getting on, bringing a chill and lonesomeness with it. Not long ago, I had served food and eaten with a man, our laughter spicing the evening. I had taken off my clothes and watched desire take over his face. But Eugene had gone home. He had to go.

I carried my bowl with its unfinished soup into the kitchen and left it unwashed in the sink that always seemed too big for the kitchen. The cliché about time and tide waiting for no one came to me all the way from idioms class at Girls' High School Aba. I forced myself to sit at my desk in my room to continue work on the lesson notes.

Before I met Eugene, I had lived. I had not pined for a man, though there were times when I'd longed for hands to brush across my breasts or even to lift them up, heavy as they were, and admire them lovingly. That was only at night. In the morning, I would get up and go about life like a man. Teach, buy a plot of land, apply to see if I could be one of those sent on full-time, paid study leave to London.

"Perhaps Julie is destined to remain single, an okpokwu," I had heard my mother confide in a low voice to her friend two weeks ago when they thought I could not hear. There was sadness and something like resignation in her voice.

"Wash your mouth out with water and soap," her friend, Mama Nduka, a woman who had eight sons, had replied. "She will still marry."

I hoped Mama Nduka was right.

- - - - - - - - - - - -

My brother was drunk. Alcohol, cigarettes, vomit, yesterday's clothes, and sweat intermingled and yet assaulted the nostrils distinctly. There he lay, his mouth open, drooling saliva on my mother's couch, his snores the sound of an old car engine.

I had come to visit my mother from Enugu, as I often did on the weekends. On my way in I had passed some firewood stacked on the red earth by our raffia fence, waiting for someone whose hands had more strength than my aging mother's to take them to the kitchen for splitting. My brother, Afam, had strength in him, but he lay slack, looking disarmed, abandoned by the universe. For a fleeting moment, I wanted to cradle his head and have him nestle in my arms as I would have done when we were young and loved each other. But something snapped in me. I stormed at him and hit his back. It was fleshy yet hard. "Get up!" I shouted. "Other men are at work." Probably not on a Saturday. But it didn't make any difference; he was often drunk in the week too.

Afam merely groaned and turned his head the other way. I pounded his back with both hands. A nut had come loose in my head, I would think later. Or perhaps it had always been wobbly and just fell off, letting hinges within my brain come apart.

"I will not let you kill my mother, you hear? I will not," I shouted like a madwoman.

Without warning, he swung out at me with his left hand. He caught me in the face, hard. The blow was painful and stunned me for a few seconds. Even when we were children, Afam had avoided hitting me, although he had always been stronger than me. Now, I retaliated by pounding him harder, all over his body, wherever my fists could reach. My hands against his body felt like a small boat tossing on the sea, helpless in a storm. Helpless against his drinking, his determination to self-destruct.

When he could no longer take it, he launched at the nuisance that was keeping him from sleep. He sat up and hit out at me with balled fists like a boxer, catching me in the stomach and on my left breast. He stopped when I screamed. Without looking at me or my mother, who had by this time come into the room and was shouting herself hoarse, commanding us to stop this nonsense, he stumbled out.

My breath came out heavy, laboured. Fighting a man was not an easy undertaking, especially when you knew from the start that you were going to lose.

"Why do you turn into a goat, into a mumu, every time you see your brother? Where do your senses flee to when you set eyes on him?" my mother asked me angrily, her index finger extended in my direction. "Will your hitting him stop him from drinking himself into a stupor this very evening? If he hit you and sent you to the hospital, who would you blame?"

I bowed my head and pressed my sore stomach where the blow had landed. She was right. I had let my fury, my frustration, get the better of me. And I knew that my mother could not abide stupidity. Women who were foolish did not survive long in the world of men, she often said.

My mother went to fetch some Robb. "Here, put that on the sore spots. I will get you Panadol."

I knew better than to say I did not need these things.

She sat on the other sofa, placed an arm on its dark wooden armrest, and waited for me to take the Panadol. I hated taking medicine, an old antipathy from childhood, but she did not urge me on. She simply waited. Her quietness told me that a lecture was coming, whether long or short, I could not tell. I put my finger into the small bottle of Robb, pulled down my skirt, and rubbed it on my belly. I winced. My mother waited. Her only movement was to retie her scarf. Since my father had died, she had worn her long, full hair short, as if there were no more point to tending it, tying it in black thread, or weaving it.

"Juliana," she began when I was done with my massage, using my full name. Because what she was about to say was important. I could remember all the times she had called me "Juliana" like that — when I was about to go to boarding school at Girls' High School Aba, when Amechi had come for my hand in marriage and I was going to turn him down because my father thought I could do better, when my father died and no one could console me.

"You love your brother," my mother stated. It was a fact, neither good nor bad. "But he is not a little boy any more. He is a man. You ..." Here, she paused and studied me with piercing, knowing eyes. "You," she repeated, "you are a woman." She stopped and searched my face to see if this piece of information had made its way home. "A woman must love herself. You must love yourself too. You must take care of yourself now." She stopped — waiting, it seemed, for this vital truth to sink in.

Then she went on to illustrate: "This brother of yours is a drunk." Her lips curled in scorn as I startled, hypocritically, at her description. At that moment, fragments of our childhood came to me. Us, playing outside the house in Umuleri when Papa taught there, building small huts of sand and then trampling them. Reading for entrance examinations by the dull light of the hurricane lamp. The small party the night before he went off to school at CKC, when we lived near St James. Afam kneeling before my father, while I suppressed envious and thus devilish and unworthy thoughts that no such party had been thrown for me or even contemplated when I got into Aba Girls on scholarship, the only child around Umuleri who had done so in the year 1951. All our neighbours cheered, with stomachs full of nicely pounded yam and egwusi soup, for the young man who had secured a place at the prestigious CKC, the school where smart Catholic boys went. After my father's hands had rested on my brother's head in prayer and pride, Afam stood and faced the small crowd of people who had gathered in our compound that evening: tall, vital, energetic, happy, looking forward to tomorrow.

That tomorrow had now become yesterday, and today my mother called her son — the bright hope of yesterday — a drunk.

"He will marry one day," Mama Afam, as everyone called my mother, continued. "Yes, a woman will marry this drunken brother of yours. For love; for money, though God knows how he will ever make any; for his tall foolishness; or for children. Why? Because he is a man. With a penis between his legs. But you are a woman. With a womb that comes with an expiry date."

Did penises have no expiry dates? a stray demon asked me. "Coming here to hit him, to shout at him, to pour anger on him will do neither you nor him any good. It will solve nothing. Go and live your own life. Find a man, any man, get married, and have children. Have children. That is what is most important. So that you can be happy and fulfil your life's purpose."

I wanted to ask if she felt that, having given birth to a drunk, she had fulfilled her life's purpose. But I lacked the power to be insolent to my mother. She had made sure of that long ago.

"You see this drunk you call your brother?" I still winced inwardly at her words and tone. "One day he will get a young thing, who will come in here on two sticks that she will call legs and tell you not to pluck an orange, an orange that I, your mother, planted. Or a pear that you planted. And what would you be able to do about it? Nothing. It will be her home after all. You will be allowed in, but only just. If you have your own home, however, you can come visit but you will go back home, where you can pluck your own oranges and pears and manage them as you please. And, most important, raise your own children.

"Children are the joy of a woman's life. Not men. Not marriage. Not money. Children," she emphasized with that extended index finger. Had my father been that awful to her? that demon asked me again.

"Even if you have one that is as hopeless as your brother — and I pray that you do not, for it is a painful experience — you will have another like you have been to me, who will love you, who will take care of you in your old age, of whom you can be proud. That is the joy of a woman's life." Here, she stopped and we sat in silence for a little. Her words were forcing themselves into my head, making sure that they would be there to reverberate when I least wanted to entertain them.

"I pray you do not miss it. For you have been God's gift to me. I pray that you will find someone soon. And that God will open your womb immediately as He did mine when I married your father, and as He has done for your younger sisters."

I had heard this sermon, or some variation of it, since Papa died. But it did not diminish the urgency with which it was delivered, nor the fear within me that she spoke truth, that it was a joy that I might never encounter. I did not say what I would have said even two years before — that one could have a child without the benefit or burden of marriage — to which she would tell me to spit out the foolish words and that it would not happen, not in that manner. I was beginning to be afraid. Afraid that I was an okpokwu, nna ja-anu, the one whose father would marry, the leftover. Afraid that I was useless as a woman, no good to anyone including myself. And now, after my mother's speech, afraid that I would not have what she thought was the best thing that a woman could hope to possess: motherhood.

She stood up and went into the kitchen at the back of the house. She returned with some okpa, one of my favourite things to eat.

While she watched, I cut it carefully with the knife she'd handed me and put a small, moist, red piece into my mouth, more out of obligation than hunger. But it was soft and delicious, and before long I was not eating out of courtesy. I sometimes would buy okpa in Enugu, just outside my office. But my mother had made this herself as always, and it tasted not only of the right ingredients mixed in at the right time, but of home and love.

As I ate, the tension began to dissipate, to leave the room and find other homes to trouble. We began to talk about ordinary things. Afam stayed in my mind and in my mother's, but we did not speak of him again. There was nothing more to be said, really. Instead, we spoke about Grace, Mama Mike's last child, who was going into secondary school. Her mother had come to my mother, she said, to ask for advice about whether they should betroth her to someone before she went. My mother told her that those days when little girls were betrothed so young were long gone. She would find a husband when she finished secondary school. Educated women were more marriageable these days than in years past, Mama Afam assured Mama Mike. I let that sink in, to ponder in solitude, reconciling the seemingly conflicting views my mother espoused.

Then we spoke of Ebenezer, a distant cousin, whose son had died and would be buried in the coming week. A house was being constructed quickly in his father's compound by his younger brother so that he could be buried properly. His father had been an efulefu, a prodigal, who had married his wife, given her three children, and moved to Lagos, refusing to come home or send what was more important than his presence: money. A Calabar woman had him enthralled, and it would require the intervention of God Himself to separate them. Now his son had died and the prodigal father had still not come home.

After some time, Ekweozo, my mother's brother, arrived and joined the conversation. I got up to fetch the firewood outside. I took it to the back, and split it with the axe, then stacked it neatly in a corner of my mother's small kitchen. I poured some water from the clay water-pot with the aluminum cup that was always left on top of it. It tasted cool and pleasant to my tongue, like nothing I drank in the township. My mother came into the kitchen and, murmuring thanks, took a piece of fish from the uko above her fire in which she grilled fish and meat. It was her gesture from childhood of thanks, of comfort, of kindness. I bit into the fish and found it as tasty as always.

Later, my mother saw me out. She was not one for gratuitous affection, so I kept my hug brief and climbed into the car. Afam had slept all the while and did not come out until I started the engine. One hand on his head — nursing a headache, I was sure — he waved goodbye lackadaisically from the veranda, our fight seemingly forgotten.

"Drive carefully," my mother said, like she says each time I visit. She still worried about my driving, worried that men would be put off, that the car would be too intimidating. I won't waste money on taxis when I can buy a car, I had told her. She had shaken her head at my stubbornness, asking the Virgin Mary to help me see sense. Virgin Mary did not agree with her, obviously, because I had bought myself a new red Volkswagen. I was guilty of too much pride over it, but my only regret was that my father had not lived to see it.

"Remember what I said," she added now after a pause. "It will be well, do you hear?"

"Yes, Ma," I said with a smile that stayed on my face for a little while. I set her lecture on the important things a woman must accomplish aside for dissection during quiet, lonely nights in Enugu.

CHAPTER ELEVEN

My heart beat fast, pounding like the drums of Achukwu in my chest each time I visited. The smell that came into my nostrils, an unwelcome stranger, reminded me that I wanted to be anywhere but here. It was the same smell from the time when Papa died. At this thought, panic suffused my being — hospital meant death.

Today, Afam was lying on his side when I came into the room. My mother was curled in a chair in the corner, sleeping. She had slept in that position every day for the past seven days since Afam had been brought in — that is, when her body overcame her will and its protests overwhelmed her desire to keep her eyes on her son. She had not showered in days, and refused to entertain my pleas to come to my flat to rest.

The doctors had said the same thing every day for the past seven days. He was in a coma. There was nothing to do but wait and pray.

I sat and stared at Afam, willing him to wake up. I thought about his tears when Papa died. "I disappointed him," he had said to me then.

I was silent — it was true.

"You know," he'd said, his deep baritone booming in our small sitting room, "when Chima died, I knew the war was over."

Chima had been Afam's best friend. A slight young man, with a deep voice like my brother's. But Chima's voice and his bravery outsized him. He served under Colonel Achuzie, and his exploits, his ability to inspire men, made many say that Ojukwu would make him a general before the war was over. But he had died at the Umuahia front.

"Julie, I wish I had died in battle like Chima," Afam had once confided in me.

Unlike so many that we knew, my brother had come back from the war. Thinner, yes — his collarbones and his Adam's apple jutted out — but without much injury that was visible to the eye. His smile, however, was gone. Something indefinable, indescribable, seemed broken within. The joy and the passion with which he had sung war songs when he'd set out as a vibrant twenty-four-year-old to join the army in 1968 had gone, a log that had burned brightly and then out, leaving dying embers slowly falling apart.

"No, don't say that," I had protested immediately. Because that was what was required: when people wished for suicide, you told them no. When they had nightmares like he did every night, you waved their fears away and told them that all was well. When I thought back on that conversation, I knew I should have let Afam speak. It was the first time my brother had spoken to me from his heart, the way we always did before the war. But I shut him down. And he kept his thoughts inside.

After the war, Afam wandered aimlessly, as if he had lost his eyes in the war. Had Afam gone back to school, Papa would have been content, retaining hope for the family line, for the future of his bright son. But he did not. He had brushed off Papa's talk about a wife. How could he marry without work? How would he feed a family, he asked when Papa brought it up.

He went to Lagos, but did not stay long; none of his friends could help him, he said. Why must friends help you? I asked. He came to Enugu, where I had returned to work as a teacher in the secondary school. He slept all morning and kept me up late talking about our childhood, anything but the war or what he planned to do with his life. I reminded him that he had talked about going to the United States, to Stanford for postgraduate studies after finishing at the University of Lagos. Papa had thought that was a wonderful idea. But that was before the war, he replied, as if that explained everything. The war was over, I argued with him. He had no answer to that; Stanford was simply another dream the war had killed. He left my house and moved around, staying with an acquaintance and then a friend. He was like a boat set adrift on the Ngene River with no one to row it.

But he was not the only one who had disappointed Papa. I had too. Even on his deathbed, Papa gave me the injunction, "Look after your brother. Make sure he becomes someone."

I prayed that Afam would wake up, that he would be all right. I could not bear Papa's disappointment hanging over me for the rest of my life.

-- -- -- -- -- -- -- -- --

When we were young, I hated Afam's nickname for me. He called me "Akpa Akpu," a heavy sack of cassava, because of my chubbiness. He teased me without mercy. We fought each other, but we stood united once we were in company. I loved this and I loved him. My brother had been smarter than me, but many people outside the family did not know this because I was the one who, through sheer discipline and determination, came first in my classes. He would get into trouble with his friends — go to the stream and play when he should be cutting grass to bring home to my mother's goats; sneak out from school to go steal fruit from other people's mango and udala trees; join the boys who followed the masquerades, those spirit beings that my father, a staunch Catholic, said were of the devil. My father's frequent thrashings with his cane, my mother's lectures and ear-pulling did nothing to curb Afam's enthusiasm for trouble or his appetite for adventure. For all our parents' strictness, he was a free spirit who kept a smile on his face and ran around with the brashness of youth.

Papa would call me into our sitting room, his chaplet in his hands, rubbing the beads. He would sit on one of the two stools that a reverend father had given him and I would sit on the brown floor before him. He would look at me and say, "You will have to take care of your brother. He is smart, but he is foolish also. He has many things to learn yet, but you came almost fully prepared for this world."

I liked the way my father confided in me and entrusted responsibility to me. It made me feel close to him. And so, although I had a deep love for my brother, taking care of him was special because it was something I could do for my father. And I knew this was something important to Papa because, after my brother, my mother had three more girls before her womb seemed to shut up shop, thus leaving my brother an only son for several years. Only sons could carry the family name, could make sure that the name of the family did not get lost.

"See, your name is Afamefuna," Papa would say to my brother. "Your other name, Ugonna, the one who will bring honour to his father, carries a similar weight. I have not failed my parents. I know that you will likewise not fail me, not fail the honourable name of our family. And when the time comes, you, and your brothers, should it be God's will to send us more, will carry on the great legacy of our family and pass it on to your own children."

Afam, diminutive for Afamefuna — "may my name not be lost" — that was my brother's name. When more boys did not come along immediately, the name became even more significant. His academic strengths and his growing height boded well for the responsibilities that rested on his shoulders. His penchant for fun and frivolity did not.

My father would call him for special sessions on our family history. Whenever possible, when I had no work to do for Mama in the kitchen, I would slip outside to listen. We would sit on a mat in front of the kitchen, Papa cleaning his ear with the tip of a cock's feather and our mother peeling egwusi, the darkness lit by the glow of the hurricane lamp and the moonlight. The bright light of electricity would have disturbed the intimacy of the evening; over time, in Umuma, hurricane lamps gave way to kerosene lamps and only occasional electric lights, and then to rechargeable lamps, and then to noisy generators.

My father had a lot of stories, and his deep voice was filled with spellbinding emotion — by turns joyful, sad, angry, but never passionless. Sometimes, it was about adventures in foreign lands, like the war in Burma. Other times, it was about our family. How our ancestors had worshipped the old gods, and how our father, one of his father's two sons, had run away from the ichi ceremony. Igbu ichi was that painful branding and scarification of the face, which formed lines that criss-crossed on the forehead. In those days, it was done to sons of noble families, starting with the eldest, to distinguish them as members of the prestigious society of Nze na Ozo, a society of men who upheld truth. The hot iron seared into the forehead while the young man, in a show of the strength given him by his chi, bore the pain with only occasional short grunts.

Papa had joined the Catholic Church, risking my grandfather's grave displeasure. As an adult, it occurred to me that he might have considered priesthood had it not been for the family trad-itions and the need to ensure that the lineage went on. Papa's own father must have done much etching and imprinting of custom, of family pride and history. For Papa was a staunch Catholic, but also a firm believer that family lineages must be continued. As we grew up, he often said, as frequently as he could find a child to listen, that we should know where we came from. He would often say, "I am a Christian. But one has to protect one's legacies. That is one's heritage. Otherwise life becomes meaningless and vain, as the wise author of Ecclesiastes says." He would pause and look intently at Afam, who always looked past him. My own eyes always stayed on Papa's face, drinking in his words and stories of who we were.

"By joining the church and getting an education," he con-tinued, "I brought light to my family. It is the duty of each new person in the line to bring something good to the family, to keep the family going."

I was proud of my father's contribution to the family line. When farming and old titles were becoming things of the past, our family stood in the new world as respected people — catechists, teachers, headmasters, civil servants, politicians.

"Do you understand what I am saying to you?" my father often asked Afam when he ended one of his stories, peering at him through the dim light of the hurricane lamps.

My brother would say yes, although he had been pinching me in the dark, playing, not taking my father too seriously, trying to get me to do the same.

"That's my boy," said my father, approval and love on his stern face.

I would make a better son of the house, I sometimes thought. But what fell to me was not carrying on the family name but ensuring that the one who was to do so succeeded. So, each morning when we were seven, eight, nine years old, I would hold my brother's hand and we would walk to the school in whichever town my father's teacher job had taken him — Awka, Nanka, Oyi, Umuleri. I intervened in my brother's fights. I made sure he did his homework.

And yet, Afam was kind. He would save his lunch to share with his friends whose parents could not afford three meals a day; he fought bullies for his friends, his height even then a great bonus. His patience for explaining school work always made me think that he would make a great teacher. Once, when I told my father this, he said, "No, he will not be a teacher. He will be a lawyer. Maybe he will become a judge like Justice Louis Mbanefo. He could even become a politician like the great Zik. You, of course, may be a teacher. But you could also become a nurse. Or even a doctor. I hear that there are doctors among Yoruba women."

It seemed we would become whatever we wanted. We finished elementary school and got into the best secondary schools. Papa found ways to inject this information into every conversation he had with the people who visited our house for counselling, advice, or to borrow money. Then we both went to university, me to the University of Nigeria to read English, Afam to the University of Lagos to study law, making my father swell with pride so much so that my mother warned him he might burst and end up in hell, for pride was a sin. He would retort that God, who had begun the good work, would let him, the man who loved Him most on earth, see the end of it.

When my mother, after having had three girls after Afam, unexpectedly conceived again and had her last child, my father called the boy Chielotam — "God has remembered me."

And then the war broke out. And everything changed.

-- -- -- -- -- -- --

Papa died of diabetes in 1972, two years after the war ended. He would have lived if not for his stubbornness. He had developed a small sore on his foot that would not heal. Then it grew. The doctor had said it was infected and that his foot would have to be amputated.

I remember standing by Papa's bedside and hearing him say, "Tell that doctor that nobody can cut off my leg, do you understand me?"

"Yes, Papa, but —"

"You do not say 'but' to me, young woman. Nwabueze Ndubuizu can never be a cripple, do you hear me?"

"Yes, sir."

"Ehen. Now, Afam" — his gaze pierced deep into my eyes — "you must take care of Afam. He is drifting now. The sooner he settles down, the better. He must marry. As soon as possible. At his age, I was married. You must help him. And Chielotam. You understand what I am saying to you?"

"Yes, sir. But —"

"Did I not just say not to say 'but'? Your mother is a strong woman, but you must stand by her and help her."

"Yes, Papa," I whispered, although I wanted to say "but" again: *But why do you talk this way? But you cannot leave Mama? But what about me?* But I did not want to raise his ire, so I kept my buts to myself.

When I returned to the hospital in the morning to relieve my mother, my father was gone.

I had little time to grieve, or to wonder at the unremitting emptiness Papa's death left in my heart, because that was when Afam began to drink. I often thanked God that Papa had not lived to see this, that he only had seen his son's inability to settle down. After drifting for a while, Afam went back to live with Mama in the village. There he drank every second his eyes were open. He stole from my mother. He robbed our neighbours too, selling their goats and chickens to feed his growing habit. He showed no remorse when he was caught, and paid no mind to my mother's weeping.

His behaviour angered me. He was not the only one who went to war. We all had scars from it. But we carried on. We put away our thoughts like carefully folded wrappers at the bottom of the clothes box and faced the business of living. Those whose houses and property had been confiscated by the government in Lagos and Port Harcourt began to figure out how to build new ones there, or moved to Enugu and Onitsha to start life afresh. Those who had buried kwashiorkor-ridden children had other children, woke from their nightmares each morning, and set off for work to feed their children. Young men held jobs in Enugu and even found time to drink and smoke while listening to new bands like Egwugwu. But Afam was determined to throw his life away. When I wanted my mother to come live with me in Enugu, Mama reassured me that Afam was a quiet drunk and that he did not bother her or act violent. Besides, she said, we could not leave him all alone, and there were always people around in the village who could help keep an eye on him. She did not say so, but I knew she feared he would kill himself. Not slowly through his drinking, which she hoped would pass, but through suicide.

Even though Afam was not a violent drunk, it was a blow from another drunk at the village drinking spot that had put him in this coma.

The doctors said to wait and pray, so I prayed. I prayed I would be able to do what my father had asked of me as he lay dying.

Breathing in fumes of Izal, I sat there in the hospital room, silently pleading with Afam, willing him to wake up, to smile at me and call me Akpa Akpu.

But Afam died. He was thirty. We buried him. And my mother entered a depression we thought would never end. For weeks, she rejected food and water, would not get out of bed, would not bathe, and suffered delusions in which she called out for my father and my brother. I had lost a father and a brother within five years. I wondered if I was about to lose a mother.

Finally, one morning, after a deep sleep that lasted almost two days, she woke up and asked for food. The next morning she said to me, "You have to marry." Her tone brooked no argument, she would entertain no excuses.

CHAPTER TWELVE

I sat in my best friend Obiageli's house, watching her lumber around the kitchen, her pregnant belly leading the way. She had insisted on serving me some food even though I was no guest in her home. Knowing that an argument would only take more time than a gracious concession, I waited for the rice and the nchanwu stew to make its slow and delicious way to the stool before me. The aroma of its scented leaves, stockfish, and dry catfish was already making my mouth water.

In the weeks after Mama recovered, a plan had come to me. A plan sent perhaps from the land of the dead because it was not something I would have conjured in the ordinary course of things. Now that I had failed my father and my brother, it was vital that I did not fail my mother. This thought kept me up at night. It stayed with me like an invisible load on my head through the day, immovable no matter which way I twisted my neck.

I needed to talk to someone about my plan, someone besides my mother, who would never approve, even though the prospect of my continued singleness kept her up at night. It was this plan that I had come to share with my friend.

"So tell me," Obiageli said, when she could see that I was now eating leisurely.

"Tell you what?" I asked, stalling. She knew me rather too well, I thought in mild irritation.

She did not respond, merely stared into my face, waiting.

"I will marry Eugene," I announced. Now that it was out in the air, it somehow seemed more real, more feasible.

"Have you gone mad?" she asked, a frown on her pretty face.

I was not fazed; I had expected this. Now that I had had the courage to say it, I felt determination like a nut finding its place on a screw.

"Look, Julie, I know you are worried," she said in a conciliatory manner — I was now a child in the middle of a tantrum who needed to be pacified. "I know that these past few years have been very hard on you." She stopped, and I knew she was thinking of Afam. Grief, she was thinking, had roiled my brains, and was now cooking beans with my best judgment.

Obiageli and I had been friends since our first year at Girls' High School Aba. We both were the children of teachers; we had made it there on brains, not because our parents had money — weren't teachers to wait for their rewards in heaven? — but through the generosity of scholarships. We took care of each other, faced the new world without parents together, challenged and competed with each other. We found each other again in Enugu after the war, and our friendship went on as if the distance of university or the war had not intervened.

"Nwannem nwanyi," we called each other. And indeed, we were sisters. I was closer to her than to my own sisters, who had gone the way of many women — certainly not like the women I thought they would be, being children of my father. They left secondary school, married low-level civil servants, and were content to keep house, one in Enugu, the others in Lagos. They were satisfied to adopt the sensibilities of happily married women focused on their families to the exclusion of anything else. When Afam was drinking himself to death, they kept their eyes fixed on their husbands and children, wringing their hands helplessly but with no intention of coming home. But they came home, eyes rimmed red, shaking and wailing, when our brother was lowered into the red soil of Umuma.

So Obiageli was my sister, my true sister. She was the only one who knew about my affair with Eugene, and she was the only one in whom I confided my plan.

"Nwannem nwanyi," she called me now, her voice soft and full of reasonableness and understanding. "I do not dislike Eugene. You know I do not. But you know the kind of man he is. Tomorrow he could wake up, after he has married you, and go looking for another woman. Men like Eugene use women and throw them aside like used wrappers." She did not need to say that he was doing it to his wife now — who was to say he would not do exactly the same to me?

Her face was worried, but I had come prepared. She would warn me that I was playing with fire and that the flames might engulf me. And I knew that I would not budge. I was already in hell, if only she knew.

"He might," I said. I was no fool. But, driven by my mother's words, could I afford to get too choosy? At thirty-four?

Obiageli thought I was making a serious mistake. She had also thought that the relationship was a mistake from the start. In the past, she had asked if I was certain this relationship was not what prevented single men from approaching me. It was easy for her to say, to speculate on the direct and indirect causes of my singleness; she was married. Already, she had secured her place in her husband's home by bringing forth two boys, one after the other.

I knew what I was doing, I assured her now.

"What about his wife?" she asked, her eyes seeking mine. "All will be well," I said.

She did not look convinced.

I avoided Obiageli's worried gaze as I ate her delicious rice. It was simple, I wanted to tell her: I was helping Eugene get what he really wanted by taking what I needed.

Eugene Obiechina — tall, handsome, if you did not mind that his mouth seemed a little too large for his face, his head a little too thick. When he was animated, one could be fooled into thinking that God had given him more good looks than he actually possessed. Owner of a construction business that had, thanks to a friendship he had formed with the governor of the East Central State in circumstances he told me were better kept quiet, picked up profitable contracts in the Eastern Region as it struggled to rebuild after the war.

He carried himself with the authority of one who knew who he was and was assured of a place in the world. Success, which he defined as money, was his chief desire, followed closely by the need to pass that and his family name on to his sons. He told me often, especially when he had downed some of his favourite goat meat pepper soup, washed down with rich, dark Odeku beer, that his father, Okeke Obiechina of blessed memory, was a great man. Okeke Obiechina, who, his son never forgot to add, had never converted to Christianity, was a great farmer who had given them everything a father could give his children, but had left them no money. The obi, the compound of the Obiechinas, would never chie, never end, Eugene would say, pounding his chest for emphasis. Not on his watch. It sounded like a solemn vow. He, Eugene Obiechina, would give his sons not only the name of the great Obiechina, who had been warriors and great farmers and titled men since time immemorial; he would give them money too. Human heads, barns of yams, large numbers of wives and titles had been good in the past. But now money could provide those indulgences, he would proclaim. Money was what people needed to survive in the twentieth century.

When he made those grandiose statements, which sounded like lyrics from Oliver De Coque's praise anthems for the Peoples Club of Nigeria, I smiled politely. It was clear that he took himself too seriously. But, after my brother passed, I remembered this sort of pontificating and Eugene's ramblings about legacy. I remembered and thought that we, he and I, could assist each other to procure what each of us needed. Eugene's wife had suffered several miscarriages after their two children, both girls. The last was now eleven years old, and his wife had not conceived at all in eight years. Eugene spoke with deep regret about being unable to father a son. Once, he wondered aloud about the possibility of having a son with me, even if I did not want to marry him. Would I be able to give him a son? he asked earnestly.

In response, I told him about my father and my brother, my father's first and, for a while, only son. Having a son did not eliminate every problem, I ventured. He looked at me scornfully when I said this. I was just a woman, he said; I did not understand. He told me that his uncles often asked if he was not man enough to produce a son. I heard pain in his voice when he said this, and I knew that I was the sole repository of this information — his wife had no knowledge of the depth of her husband's feeling of humiliation at his seeming inability to sire a son. I had offered no more words of consolation or encouragement, no pretty little speech that every child was worthy, regardless of gender. Did I not know what it had meant to my father to have Afam and Chielotam, his sons?

At the time of that conversation, it had seemed beyond me — even worried about my single state as I was, desperate as I was to move to the planet of married people — to think of extending our quiet affair into an awkward polygamous marriage. What would my father, he of truly blessed memory, fervent Catholic, think of me? I wondered then.

But that was before Afam died.

My plan was easy and feasible. I would get pregnant and then tell Eugene. He would ask to marry me. And I would agree. It would not be difficult. I knew that it would not be about me. It would be about that son of the Obiechina house that he wanted, like a gambler wanted to win the lottery.

It was not a novel idea, to trap a man with pregnancy. It was even less original when the man in question would be happy to be so trapped. Yet my heart shook. In all the romantic fantasies I had ever had, or the realistic musings of these later years, never had I thought of marriage as a second wife.

CHAPTER THIRTEEN

After I made my plan, I sought out Eugene, who was happy to continue our dalliance. He had kept away while I had been caring for my mother in my flat. Eugene could come to the flat again now that Mama had had her way and gone back to live in the village, in her own house with her own things around her.

I had nothing to do really except wait and, in a reversal of my ways from the previous three years, do nothing to prevent pregnancy from happening. During the next few weeks I let Eugene complain about his wife. I made love with him as often as he could find the time away from her. I prettied myself as much as my plump face and figure would allow.

When I'd waited for three months and I was still not pregnant, I told myself there was no need to wait. Would I not focus on getting pregnant the minute I became Mrs Obiechina? I had promised my mother that the year would not run out before I brought home a man. And so I went ahead with my plot.

I made Eugene his favourite onugbu soup, loaded it with pungent ogili, azu asa, stockfish, and spicy goat meat, and prepared soft, pounded yam to go with the soup. I could see his mouth water when he came to my onugbu soup–smelling flat that evening. He ate eagerly, noisily; as he chewed the meat, he patted his belly that had begun to shoot over his belt. A little distaste came over me. You cannot be too choosy, I warned the dying romantic in me.

I waited until we were in bed. Afterwards, I watched him sleep. He was a good lover, even if unfaithful. His face remained handsome, if imperfect in repose, although it was slowly being swallowed up and softened by fat and middle age. His hair was starting to recede, but he still proudly let the remainder grow out in the afro that men favoured these days. He carried a charm, a charisma and smile, that few women could resist, especially in conjunction with his obvious success in life. His construction business was doing very well, and he spent money on me to prove this, buying me gold chains and pendants. He was still young at forty-two, I thought, although his first child was thirteen. I could see he would do even better than he did now; he would climb further up the ladder of success.

Our first meeting had by no means been romantic. Three years ago, he had come to the school where I taught. His wife had been by his side; they were looking to transfer their first daughter, who was having trouble at school. He did not look like the kind of man who went school hunting, but his wife had failed in the first bid, and he thought it important that he accompany her on this one. I had entertained no ideas and, by his own admission later, he had not really taken much notice of me. I had pointed out the principal's office to them, for which they had thanked me. I dismissed this from my mind, along with all the other insignificant things that occurred in one's day. Until I met him at Kingsway Stores the following week. His "Where have we met?," my attractive red dress I had worn that day out of fear that no good occasion would ever require its appearance, and my willingness to fling caution into the dustbin for a few minutes had ended in what was now an almost three-year affair.

I nursed guilt for only a little while before I settled in to enjoy a fling that I was sure had nowhere to go. I pushed away fears of what might happen should his wife find out, what my father would have thought about my lack of integrity, my mother's cautions about how foolishness could be the downfall of any woman, and the teachings of the church. I soaked myself in the masculine attention that had long bypassed me, in cooking for a man and making love with him, albeit in near secrecy. It was not awful. Indeed, it felt very good for a time. Eugene was the type of man who could keep both a mistress and a wife happy, if they did not hold on too tight. I was a mistress who wanted to be a married woman, preferably the only wife of a man. Despite the occasional irritation, the subterfuge was protective for a woman who wanted to marry one day. It was the perfect affair.

Until my mother, who knew nothing about my relationship with a married man, reminded me of my need to marry. Until I failed my father and let my brother die.

I breathed deeply now and sat up to wait.

The crackle of thunder, the smell and the coolness of coming rain, and the satisfaction of a good orgasm almost lulled me to sleep. But there was a task to be accomplished.

I let him sleep. He could go home later than he usually did, even tomorrow morning. His wife and daughter had gone to visit her parents, he had said. A sign that they had fallen out yet again. In the nearly three years I had known him, they went through these cycles. They quarrelled, she went back to her parents, he would go and plead with her parents, and she would come back. Yet they had stayed together somehow, I reminded myself. I hoped now that I had not overlooked the strength of that relationship.

He wants a boy, I reassured myself.

It was a few hours before he stirred. He frowned when he saw me sitting in the chair across from the bed in the dark.

"Are you all right?" he asked, groggily. He stood up and went to the bathroom before I could say anything. I heard his water flowing into the toilet and knew that this was what had woken him up. He plans to spend the night here, I thought.

"Are you all right?" he asked again. His voice was clear this time, his eyes alert.

I smiled.

"Yes," I said, still smiling. How did pregnant women tell their husbands that they were carrying within them heirs to their name? I looked down and rubbed my belly a little; then I smiled up at him.

I saw the question in his face.

"I am pregnant," I said.

"You are?" he asked.

I felt a frisson of fear. Had I miscalculated?

"Yes," I said softly.

He ran to me. He picked me up; the many pounds of me that I had sometimes thought were keeping men away from me seemed only featherweight to him now. I felt the strength of his grip and thought it would be all right. I was relieved. And then I was afraid.

"You are pregnant. I know it is a boy!" he shouted. "I know it is a boy. I knew you would bring me luck. I knew it!"

"Please keep your voice down," I begged, smiling. My neighbours, I thought.

"Thank you," he said. "Thank you." He said it over and over, as if this were something he had begged me to do. I pushed away my guilt at my deception; I was becoming an expert at it. Hopefully, the baby would come once we married.

"We will have to do things fast," I said.

"What?"

He had not been thinking that far ahead, I could see. I said a little prayer.

"Well, in our place, they will claim the boy if the pregnancy becomes apparent before the marriage rites take place, before the bride price is paid," I said.

It was a big presumption. But he was from an Igbo village too; the customs must be the same.

"That is true," he said with a frown. He let go of me and went to stand by the bed. He did not speak for a while. It must have been a full minute, maybe even two. My heart did a dance of suspense while my head warned me that I had overreached.

"We will have to do things fast," he said then, repeating my words.

I smiled at him, a little weak with relief. I was going to be a married woman. For a minute, I put everything else out of my mind — the baby who was yet to reach my womb, his wife, what my mother would say when I told her he had a wife already — and focused on this. I was going to be a married woman.

And then I returned to reality.

"What about Onyemaechi?" I did not want to say, "your wife."

"Ehen, what about her?" he returned harshly.

I was silent. I was not sure what to think about this change in tone. Even though he had been unfaithful for years, I thought, he must have feelings for her. They had been married twelve — or was it thirteen? — years by now. I did not know if she had any inkling about her husband and me. This would come as a shock to her. I took a deep breath and ground my teeth together. I could not afford to be soft now, to think of her as a woman, perhaps even a little like me.

After our affair began, I had seen her again. She and Eugene had come to shop at the Kingsway Stores. I almost walked right into them in the cosmetics aisle. Eugene looked away rather too quickly when he saw me. I walked past them, as if I had not smelt his sweat on me the evening before. But I took a good look at his wife, more than the passing glance I had given her when she had come to my school with Eugene that first day. She had kept her figure, her fairly pretty face, even after several pregnancies. Her voice when she spoke to him was soft, feminine. And yet he found me attractive? There was no accounting for the tastes of men.

Seeing that his tone had upset me, he came to me, placed a hand tenderly on my belly. This frightened me. My womb was empty. And even if anything came into the belly, it might be a girl.

I shook myself inwardly. It would happen soon enough, I thought. And then we would be a family — me, Eugene, and the baby. I already knew his name. His name would be Afam.

CHAPTER FOURTEEN

I was firmly set on my course. But first, I had to tell Mama Afam, my mother, the woman who had maintained integrity all her life, chastised errant women as part of her duties as the wife of a headmaster and catechist, and who, in her later life, began to propound the theory to her daughters that men had things too easy and it was no duty of women to make them even easier. As I prepared my speech to her, I deliberately removed the excuses: he did not love his wife any more, I did not know he was married, I was crazy about him and could not help myself. Obiageli and I had laughed over that last one. It was untrue, of course, but more importantly, it was one of those things that one read in books, even said to one's girlfriend, but certainly not to one's parents — not in our time or place. So I had prepared a bare-bones speech during which I would permit no interruption until the end.

I delivered it one Saturday. "Mama," I inserted in the lull that reigned between the sharing of tidbits of all that had happened in the village in the past couple of weeks. She looked up from the dry fish she was picking apart in preparation for soup, her expression only slightly quizzical.

"I have met a man."

Mama Afam did not jump for joy immediately — not that that was her way of doing things. She waited, while my heart thumped.

"He lives in Enugu," I said to break the silence.

"Where is he from?"

I told her, and then blurted out: "I am going to marry him."

"Hmm," she said.

Why was she not smiling, and jumping up and down?

But in my heart I knew that she was thinking it was soon.

And then I said it: "I am pregnant."

"Hmm," she said again, as if she had run out of words.

I waited.

"Have you told him?"

"Yes, Ma."

"And he is coming with his people?"

"Yes, Ma."

And so my mother, whose reaction I had dreaded, accepted my decision with composure, if not jubilation. I watched her face, calm as always, break into wrinkled concentration. Her equanimity remained constant through life's struggles, through moves from one village to another following my father, through the financial hardships that accompanied a man whose profession was adequately compensated only in heaven, through raising children who grew up to disappoint her, through the death of a husband and a child. She had aged a lot since Afam died; her strength had wavered substantially. A weakness had come over her frame, and she lost weight, freshness, and the remainder of her youth. Her wrinkles were more pronounced, as if the town crier had suddenly called them forth, her cheeks more sunken.

"You say you are pregnant?" she asked again.

"Yes, Ma," I said, and looked down at my feet. I could feel the steady gaze of her tired eyes on me. Years ago, she would have screamed and pounded me wherever her hands could find. Today, she only stared at me. The weight of telling such an enormous lie bore down on my shoulders. I waited for her to ask how far along. She did not.

"He has been married," I added, wanting to get all the awkward news out at once.

I expected surprise, disappointment. But her face was thoughtful. Instead, she said, "Where is his first wife?"

I said that he intended to give her a house in which she could live. I did not say Onyemaechi sometimes came to me in my dreams, warning me, her index finger reaching between my eyes, pulling out a cutlass that was not there, the type that people use to split firewood, raising it to split my head open, causing me to scream out loud in my sleep.

"Does she have children?"

"Yes, Ma. Two girls."

"Hmm," she sighed, "he will provide for her and the children?"

I said yes.

She nodded.

"You say he has no son."

I said yes.

"Eheennn," she nodded again. She could see how that might make sense: a man, an Igbo man, needed a son. She closed her eyes briefly and I knew that she was thinking about our own family, our compound that might be taken over by extended family if Chielotam went the way of Afam.

"And you are satisfied with this man?"

I knew now that the tricky part was over.

"Yes, Ma," I assured her.

She sighed in resignation. This, a polygamous marriage, would not have been her preference. Unspoken went the worry about the parish priest's opinion of her, of me. I knew she understood that I could do this only because my father was no more. And that this last factor was the most significant. But any marriage was better than singleness in her eyes, and so she quietly acceded once she saw my unshakable resolve. Besides, I was pregnant. The choice was clear between bringing a child into the world with no name and bringing a child into the world with a father. So, instead of launching into a lecture — her style only in the direst of circumstances — she gave me a few chosen words of advice.

"Men don't like to be told that they are stupid. They can be foolish, but put a guard on your lips when it does not involve something major. I have never seen a man who does not like domestic peace."

- - - - - - - - - - - -

I pushed for quick marriage rites. I did not want to show, I told Eugene, echoing my mother's sentiment. Besides, my people might make greater demands, seeing as they would be selling the cow with the calf in its belly.

"Do not worry," he said, his smile as wide as the Niger and Benue Rivers. He did not care if I showed — what could be better evidence of his masculinity? As for demands and long marriage lists, "Am I not Ozukaome?" was his laughing response. "Am I not well able to marry ten of you?" I felt a mild irritation at this, but I did not turn back; common sense was my middle name. But he did acquiesce and was quick to inform his people. His kinsmen supported his decision, he told me. He did not add that it was unthinkable to die without a son to take over the family name — especially for an illustrious man whose business was booming — even if hapless Christian fanatics were beginning to say otherwise.

A date was chosen, marriage lists — goats, fowls, kegs of palm wine, wraps of tobacco for the umuada, umunna, and other groups — were provided. His people's joy was clear on their faces when they came to my village to pay the bride price. It was obvious in the way they took care to address me, the way a woman came forward to help me kneel when it was time to present the cup of palm wine to my husband-to-be, in the way they asked how I was feeling, in the way they rushed to take the tray of kola from my hands like I was carrying a four-gallon container of water up a hill. They met and exceeded the expectations and requirements for taking a bride. They drank good palm wine, nkwu enu, ate ugba and abacha, and danced to their akwunech-enyi into the night before taking me home with them. I wondered briefly if they had done the same for Onyemaechi, and then I put the thought away. The day was for joy.

A church wedding had been out of the question since there would be no annulment. There would be no white wedding gowns, no flower girls throwing confetti at the bride and groom, no bridesmaids in awkward colours and styles, no church photographs that we could display on the wall. This was painful for my mother, who had given away both her other daughters in marriage in the Church. But she said nothing, not even when her parish priest said that she might be denied Communion because I was in sin.

A marriage under statutory law, a marriage at the marriage registry, was also impossible, as there would be no divorce. I did not seek it. It was enough that everybody recognized that this man was mine. Once the traditional marriage rites were done, I went to Asata to my goldsmith and made myself a gold ring. My ring was a little fatter than the regular-sized wedding band, the type my friend Obiageli wore. It was broad enough for anyone whose glance touched my hand to notice. I put it on my finger with satisfaction. I did not make one for Eugene; he was not interested. Having worn one and ceased to once before, I supposed, he was over the thrill. But secretly I wished he would wear one for me, for us.

Seemingly, Onyemaechi had given up much easier than I thought, and my nightmares had not come to pass. She had not fought, at least not with vigour. Perhaps she had cried and begged, or perhaps she had remonstrated and threatened to pluck out my eyes and pour hot water on me — things that a scorned wife would wish to do. If she did any of these, Eugene did not mention them to me. She had not, as I had feared most, come to my school to shame me, to ask why I had chosen to dig my greedy, chubby fingers into her husband.

What she had done was go back to her parents' home, as she often did when they quarrelled. According to Eugene, this time they had simply begged him to take her away. Even if he chose to marry a new wife, that was not reason enough to send the first away. They must have understood her fragile position — a woman without a son, after more than ten years of marriage. If she did not understand, her parents and relatives must have explained it to her in detail. "Your hold over a man is a son," I imagined them saying. "Without that, your place in his house is not secure."

Still, I did not want to run into Onyemaechi at the store or elsewhere. It was uncomfortable even to think about. One night, after I had met his needs, I told Eugene I did not want to share. I could not stand to share him; I loved him too much. More importantly, his son could not be expected to share. But I did not want his daughters by Onyemaechi to suffer by not attending a good school in a city. Perhaps, I suggested, kindness coating every word, perhaps they could move to another town — Onitsha, Owerri, even Port Harcourt. With little reluctance, praising my sensitivity and kindness, he moved Onyemaechi and their daughters to Owerri, leaving us — him, me, and our coming baby — in Enugu.

I stood back and let him make arrangements. I had not really cared about Eugene's money at the beginning of the affair, but now I clambered into the lap of luxury. We moved into a lovely flat in Tinker's Corner, while he started to make plans to build us a house, for I had told him that I could not abide living in the home in which he once had lived with Onyemaechi. We were one of the first families to purchase a colour television. I was soon gifted with a brand-new Peugeot 504; its grey leather seats were the definition of luxury. I went to London for the first time with Eugene and became a "been-to." I watched the quiet envy in fellow teachers' eyes, and heard their loud congratulations. If they gossiped behind my back, I paid no heed.

Eugene spent more time at home, and I discovered that my fears of sharing my space were for nothing. There was something pleasant, rather enjoyable, about having a happy man around. He pampered me the best he could, but this was not what brought me pleasure, for he tired easily of taking care of me, and before long reverted to demanding to be looked after. I did not mind. I liked the smell, the sight and sound of a man in the house, even the take-charge attitude he wore like an invisible cloak. Marriage, I learnt, could be good.

A crib imported from England soon arrived, along with a rug for the child's room. Eugene was going all out. This child would have nothing that could not be called the best. He took me to the village and showed me an ite-otu, its roundness reaching up into a small snout through which good palm wine, nkwu ocha, was poured for brief storage. It had been his grandfather's. The round ceramic pot must have been at least a hundred years old. His grandfather had passed it on to his father, who had given it to him. And now, he would have a son to give it to when the time came.

I marvelled at his excitement at this baby who had not even shown himself, not even in a bigger swell of belly. Some children took their time, I assured him when he mentioned this. My mother said it was the same with her, I lied; women in my family showed very late. I told myself that time was on my side, three months at least. Sometimes, Obiageli had assured me, first-time pregnancies did not show for seven months. Seven months, by which time I should be well and truly pregnant. I soaked in Eugene's attentions and deliberately, consciously, folded my guilt away deep in a metal box, into which I also packed my father's words about integrity. And I tried to get in as much lovemaking as possible, even against my husband's wishes, for he was afraid we would hurt the baby.

Yet, by the fifth month, when even a one-month-old fetus had not found its way into the folds of my belly, it was clear to me that a baby was not coming as I had hoped. With difficulty, but knowing that it soon would be impossible to keep up the pretense, I summoned the courage to inform him that I had had a miscarriage. It had not been difficult to manufacture the tears and the hysteria. I was truly disappointed. I stayed in bed. I accepted his pampering and pretended not to see his own disappointment in his eyes. For two months, he travelled to Owerri on business. But I knew that he went to visit Onyemaechi and her daughters.

It had been more difficult to lie to my mother, to watch her making supplications to the Virgin Mother to open my womb as the first year came, then the second, then the third. I sat by her and held her hand in the same hospital where Afam had died. The prayers she sent out to heaven, the blessings she bestowed in a feeble voice as she lay dying, were for me. For my womb to open up.

On the day that Dimka shot Murtala Muhammed while everyone, including the nurses at the hospital, wondered why he had done it — whether he acted alone or in concert with others, and whether the Igbos in Lagos now would have to flee again even though it had nothing to do with them — I was sitting with my mother, watching her open yet unseeing eyes, and wondering why the ever-present numbness in my soul was so invisible. Her death left me alone, bereft of comfort, orphaned in heart and soul.

— — — — — — — — — —

Eugene became frustrated, then distant. Long gone were the days when he held me and we danced to Bobby Benson's "If You Marry Taxi Driver," our laughter ringing out at our own silliness. By the time Nelly Uchendu's sonorous "Love Nwantinti" became the song of the day, love no longer came up in our conversations. Long gone were the days when we went to watch the Rangers play in the stadium. Success, not man or woman, was Eugene's first love. He threw himself into work, travelling inside and outside Nigeria, pursuing building contracts. Distance meant fewer chances to work towards pregnancy. And when distance did not intrude, lovemaking became work, not pleasure. I could not know if I was truly infertile, as I began to fear. Almost four years after a marriage that had commenced when I'd lied to my lover, now husband, that I was pregnant, I had yet to conceive a child.

Why was everything difficult for me, I tearfully asked Obiageli. A husband, now a child? She spoke words of comfort, but I was not mollified.

One Saturday, Eugene's sisters, all eight of them, came to Enugu with the specific purpose of insulting me and perhaps shaming me out of their brother's house.

They crowded our sitting room, each jostling to hurl abuse faster. "Ashawo. You saw a rich man and you thought you would get your fingers on his money." This one came from Adaku, the eldest sister, who had welcomed me with open arms in the beginning.

"Ndakakwa," Chinyelu, the feisty middle one, who was said to slap her husband on occasion, called me.

It was true that I had gained even more weight in recent years, but the name hurt. I might need to squeeze myself into some seats, but there was no way my weight could break a bed.

"You have sent away the one who could at least produce children, even if they were female. And what have you brought in but your fat buttocks that could break a couch? What do you do all day but plot ways in which to spend our brother's wealth on choice foods?"

I stood by and let them expend themselves. It would be worse if I responded — eight against one was an uneven match. I did not want to give them an excuse to fall on me and do me physical harm. I could tell that Chinyelu was itching to give me a beating.

When they were done, they left, promising to come back soon and throw my things out if I did not have the good sense to show myself out of their brother's house.

Eugene came back from his business trip and I told him what had transpired. After a little silence, he responded by asking if I did not think I deserved it. Soon, our voices were rising in anger.

"Anuofia."

"Nwanyi aja."

"Efulefu."

"Ashawo."

"Uregurenshi."

The invectives were hurled out into the night, where they must have reached the ears of our neighbours. But we did not care. We shouted ourselves hoarse until he got into his new Mercedes and left.

The insults hurt. And it was in the hurt that I realized how much I had hoped to convert an inauspicious beginning into a love story, deception into truth. And it was in the depths of that hurt that I came face to face with the knowledge that this was not to be.

Though we did not quarrel like that often, domestic harmony had become a distant memory, and I began to realize that a single life was better than a life lived within the prison of a loveless marriage. Especially when you had put yourself there willingly. There was a little death in the way we now lived, an emptiness, a nothingness of spirit where something — perhaps not true love but at least a certain kind of friendship — had existed. This death stood side by side with the vexing truth that I had brought this on myself. I was surprised that I could not decide what I wanted: to stay or to go. Resolve, once my strongest virtue, had gone missing, like the old woman who went to the market and forgot her way home.

As I pondered all this, I did not know that I was about to engage in a bigger lie than the one that had brought me into the marriage.

CHAPTER FIFTEEN

The opportunity for the lie came late in 1978, amid Lt General Olusegun Obasanjo's regime, his call for Nigerians to tighten their belts to prepare for austerity, and his promises to hand over power immediately to the civilians. The opportunity came in the package of a baby in Obiageli's small apartment.

Obiageli had remained my constant friend, wiping the tears that flowed freely and unceasingly after my mother passed. She encouraged me when barrenness rose like a wall of shame around me. I made her laugh when she complained about the difficulty of her marriage to Emma, the man who had a senior position in NEPA, the electricity corporation, but lived like a mason who could not find work. When Obiageli complained about his stingy ways, I would say, "Ah ah, Obiageli, nwannem nwanyi, you would not want a man who gives away his money like an aching belly gives away shit. Believe me, I live with one of those."

My husband's generosity was legendary. Once he had given a man the keys of a car he had just alighted from because the man, a taxi driver, had lost his car when it was engulfed by fire and he had no money to pay hospital bills to secure the release of his wife, who had delivered by Caesarean section, and his baby, both of whom were detained at the hospital until he could raise the money. At Christmas, Eugene would host a party for the Enugu branch of the Umuma Town Union. Back at the village, where we spent every Christmas, he would buy goats and cows for the people in the village, and on Christmas morning, people trooped into our compound for their portions of rice, onions, tomatoes, and the meat of freshly slaughtered goats. I often worried that he was not saving enough and reminded him that we would have lots of responsibilities throughout the year.

"Orimili agwu agwu. The ocean never runs out of water," he would intone in a booming voice.

"But he takes good care of you," Obiageli would retort. "If Emma would give me a tenth of the gold Eugene has bought you in a lifetime, I would consider myself a queen. My husband does not look after me — even worse, he does not look *at* me. Whether I wear rags or the most expensive george in the market, it is all the same to him."

"But you know you are beautiful, Oby nwannem nwanyi," I would tell her. "Your beauty would make rags the fashion of the week." She was in no danger of wearing rags; she had a job and she was learning to hide her money from Emma. Plus, I had given her several of the georges I had bought in that first year when things were good between me and Eugene.

Obiageli would laugh, appreciatively. She was indeed beautiful. She was one of those people whose smile made you smile back automatically, her eyes lighting up her evenly brown and wrinkleless face. She liked to flirt too, and had the eyes of the male teachers in her school glued to her. Even Eugene was susceptible to her charm and made sure to enquire about her health often. I had on occasion heard other people wonder what had drawn her to the short, nondescript Emma.

"Besides," I would continue, "if money is all that Emma is stingy about, you must be a happy woman." At this reference to his sexual prowess we both would laugh helplessly.

Still, my friend had the one thing a woman needed: I envied her the two boys she had borne for Emma.

When I complained about Eugene's lack of attention, his partying, womanizing ways, Obiageli would say that powerful men like my husband needed a few vices, but that the important thing to remember was that he always came home. She did not remind me that she had warned me before I married him. She would say in a soothing tone that, when I had children, I would not mind his occasional misbehaviour. When would that be, I would ask in despair. Soon, she would reply, confident.

But she, too, had begun to worry. When Obiageli one day told me about an Uwani woman who was said to help women in my predicament, I laughed hard.

"Have you forgotten who I am? Imazikwa m? The daughter of the catechist?"

But Obiageli was bent on a course. "I am telling you. She is good. I have heard lots of good things about her. Very effective."

"I want a baby, Obiageli. But not enough to see a dibia. I am Catholic."

"Nwanyi na-acho nwa na-agboto aluru ula," she said. *A woman who wants a baby goes to bed naked.*

I sighed. She smiled.

We got into my Peugeot and drove to Uwani to see Eze Nwanyi.

- - - - - - - - - - - -

Number 8 Chiene Street was a block of several flats. We stood outside, wondering which was Eze Nwanyi's. Obiageli knocked on the first door.

A young boy, not more than eleven and still in his school uniform, opened the door and greeted us politely. "Good afternoon, Mas."

"Good afternoon," Obiageli responded. "We want to see Eze Nwanyi. Do you know which is her flat?"

"It is this," he said.

"Ah, that is good." Obiageli smiled and glanced at me reassuringly. "Can we see her?"

He nodded. "Who shall I tell her wants her?"

"Mrs Nwajei," Obiageli said, giving her name. He stepped back and closed the door on us.

Soon after, a woman opened. She was wearing white jeans and a frilly long-sleeved red shirt. Her hair was a big, big afro, and her mouth coated with red lipstick. She should have looked loud and brash, but she didn't.

"Good afternoon. Kedunu?" Her voice was soft.

"We are well. We are here to see Eze Nwanyi," Obiageli told her.

She studied our faces, from one to the other. She must be wondering what brought us on this journey.

She invited us in. A medium-sized room, with family pictures on the wall and comfortable-looking seats. "What do you want with Eze Nwanyi?"

She looked at us, waiting for us to speak. Obiageli looked at me.

"We would like to see Eze Nwanyi," she repeated.

The woman smiled. "I am Eze Nwanyi."

I was surprised. I had expected someone different, perhaps wearing white marks on the face and a wrapper across her chest — not this sophisticated-looking lady.

My tongue was strangely tied, and as I moved it around in my mouth, Obiageli spoke.

"My friend," she said, glancing at me and then back to Eze Nwanyi, "has had some delay in child-bearing."

"Hmm," was all Eze Nwanyi said. She invited us to sit, went to the corner and unrolled what turned out to be the skin of an animal, goat or cow, I could not say. She sat on it, facing us. She asked for two naira, the consultation fee. I fumbled in my bag and brought the money out. She gestured for me to leave it on the floor.

She took out some beads and, placing them on the carpet, turned them this way and that.

She studied them.

"It is well. Soon you will have a baby boy. Do not fret. He will come to you soon."

Obiageli asked, "Is there anything she should do?"

Eze Nwanyi stared at her. "No. When the baby comes, she will come and say thank you with whatever pleases her." She stood up. It was a dismissal.

We thanked her. But I was dissatisfied. Was that it? Not even a fast, a potion? Soon? How soon? I felt deflated, and only then realized how hopeful I had been.

-- -- -- -- -- -- --

By October 1977, Obiageli had become pregnant again. She told me, almost apologetically. Her hands were full with her two young boys when her aunt, Mama Nathan, arrived without notice. She brought a little baby boy with her, very young, about four months.

Obiageli was put out: her aunt's visit would make relations with Emma more difficult, and she could not fathom why Mama

Nathan had come to visit, surprising her. She had not seen her aunt since Mama Obiageli, Mama Nathan's sister, passed away three years before. As a girl, Obiageli had gone on holiday to Mama Nathan's when she and her husband lived in Ajakurama. Then, after she started to work in Enugu, both Mama Obiageli and Mama Nathan would come to visit together. But Obiageli had not seen Mama Nathan when she lost her only son, Nathan. She had been ill and unable to attend the burial.

Mama Nathan called the baby her son, referring to him as Nathan, and would add nothing more. Obiageli speculated that the boy was her grandchild, a child of her late son. But where was his mother, I wanted to know. The boy was entirely too young to be travelling with Mama Nathan, Obiageli said. She had come with wraps of akamu, which she fed the baby on the first day. Obiageli thought this was not the best food for a baby that young, and bought some baby formula, which Mama Nathan was all too happy to give the baby. She smiled as she fed the baby from the feeding bottle, calling it nni ndi ocha.

Emma also wanted to know why Mama Nathan had come to visit, and with a baby, but she gave no satisfactory answer, repeating only that the baby was Nathan come to life again. This made little difference to Emma; he could not understand why he had to spend extra money to feed people he did not know. It was true that he was required to open up his home to his in-law — after all, a man was the chi of his in-laws, ogo bu chi onye. But, as Obiageli often told me, it almost seemed as if he experienced a physical pain when money came out of his pockets.

It took only a week of Mama Nathan's visit for Emma to begin to hint that Obiageli's aunt and the baby had to leave. It was unheard of to send an in-law away, especially one who might now be argued to be one's wife's mother. But Mama Nathan was in no position to leave. A few days after she came, she fell sick.

Obiageli thought she had malaria because she had a high temperature, complained of a sour mouth, and had no appetite.

The only truly content person in Obiageli's home was Tata, the baby. We called him Tata, the name for every newborn baby. His little cheeks filled up to bursting point with laughter whenever I picked him up. It was uncanny, the way I made him laugh.

While Obiageli juggled her boys and her husband's irritation at having extra mouths to feed, I helped with the baby. Twice, thrice a day, I stopped by Obiageli's small flat in Ogui to see and touch the little boy. After a while, I got into a routine. I bought tins of formula for Tata, and fruit for Mama Nathan. I stepped into the room where she lay on the bed to ask how she was doing. I waited for the short time it took her to say her feeble thanks and observe that life was in the hands of God. I then escaped to pick up Tata. I fed him, I burped him, I sang him silly songs, and made funny faces as I walked around with him. Once, when he spurted milk all over me, I wiped it with tissue, asking myself if this was how all mothers felt — this tightening of the chest.

Obiageli watched my attentions with concern, but she did not stop me. I felt her eyes on me, but ignored the unspoken queries.

"This one must have some kind of magic," she finally said one day as I sat down on a small kitchen stool, resting from my exertions with the baby. "Not even your godson got this much attention from you." She looked up from the stove where she was stirring some delicious-smelling ogili-and-okporoko-filled onugbu soup. The smile on her face took the sting from her statement.

I knew what she meant. I had been good with Ife, her first boy, my godson, and Uzoma, the younger one. But my attentions to Tata were extraordinary. He filled an emptiness in my heart. My mother was right; children were the best things in life.

"He is a lovely baby," I said to her, smiling.

Obiageli and I understood each other well, so I knew what she was thinking: that I needed a child of my own; and that coming to feed and play with Tata would not give me what I desired. But brooding at home, mooning after my husband, even visiting a dibia had not solved my problem either. So I took care of Tata, and she watched me with anxious eyes.

- - - - - - - - - - - -

Mama Nathan did not get better on the tablets of chloroquine. She was sick for over a week before Obiageli sought help from a doctor. The doctor said she had to be admitted immediately; her blood pressure was very high. Emma murmured that he knew that no good would come out of this visit and that they would be packing their bags to the village, such poverty would this hospital visit bring upon them. He was wrong: two nights later, Mama Nathan died, the victim of two massive strokes.

Obiageli was distraught; the poor woman, she kept saying, the poor woman. She must have known that she was dying and sought out a relative, Obiageli said through tears. Emma was furious: expenses, from the doctor's bills, to the mortuary, to transporting the corpse back to Nwokenta, Mama Nathan's village, to buying milk for the baby.

Arrangements had to be made for the funeral. A week and a half later, they took her home to the village to bury her.

I could not go with Obiageli, for Eugene came home unexpectedly, angry about a business deal gone sour. He had been away for a month and fell ill with malaria on his return. He was one of those people who became babies when a touch of fever attacks them. I counted "one, two, three, set, go," to get him to gulp down his medicine. He expected an "ndo" every time he moaned, which was often. In short, it was not a good time to mention that my friend needed help. Our relationship these days had a fragile quality — a soapy glass that could slip and splinter at any time. I stood to gain nothing if it shattered.

Instead, I stayed home and mourned yet another loss, an unexplainable one this time: the departure of the baby to Mama Nathan's village. The sharpness of my grieving surprised me. I woke up each morning with the heaviness of a rock in my chest. I went to school with dread and taught my classes with unwillingness, knowing that my usual drive from my school in Emene would not end with my regular stop at Obiageli's before I went home to Tinker's Corner. Obiageli had marvelled at my willingness to drive all around Enugu each day just to see Tata, even if the driving was in a brand-new Peugeot 504.

I expected that Obiageli and Emma would come back without Tata. But they brought him back. He was his sunny, chubby self, unaware that he had lost his closest relative. And my joy came back.

At Obiageli's house one evening, I rocked the baby to sleep. I put him down in the crib gingerly. It was the same crib that had lulled Obiageli's children to sleep when they were his age. The crib stood in the sitting room — it had been in the bedroom when Obiageli's boys slept in it, but Emma would not hear of Tata sleeping in their room.

I stared down at him, half listening to the sounds of the news on NTA. I was not eager to go home, although it was past seven and darkness had taken the place of day. But Emma's dour face and occasional questions about Eugene meant to remind me that married women did not stay out of their homes after seven o'clock made me stand up and announce my departure to my friend.

"Is Tata asleep?" she asked from the kitchen.

"Yes."

"I will see you out." She came minutes later and we walked down the stairs in the silent companionship of friends who did not need chatter as reassurance.

She followed me into my 504. She loved my car and took every opportunity to sit in it. Just the car alone made Eugene the husband of the century, she often said, which never failed to elicit a laugh from me. I too liked the car, even though its grey leather seats had been the recipient of many tears.

That night, as we sat in my car in Obiageli's yard, she turned towards me with a serious expression, and laid out the plan to me.

I listened to her in shock; I could not believe my friend capable of such cunning.

"I can't do it," I told her. It was impossible. I would be found out.

I had stolen a husband. Stealing a child would be impossible.

"Hold on," Obiageli said, raising her index finger. "Think. Just think. What do you stand to lose by thinking about it?"

When I said nothing, she added, "Perhaps it was meant to happen this way. Perhaps this is the way your chi meant to send you a child."

"That is not how the chi of others send them children," I retorted. "That is not how your own chi sent you yours."

"Yes," she said. "You are right." There was a pacifying quality to her voice. But she persevered. "Everybody's chi is different. You know that. Even this little boy's chi. Remember what Mama Nathan's husband's relatives told us about the mother of this child? How she ran away from home? No one knows where. I told you, the girl's family does not want him; Mama Nathan's family does not want him; Mama Nathan herself is dead. Even at the burial, Mama Nathan's family avoided the subject. You should have seen the shifty looks they had on their faces!"

Obiageli had told me these things before. The mother, a young girl married under circumstances that sounded like something out of the last century, had run away. The men of the family did not want to know about the child. He was an extra mouth to feed, one who would grow up and demand land that had been in their family for years. He was an unwanted child, almost like the ones abandoned on the streets by hapless young girls who sought to hide their shame. It would be tragic to send this baby to people who did not want him, I thought. Would he even survive?

Maybe this *was* my chi at work. My chi had not been very kind, not in matters of marriage, not in matters of child-bearing. Perhaps it was changing its mind.

Obiageli, intuitively picking up on my easing resistance, said, "You don't have to give me an answer now. Think on it. Only remember that Emma says I have to take him to Mama Nathan's people next week."

"But what will you tell Emma?" I asked. How did my friend think we could get away with this?

"Leave that to me," she said confidently. "Will you be the one to say I did not return him to the village?"

"What about Eugene?" My husband who was halfway out the door, who had reminded me the other day that the clock was ticking on my presence in our home?

"Did I not say to leave that to me? You ask — what about Emma? What about Eugene? What about this man? What about the other? But what about yourself? We women have to think about ourselves too. I said go and sleep on it. Tell me if you want the boy. And we will figure out the details. You have a week, not more."

- - - - - - - - - - -

I did not sleep that night, and for many nights after. I stood before the river of decision again and pondered Obiageli's proposal. Four years was not a long time, but in the life of a barren woman, it was a lifetime. I had not conceived even once. With the months growing longer between lovemaking, it might be a long time before it happened, I told myself. That is, if Eugene did not send me away, as he had his first wife. The child, Tata, had woken up the spirit of motherhood in me. He had opened my eyes to see what my mother had said — the heart of every woman longs to hold, to love, a child.

I longed to hold him, though he had not grown in my belly. Who would look after him in the village? The relatives who had been so quick to let Obiageli bring him back to Enugu? I thought about Obiageli's assurances that I would be doing Tata a favour.

How did Obiageli think we could deceive my husband? I wondered. The man whose only sorrow was that his raging masculinity had still not produced a son? Should he even imagine that I was suggesting he adopt a child, one who did not spring from his loins, I would be out the door. Should he discover that he was tricked into accepting a child who was not his, I would find myself in the netherworld telling my ancestors why I left the earth so soon.

Many thoughts made their stop in my head, but instead of moving on, they stayed to join the din of confusion in there. So, for three days I said nothing about it to Obiageli. Three turbulent nights and days of pretense, pretense at ordinary tasks and conversation, while thoughts churned on the inside. I kept telling myself that it was impossible. Impossible to accomplish. I would be found out. Then divorced, disgraced, detained.

She did not press. Every time I went to her home I held the chubby, happy little boy to me and wondered how anyone could consider him a liability — how anyone could not want him. My desire grew with each visit, and I imagined that his smile widened each time he saw me.

When I came back from my visits, I spent restless nights, between nightmares filled with retribution.

I did not think I could pull off the deception this time, I told Obiageli. She disagreed. "Where there is a will ..." she reminded me, waiting for me to complete the idiom we had learnt in our English class in our first year at Girls' High School Aba in 1951. "There is a way," I chorused back to her. This time she could help me, she said. I wanted to be infected by her confidence, but my heart still quaked within me.

In the end, it was not a difficult decision. If I was honest, I had made it the minute Obiageli asked if I wanted Tata. I wanted him. With all my being.

PART THREE
IN THE HOLD, 2011

CHAPTER SIXTEEN
NWABULU

I got ready for work in the dark; my movements were deft and quiet. Ifechi often wondered why I did this. He would not have minded being woken up, he used to say. But it was an old habit learnt during many years of domestic service with the rich and the poor. Accommodating others, containing issues, and making sure no problems arose. Putting others first and your needs last. I was learning to value myself, but it was work that I would do the rest of my life.

Work, hard work, was also ingrained in me. If by chance he awoke to empty his bladder while I was getting dressed, Ifechi would stare at me and say, as if this were a truth universally acknowledged by reasonable people, "Nwabulu, there is more to life than work." I believed many things he said; honesty and integrity were engraved in him and showed on his face so everyone could see. Like those marks that were put on children in the old days to prevent convulsions — small, yet distinct, and visible to all. But I did not believe this one. If there was more to life than work, it was work that was the foundation of everything. At least for those whom life had handed nothing, for those from whom life had taken important things. Like a child.

All dressed — a long skirt made from a beautiful green Ankara fabric that I had bought in Onitsha and made in the flowing mermaid style that had shown no signs of waning since the early 2000s; a chiffon sleeveless shirt that showed off my still firm and toned arms; flat, fashionable slippers for comfort; a head scarf because I felt like it, all picked out the night before — I turned towards where Ifechi slept. He still had not moved. He was one of those lucky people who slept like the proverbial edi; I awoke at the slightest sound. I smiled at him in the darkness even as his gentle snores punctuated the quiet.

Then I stepped outside the room and headed to the kitchen, walking quietly in the darkness. This was our routine: I went to work and he would come by on his way to his; he said he could not afford to spend so many hours at work without setting eyes on me in the morning. I smiled again. Routines like that had the deep comfort of a blanket in the harmattan cold.

I turned on the light when I got to the kitchen. Although one of the workers could have made me breakfast, I always got this myself each day, and on the weekends I got Ifechi his. The reason was simple: I woke up before everyone else and my stomach woke up with me. I used to wonder if my stomach did not quite trust that the days of hunger pangs and insufficient food were over.

I sat down on a stool, pulled a novel from my bag, and left it on the table. I made myself Milo, scooping large spoons of Peak milk into my mug. I took a sip of my tea — as we call every drink made from hot water around here — put some slices of bread on a plate, and picked up my book. Ifechi had bought me an iPad last year and my son, Chukwuemeka, had downloaded books on it. But I was old-fashioned. At least Chukwuemeka thought so. If it was old-fashioned to flip brown pages, turn the book face down while I stood up to go to the sink before returning to the familiarity of my brown pages, then old-fashioned I was and always would be.

I proceeded to eat without style or grace. That was one good thing about my early morning eating — I did not have to watch my manners and behave as though I were a well-brought-up person, chewing my food quietly, not letting the saliva from my mouth touch anything outside it, as Daddy insisted in those days. I breathed deeply and wished that no one would wake up for a while. The smell of last night's ora soup had clung to the walls and now climbed into my nose.

I had been up an hour, buried deep in Colombia, before one of my girls came in. "Good morning, Ma," she said, the night's sleep still in her voice.

"Good morning, Nkechi. Did you sleep well?" With those first words to another, the day had truly started. I mourned a little as I became an adult again, putting the book in my bag and arranging my features to suit my voice, the madam of the house.

"Yes, Ma," she replied. I could see that sleep had not completely left her. I stood up. She only came up to just below my breasts. She would never be tall, I thought. Her legs were short and stocky, planted solidly on the ground in a little bow, like they had no idea why those of us who pursued the heavens with our frames did that. She was from a village in Udi. She had come to live with me two years ago and, at first, had eaten as though food was a new thing, a novelty invented in my house. It showed in her girth but not in her height. Nnenna, the other girl who had been with me a year, would complain to me. I tried not to let my irritation show — Nnenna had no way of seeing back into the past to know that I could not be put out by a young girl eating too much, that I knew, like a wife knew what a dear husband does in the wee hours, what hunger felt like. I let Nkechi eat and I was rewarded with a hard worker who woke up to start her chores each morning before everyone else.

"When Nnenna comes in," I said, "let her make Papa Onyinye's breakfast. Then come to the shop as soon as both of you have eaten."

"Yes, Ma."

"If the carpenter shows up this morning before you girls go, call me on your phone so I can speak with him." As I said this, I felt in my bag for my mobile phone.

"Yes, Ma."

"Tell him I said not to start work on that poultry house before he has spoken to me or Ifechi." I pulled on my ear for emphasis.

"Yes, Ma," she answered again, patient, acquiescing, much as I would have been years ago.

I was different, I reassured myself. I was a better mistress than some of the madams had been to me or to the housemaids I worked with. I did not overwork my girls. I let them go home every other weekend. I fed them well, gave them comfortable beds to sleep in. I did not raise my voice too often, nor did I ever raise my hands to them. I did not make them do anything that I could reasonably do myself. I got myself water when I wished to drink, searched out missing trinkets from under my bed, served my husband his food when I was home, and cleaned up after myself. I permitted them rest, especially on Sundays. Most importantly, I taught them my tailor's trade so that, when they left me, they could depend on themselves and help their families. Unlike many madams, I talked to them frankly about sex and love, menstruation and womanly desires, birth control, sexually transmitted diseases, and the value of waiting for the right person and the right time. I ignored their horrified expressions and their shamefacedness, and told them what someone should have said to me at their age.

"Should we bring some okpa with us?" Nkechi asked.

"No." I felt too full to contemplate eating anything else, although from experience I knew that my belly would wake up again around brunch time.

When I stepped out, the sun was still trying to make up its mind whether it had to work yet another day. The car sputtered a little, also trying to decide whether its ten years on earth — that is, if you believed Innocent, the mechanic who had sold it to me — did not yet qualify it for retirement.

The drive from our house to my shop was short. Our house. That phrase felt so good, as good as anything that had taken its time coming. Although it was not the Independence Layout I had dreamt of, it was mine, ours. A house in Trans-Ekulu was not something anyone could turn their nose up at. There were three neighbourhoods that were the best: Independence Layout, GRA, and Trans-Ekulu. Initially built by the government and acquired mainly by civil servants — in those days when civil service was the place to work, the place where salaries were paid without interruption, and you had a guaranteed pension — Trans-Ekulu lay between Independence Layout and GRA. Independence Layout was the place for the rich, where I first served in Daddy's house as a housemaid; GRA, the government-reserved quarters, was where the colonizing Europeans had first lived and where top civil servants lived until they retired from government service. But things had changed. Trans-Ekulu had become commercial-ized, as I imagined most places in Nigeria were now becoming. The playground had been converted to a shopping mall. And all along Dhamija and Federation Avenues you would find shops selling everything from fresh vegetables to children's slippers and electronic appliances, the red dust that no one could escape coat-ing the wares. That was where I had my shop, hanging up the creations I made for rich and, sometimes, poor women.

Our house stood in one of the still-quiet streets. Hopefully, I told Ifechi at the time, the market would stay where it was, and we could have peace. It was not a new house. But the pride that swelled in me whenever I drove my car into its good-sized compound rivalled the happiness that I felt at other blessings my life had enjoyed. Me, a house owner. In Enugu. Who would have thought it? Who? The housemaid from Nwokenta? The tailor in Abakpa? I wished my father could see me, see our house.

It had needed lots of work when we bought it. The previous owners had abandoned it, allowing it to become dilapidated even while still living in it. I insisted we move in and then begin to renovate gradually. Ifechi acceded. He was almost as excited as I was. I remembered the houses I had worked in, the houses I had carried my measuring tape to or brought the finished product to, and I determined that we would live like that too — gold-plated vases, sweet-smelling candles, and rich-coloured curtains. I was forever looking for decorative items.

When we first moved in, three years ago, I wondered if we would ever get the incense smell of the previous owners out of the house. But, as we began to live there and fill the place with our own smells — the smell of the ora soup that my husband needed almost like air, the smell of the goats and their droppings and their pee, the smell of the new furniture that we had made to fit the sitting room downstairs, the smell of our candles that were never lighted for fear the house would catch fire, and the lavender Air Wick that I sprayed round the sitting room so that our guests could breathe something nice — the suffocating aroma of incense slowly dissipated, perhaps seeking the people who had originally put it there. Soon, I would add the smell of the poultry chickens that I planned to put in my new poultry if Mr Emmanuel, the carpenter, finished it in this lifetime.

My husband was not looking forward to the last. The smell of poultry could wake the dead, he said. And why did we need that? His computer business and my tailoring business were enough to feed us. Why did we have to add the smell of chicken poop to tell God that we were working hard? I ignored him. I knew the trick: Never argue too hard when you wanted something. Ifechi loved to argue and then to win. After almost two decades together, he knew better. But it was hard to change old habits. It did not matter how many times he lost — and lose he had many times — he had to argue. So long as you did not get into an argument while he walked about the house pontificating on any issue, so long as you waited until he came into a room where it was only the two of you, with no outsider listening in and hearing you win the argument, you could do anything you wanted. So I was ignoring him and going ahead with the poultry house. As the Igbo people would say, you do not stand in one spot to watch the masquerade. Putting one's hands in various businesses would tell poverty that we were really serious about not making friends.

I parked in front of my shop, got out, and unlocked the heavy padlock. Stepping inside, I took a deep breath: time to make the clothes of the rich and not-so-rich.

As I sat at my table, before I reached down for the bag of fabric I planned to begin work on that morning, something told me that the day would bring surprises. The feeling was so strong it made me keep quite still. One could be forgiven for thinking I was meditating or praying. Neither was a pastime in which I indulged; I never could find time for sitting idly. But the sensation was so strong, knowledge like a great shaft of wind to my consciousness. I took a deep breath; God knew I was not deeply intuitive. If I was, I would have known not to return with Ezinwa to Mama Nathan that day. Yet sometimes too I had these feelings. Like when I met Ifechi, over twenty years ago now.

We met at a Rotary function at Hotel Presidential, not an event I would have attended in the ordinary course of things — I did not care much for rich and middle-class men and women enjoying one another's company at an upscale restaurant or hotel, wearing their nice clothes, perhaps doing some charity. But a customer whose clothes I made was being sworn in as something or other and requested that I come and I ended up sitting next to Ifechi. The attraction had been instant. The mutuality of it took me entirely by surprise. Men were often attracted to me — something about my tallness, and my dark, perpetually youthful skin I inherited from my father. But it was not often that I was attracted to them; arrogance, an assurance that the world and its women were men's — a feature most masculine packages came with — held little appeal for me the older I got. A man like this, who most certainly had a wife at home or abroad, appealed to me even less. Yet I found something about this man attractive.

I could not imagine the attraction going anywhere. He was a cultured, educated, well-off man, ten years older than me. I had educated myself, made a little money. But I was still only a seamstress who had done well. He had been a senior officer in the state, running different small businesses on the side.

I ran; he pursued. Nobody thought it was a good idea. Not his people, who said I was beneath him. Not Uzoamaka and her husband, who said it was impossible that his intentions were good — he was too old for me, too educated, too everything we were not. It took him two years to convince me. Once he did, we were married. That was the last time I went to Nwokenta. As soon as he paid the bride price, I closed the chapter on my hometown.

My thoughts returned to the shop and the customers who were due to pick up their clothes that day. I picked up a bright red fabric with a wild print that looked brash, but which, by the end of the day, under my eyes and hands, would be tamed to grace a curvy woman's body. So strong, however, was my feeling of disquiet, that working on the fabric in the quiet of the early morning did not bring the usual feeling of peace and productivity.

Ifechi came by on his way to work. He brought Nkechi and Nnenna with him. I sent them to run errands before pausing to look at him. I would never tire of him. Time would cause everything else to fade, but not my intense love for this man. I smiled at him. He smiled back. In that exchange was everything — comfort, safety, bonding, friendship, even desire, all the things a good, long marriage could hold.

Ifechi stepped out, but returned with Wedgeman, a distant relative and one of Ifechi's basketful of good deeds. Wedgeman had stopped at home but, meeting an empty house, had decided to come by the shop. Given that it was only eight in the morning, I wondered when he had risen from his bed. He must have taken the first bus from Okpatu to arrive so early. I wondered what he wanted now.

"Madam, Nwanyi Nwokenta, ezigbo Oriaku Mazi Ifechi." He called out my titles, those that he had bestowed on me, grinning, his black cheeks stretched in the effort, his eyes shining. He must have got some money out of his relative already, I thought. I wondered what the reason was this time. If his wife was not ill, one of his children would be in trouble for not paying for something or other at school, or the workers who cultivated his farm would be threatening to cut off his good leg for failing to make good his promises to pay, or his belly would be growling, having done so for two days running and now threatening to jump out from where the creator had so thoughtfully put it. His tongue was fluid, darting in and coming back out with stories.

Many years before, Wedgeman had worked as a helper on the long, heavy trucks that ferried foods from the fertile north of Nigeria down to the east. His job was to put the wedges, two big slabs of wood, behind the tires to prevent the lorry from rolling down a hill both in busy traffic and on lonely highways. A wedgeman's job was an important one, he liked to tell me, unaware that he had told me the same thing many times since I married Ifechi. A lorry could throw out all the food — fresh vegetables, corn, yams, potatoes, pepper, tomatoes — smashing it to pieces, causing a huge loss of money for everyone involved. It could smash into another lorry and kill people — one of the drivers he had known had died this way, not something to look on, and the nightmare of witnessing it still kept him up nights. So, to be a wedgeman was to have the most important job in the world, he would say. I wish I could be a wedgeman, my son Chukwuemeka would say when he was younger. Wedgeman would laugh and say that he was sure that his parents — Ifechi and I — had better plans for him. Plus, he would not wish what had happened to him in that job on anyone else.

He did his work well and had become Wedgeman to all. His given name, even after that job ended, vanished from the memories of those who knew it. One day, the bad luck that had followed him out of his mother's womb, killing her as soon as he exited, caused him to be slower than usual in jumping out of the lorry. By the time he came down, the lorry was already rolling back, and another whose brakes were bad was coming forwards. The two smashed into him, mashing him up like a squished sardine in a sandwich, the kind he liked to eat when he came to our house in Enugu. When I heard this story, I tried to imagine him, small, shiny black, with even darker hair, squeezed between two white lorries, screaming in his voice that was higher than a man's should be.

He was brought to the National Orthopaedic Hospital in Enugu. Ifechi, his cousin, visited him regularly and took care of him after he left the hospital. When his first child was about to be born, Ifechi went to the village and brought his wife to the hospital because she needed a Caesarean section. Wedgeman loved my husband and, as soon as the new yam came out, would carry bags of yam to our house, his lame leg dragging behind him. Ifechi at first tried to dissuade him, but seeing that this hurt Wedgeman's feelings, he stopped. Thus, Ifechi would wait for him to arrive with the crop before eating new yam for the year.

Now, Ifechi handed him over to me and, smiling at me in the only kind of public display of affection he felt capable of showing, told me that he would call me later that afternoon.

When Ifechi left, Wedgeman stayed behind. I hinted from time to time that the bus to Okpatu must be leaving the market, but he ignored me. He had come into the city today, it seemed, and he intended to stay as long as he could. He liked to talk and he began to tell one of his many stories to the staff. I was worried he would distract them from their work. But many of them knew him and his propensity for talk, and they ignored him. His words went up, up, up, and then down, up, up, up, and down again as if he was singing a song.

The day proceeded to make its way from morning to afternoon in an ordinary way. Nothing exceptional happened. Even Geoffrey's absence from work was not unusual. He sent a text saying his mother was sick. I had discussed firing him with Ifechi, but as my husband pointed out, he could do the decorative stitching for men's caftans better than anyone else we knew. My male clientele was nowhere near as extensive as my female clientele, but the men were quicker to pay, slower to abandon their clothes.

The only slight bump in the day was Wedgeman's long visit. He stayed until one o'clock. But just as he was about to leave, and we had walked from the workroom to the showroom and were out in the reception, a woman came in.

I could tell that she lived well. Her skin had felt the luxury of expensive creams. Her perfume went before her, sweetly drawing attention to the buxom woman who was knocking on the doors of old age, but only just. She was wearing Chanel sunglasses, which she now took off to peer into my reception area.

I followed her eyes as she looked around, her expression appraising. The plush burgundy sofa, where people could sit and wait while the receptionist sent for me, was still lovely after two and a half years. It had taken me months to finish payments to a customer, a woman who had made a fortune running an imported furniture company. The console, which came with a mirror, I had bought on impulse on a trip to Lagos about two years ago. Finding a way to bring it back had been difficult, my regret at parting with so much money on one item so great, that I had almost given up and taken it back to the vendor in Victoria Island. But it had been worth it, for when I put it up in the reception area, it looked so elegant. The shine of the wood of the receptionist's desk, the brown stucco paint I had chosen over wallpaper, the chandelier, all gave the impression that you were entering the most luxurious fashion design and tailoring shop in Enugu, no, in the east of the Niger.

"Good afternoon, Madam," I said, recalling my good manners. I was about to get a new customer. That always made me happy.

"Good afternoon, my dear," she responded. Her voice was gentle but also firm, the voice of someone who knew what she wanted, and expected to be obeyed. It took me a moment to bring myself back to the present. I was no longer a housemaid, but a madam in my own right. I breathed in deeply and came out with a smile.

"How can I help you?" I asked in English.

She smiled at me and said, "A friend of mine recommended this place. Mrs Nwajei."

"Oh yes. Mrs Nwajei is one of my good customers," I replied. "Please sit." I showed her to one of the couches. I was getting ready to hand her one of my style magazines. And my feeling of inferiority was giving way to excitement. "Would you like a drink?"

"Yes, please. Some cold water if you have any."

Elizabeth, the receptionist, went to get it. She returned with an unopened bottle of Eva and a dry glass.

The woman drank the water deeply. She was not being polite; she had been thirsty.

All the while Wedgeman had been standing quietly towards the back of the showroom. I wondered if he was still leaving and hoped he was. "Ah, it is you, Madam!" he suddenly exclaimed.

The woman looked at him, confusion on her perfectly made-up face.

"Is it not Mrs Obiechina?" he asked.

"Yes, it is." She was smiling slightly now, though her eyes were still puzzled.

"Madam, it is Wedgeman." He was excited, it seemed. But every little thing excited Wedgeman.

"Oh my!" she said. "Wedgeman! Such a long time. Where have you been?"

Wedgeman turned to me and, beaming, said, "This is my Big Madam. I used to work for the driver that drove one of the vehicles of her husband's company."

"Hmm," I said, smiling back at the woman, who had now turned to me.

"Madam, I have been in the village o."

"You look well," she said.

He smiled, preening a little. "Madam, what about Oga?"

Her face fell. "He died."

"Hey," Wedgeman shouted. "Ha, mbanu. Oga was not an old man. Ndo. Ndo. I would have come if I heard."

"It happened about eighteen months ago." Her voice was still gentle, the pain more in her eyes than anywhere else.

"Ndo," he repeated earnestly. "May God comfort you and your boy. He must be grown now."

"He is," she said and smiled, a genuine smile. "In fact, he is getting married. That is what brought me here. To make some clothes for the wedding."

"Ah ah. You mean Afam has grown that big!"

"It has been a long time," she said, still smiling.

"This is my brother's wife, Madam. I call her Ada Nwokenta. My brother travelled all the way to Nwokenta to bring her to Okpatu, our village. She is the owner of this place." He looked proud and happy with himself, as if he had climbed the seven mountains with his brother.

"Nwokenta?" she asked.

There was something in her voice. Indefinable, barely there, but her expression revealed nothing.

"I know someone who used to have relatives there," she said, her eyes upon my face, a little quizzical. That must be it, I thought, perhaps she was no longer friends with this person who had relatives there. I could have reassured her; Nwokenta was not my favourite place in the world either.

I smiled at her. "You mentioned that your son is getting married. That's good news! Congratulations, Ma." Was Wedgeman ever leaving? I wondered.

"Yes, he is," she said, smiling back at me. "I want to make some clothes for the traditional wedding and for the white wedding. Obiageli said you were very good."

Obiageli would be Mrs Nwajei, the woman whose clothes we had to deliver only when she called on the phone or sent a text message so that her husband would not see. Once, I had had to leave with the clothes I brought to her, pretending I was looking for another house, because her husband had come back unexpectedly and opened the door when I rang the bell.

"We do our best," I said.

It was true. Perfection was what I sought in any fabric that made its way into my shop. I studied the styles in the magazines I got from Lagos. Onyinye, my daughter, bought me some on the internet too. She had a great eye and she wanted to try modelling. With her height, inherited from me, it did not sound like a far-fetched idea. Fashion was becoming such a big thing in Nigeria, I often said to Ifechi, and perhaps our daughter would become somebody big in it. But her father was adamant she would not. It was one of the few things we could not see eye to eye on. I kept my counsel and waited; what would be would be. In the meantime, I let her play around with fabric when she came from school and took her advice on my designs.

I cut most of the fabric that came into the shop myself. I had been known to stay up all night undoing and then remaking clothes that did not meet my standards. Deadlines must be met. Tailors who came to work for me knew this was a rule that could not be broken. They also knew they would be paid, on time, and that my rates were competitive.

My meticulousness had been rewarded by contracts to make costumes for Nollywood sets, clothes for the stars themselves. Recently, a prominent young musician had patronized me and left satisfied, promising to bring her friends my way.

"Yes, she is good. Very good," Wedgeman gave his own endorsement.

I smiled at him. "It is getting late."

"It is," he agreed, but made no move to leave.

Mrs Obiechina took the hint, dug into her bag and brought out some money, which Wedgeman accepted with profuse thanks. This had been a good visit for him, I mused. First Ifechi, now this lady. Still he didn't move. I would kill him the next time he dropped by, I fumed as I felt around in my bag for cash.

After he left, I examined the fabric that the woman had brought in. They were two expensive laces, one green, the other purple. I praised the fabric; there was nothing that customers liked to hear more than that they had picked out the right material for their special day, but hers were lovely. We agreed that the green would be made into buba. I suggested that she do a george and blouse combination for the traditional wedding. We had a selection for her to look at. We did head-ties, too, I told her, so she was not to worry about going anywhere else for that. One of the girls had just learnt to do makeup. She could do everything in one place, then.

"Obiageli told me about this place a while ago. I should have come before now," she said.

"You have come now," I responded, taking her measurements. She needed to lose some weight, but I would make her clothes look good on her.

"When is your son getting married?" I asked, partly to make conversation, but also to find out how much time I had for the project.

"In three months, at Christmas."

That was good, sufficient time to make the clothes.

"You must be very excited," I said. She must have had the boy as an older woman, probably her last child. I thought she must be at least sixty-five, and I was usually right about those things.

"I am. Very. He is a good boy," she said, and I heard the honesty in her words. When the time came, I knew I would feel as proud of my children.

As she was about to leave, she asked, "You say you are from Nwokenta? Do you go back often?"

"No, not really," I replied. The true answer was never. I had not been back since I married Ifechi. "I have not been back there for a long time," I said, then wondered what made me volunteer that information. "I go more often to Okpatu, my husband's village."

She nodded. "Oh. I used to know someone from there many years ago," she said. "But you would not know them, you are a young woman."

I smiled. Almost fifty could not be said to be young anywhere.

I stepped outside with her and waved goodbye as her driver drove her off in a Mercedes SUV, the type I hoped to drive one day.

- - - - - - - - - - - -

It was soon evening and I left for home. It had been a good day. Deadlines were met. A promising new client had come in.

Outside, in the still-balmy evening, I got into my car. Driving was one of the joys of my life. Ifechi had tried to teach me at first, after we had been married two years. We would often joke afterwards that our relationship almost ended then, he guffawing with loud laughter long after the joke had become old and stale. I did not learn to drive until five years ago. A woman over forty learning to drive beside a twentysomething-year-old who thinks that death is only a word in the dictionary is something to behold. I survived the experience and grew to love driving so much, I wondered what had taken me so long.

I turned on the radio. A report had been submitted to the president on the terrorist attack on the United Nations building in Abuja. A group, Boko Haram, was claiming responsibility. The leader of this same Boko Haram group had been killed a few years before. What is the world coming to? I wondered. The government did not seem to have a clue what to do. Instead, they were holding town hall meetings to persuade Nigerians that removal of the fuel subsidies that had kept fuel prices low for many years was a great idea. They could not expect us to take them seriously, I thought. No one trusted the government to do anything worthwhile with the funds. It was just another way to siphon money into the private pockets of public officers.

I switched to the CD player, and Onyeka's "One Love" came on. A deep wave of satisfaction washed over me. Life was hard, but if you took it in little chunks, you could find some chunks that were good. My eyes looked around the busyness of Dhamija Avenue and found a young boy, his jeans sagging, his walk a dance of sorts, a caricature of something he had seen on some music video. I wondered if he ever irritated his mother leaving the house looking like that. But maybe she was just grateful he was alive, able to do the foolish things that young boys of his age did.

Ezinwa came into my mind unbidden, as he often did when I felt satisfied with life, as if to remind me that uwaezuoke, the world could never give one everything. You could never have all you wished, not at the same time anyway. That hole would be there forever, that dull thud of pain, the memory of him, vivid and clear in dreams, but hazy on awakening.

I knew that Ezinwa was dead. I had heard many years ago about Mama Nathan's death. Not long after I ran away to Enugu, I had run into Mama Odinkemma, Mama Nkemdilim's friend, at New Market. Her daughter had married up, she told me, and now lived in Enugu. She was here for omugwo, to tend to her daughter and her new baby. Did Mama Nathan come back with my son? I asked her. The answer was no. Some of her people had brought her back from Enugu, she told me, and buried her. Nobody saw any baby.

It was as if he had never lived and that was most painful. No one could reminisce with me about his smile, his antics, his dimples. I carried pictures of my children and Ifechi on my phone, hundreds of them. It was not really my style to spend time gazing at photos of myself, or even of the children. But I would give anything to have one picture of Ezinwa.

I closed my eyes for a second and shook my head. I would not think of Ezinwa. In that moment I hit the bumper of the car in front of me. It was a slight bump, but I still screamed, "Jesus!" involuntarily. The driver of the car, a blue Toyota Prado, stepped out. In his white T-shirt, he looked like what he was — a driver. He would check his car, see that there was no dent, and get back in.

I set my face, preparing myself for some rude gesture or saucy warning finger. It had happened to me before, years ago when I first started driving. Looking at that boy with his jeans under his buttocks had turned me into a novice this evening. As the driver turned to get back into the car, having indeed satisfied himself that there was no damage, somebody — his boss, I presumed — also got out from the back seat to look. He was short and stocky in a white traditional outfit. His gold watch seemed outsized and rendered his arm shorter than it probably was.

Shock went from the strands of my hair to my feet. It was Urenna. Heavier than I remembered but still short, perhaps shorter because of the extra flesh. His cheeks were folded and his hairline was receding, his face was annoyed, but it was still Urenna.

For a moment, he looked me full in the face. I expected the same shock to come over his face as he slowly recognized me, the shock that must stand plain on mine. But there was nothing, only a look of annoyance at a woman who did not have the common sense to look where she was going. His eyes went derisively over my jalopy and then away, as if I could be of no more interest. Get out and tell him who you are, a voice in my head said. Instead, I sat glued to my seat, my hands sweaty on the steering wheel, staring at the man as he walked to my car.

My eyes stayed on him as he made his way to my open window. Did he want to know about his son? But how would he even know that it had been a boy? I kept gripping the steering wheel.

"Madam. You have to be careful," was what he said. "Very careful. You are lucky that car is not scratched." He sounded angry, unreasonably so, given it was only a slight bump.

"Urenna" came out of my mouth.

He frowned at me. Did he know me? his expression queried. Maybe once, when I was a girl still, I had wondered what it would be like to see him again. That was a long time ago. But even then, I had not imagined it in these circumstances.

"It is Nwabulu," I said, a little more confidence coming into my voice. I was no longer a girl, no longer a housemaid. I was a woman, a business owner, riding a car — a not-so-new car but still a car — in Enugu.

I saw him falter, reach into memory, and finally retrieve me. If I expected something, I was bound to be disappointed.

"I see ..." he said. "Kedu?" The curiosity that should have accompanied that question was missing.

"I am fine. And you?"

"I did not know you lived here." Had he wanted to know, searched for me all those years ago?

"I do. Not very far from here. And you, do you live here?"

"No," he said, a look of distaste coming over his face. Was Enugu now beneath him? "My parents still live here, in the old house in Independence Layout. I come to visit occasionally. I live in Abuja."

I smelt money on him; perhaps he was a politician. I did not ask. Such interest seemed out of place with his stiffness.

When was he going to stop being formal and ask me about his child, our child? What would I say in answer, some other voice asked me. That he was stolen, that he was dead — or worse, that I did not know? I was not sure, but I wanted him to ask me.

He did not. Instead, he said, "I have to go now. I am late for a meeting. Jisike."

And with that he went out of my life again.

Had he ever truly been in it, or had I merely been acting out one of Ikenna's fairy tales? He had not wanted to know anything about me, what my life was like now. He had not asked for my number nor given me his.

The traffic held them up for a minute or two, but after a bend they sped off. I shook my head gently, trying to get my bearings as I slowly drove home.

Why did he not ask about the baby? I wondered. Did he think I'd had an abortion? Had he scrubbed his memory clean of me in their sitting room, staring by turns at my feet and at him, while Mummy and his mother had asked accusing questions, to which he had kept saying calmly, "I don't really know the housemaid. In fact, I can't recall ever really talking to her before." Remembering the way he kept finding ways to interject "the housemaid" into his responses made my eyes watery.

I was reluctant to go in to face my husband and delve into what had happened. Or not happened, depending on how you looked at it. We had lived and loved for too long for him not to see that I was shaken up; he would notice it on my face. So, when I turned into my street, I drove past the big mango tree that had started pulling on the wires but which the owner of the house refused to cut down. I drove past my house and then the next house with its sign that said, "BEWARE OF 419ERS. THIS

HOUSE IS NOT FOR SALE." All in capitals, as if we could not read or obey the words otherwise.

What if he had asked what became of the baby? What would I have said? That he had died? That he was lost? That he was over thirty but was still lost? Ifechi was convinced that Ezinwa had died, perhaps of measles or malaria — many children died in those days, he said. He made 1977 sound like 1877. But what if he did not die? I would ask. What if he was alive somewhere? What if Mama Nathan gave him to someone else? Who? he would counter. Sometimes he sounded harsh. I knew what he was doing — my husband was trying to make me, a fifty-year-old woman, accept reality, accept that fairy tales were just that: fairy tales.

Only yesterday, I had bought a paper on the way to the shop. On the second page were pictures taken at a baby factory — teenagers, their bellies protruding as if they had eaten too much, some holding babies. Babies played on the floor, oblivious to the cameraman or to all the fuss. My chest tightened. Some of the babies had been sold already, I read. Could that have happened to Ezinwa? I asked my husband. Ifechi said no; baby factories were a new phenomenon. Ezinwa likely had died before Mama Nathan.

The meagre evidence was on his side. But sometimes, in my head where I resided by myself, I played the "what if Ezinwa was still alive?" game. What if he was still alive somewhere? What would he be like now? He would be thirty-three. Did he look like me, tall, dark, handsome, or like Urenna, not so tall, fair-complexioned? Had he gone to school? Was he suffering some-where, having little to eat? Would he be married, or about to get married, like that woman's son, the woman who came in today? Maybe. He might even have a child already. Imagine, I could be a grandmother and not even know it.

The ache grew wider, the hole deeper, and I knew I would have a nightmare that night, the same one I had had for years. It came and went, but it was always the same: Mama Nathan running away with Ezinwa. Always at first it seems that I can catch up with her, then it becomes more difficult: my legs are making the movement of running but I am not moving. And she is going further and further away, and then she no longer has a head, and I hear Ezinwa screaming. Ifechi would often wake me at this point. You have been screaming, he would say. He would hold me and wipe my tears. He would not speak the encouraging words he used to in the early years. His arms around me, his silent compassion, were much more comforting.

I gripped the steering wheel hard. I would never forget, I acknowledged to myself now as I had done many times. Not even if the man who fathered him had blotted out the times that had brought my child to this world. The pain was a small price to pay for remembering. I sighed deeply, my chest rising with the seat belt. I turned up the volume of the CD player to try to drown out the sadness. I shook myself. This was life, and I had been dealing with it for a while; the surprise was that I still let it master me.

I knew what to do. I would go and see Chidinma. My best friend would know what to say to me now.

As I drove to Uwani where she lived, my mind took a brisk walk through the day's doings: the clothes that had gone out, the new customer who was going to her son's wedding, my car incident, Urenna. My intuition had been working this morning, I admitted. Who could have thought that I would see Urenna again? Yet, he had not asked after his child.

CHAPTER SEVENTEEN
JULIE

"She said she was from Nwokenta."

I shifted and adjusted myself on my rocking chair. I had acquired it many years before on a trip to England. In those days, when my husband wanted to hurt me as people sometimes do when they have been together long, maybe too long, he would tell me that he was surprised it could still take my heavy frame. Once, those words, ndakakwa, had the power to wound, but no more. My heaviness was an old scar, familiar, worn, a part of life. I knew now that exercise videos were a waste of money, that sucking in my belly was a waste of precious time, that I would be heavy until the grave called me. Until it did, that chair was still one of the good things of life for me and my bad knees.

"Nwokenta?" my best friend asked now, no perceptible strain of curiosity in her tone.

I was ready, had been for the last half hour, but Obiageli had kept us from leaving. As usual. She was not sure the necklace she had on went with the gold blouse she was wearing; the shades were too close, yet not close enough to look good together. We were merely guests, but the way she was going on, you would think that this wedding at the All Saints Church was her child's. She kept plucking her eyebrows, peering into the wall mirror in my bathroom.

Aging gracefully was yet to enter Obiageli's lexicon. She wanted to stay beautiful until God called her home and she was working hard at it, she told me. At a little over seventy, though Obiageli would die rather than admit to that age, I thought she was a little too old for that fluffiness. But when I looked at the folds in my neck and my sagging jowls, I thought she might have a point. Fortunately, unlike me, she had good genes, and her skin did not show the many lines that my expensive creams and makeup did not succeed in concealing. And, more importantly, as I often told her, she could still laugh at a good joke — her brain still worked. Even so, she had told me just this past week that when she went over to the States to help Ifeoma, her daughter, when the baby came, she would see about the possibility of getting a facelift. Her husband might kill himself over the cost, but if she could get Ifeoma to keep a secret — a tall order, for Ifeoma was especially close to her father — she could get away with it. Her eyes had glowed at the possibility.

Obiageli should have left Emma long ago, I thought. His miserliness had not improved. Indeed, it grew worse with age. When the children were still at home, he would deliberately pick fights with Obiageli, which ended with him acting offended and rejecting food cooked in the house. He could do this for a month, two, three months at a time. During that time, he would bring no money home for the upkeep of the house, including the feeding of their children. When regular electricity became a luxury meant for people living in other countries, even Ghana, everyone acquired a generator. *Gbo gbo gbo gbo*, the sound went from every house, every shop, little and big. Even the barber's salon, the place in the market where we bought okporoko, and the man who lived with his family of seven in one room acquired a generator, the small I-Pass-My-Neighbour variety, which could not carry a lot of household devices. Even then, Emma insisted that his household keep using kerosene lamps. Eventually, Obiageli gave in, abandoned her stance that it was the responsibility of a man to ensure that his family did not stay in darkness, and bought a generator. Emma promptly stated that he could not buy fuel for the generator because he was not the one who chose to acquire a needless and expensive gadget. Also, he loved the word "ban" and sought every possible occasion under heaven to use it. He purported to ban her from wearing nice clothes. From seeing me, the wife of a rich, corrupt fraudster. From making soups that were too delicious and filled with meat and fish. From sitting in the living room, the only room that was air-conditioned in their house. She never paid him any mind and simply carried on living as well as she could under the circumstances.

The result of all this was that Obiageli learnt to rely on herself and no one else, except perhaps me. These days, Obiageli told me, Emma would hoard food in his room. This started after his retirement. I thought he might have a mental illness and I told her this. He would never agree to see a psychiatrist, she said. Yet she stayed with him, as she had for over forty years, proudly answering to Mrs Emmanuel Nwajei, speaking up for him in the village, in church, at neighbourhood meetings, explaining why they could not pay for this or that, and then going behind his back to make the payments. To this day they still fought over housekeeping money, how much Obiageli spent on her dressing — which I had to admit could get out of hand. Obiageli would laugh and insist her extravagance was justified by saying that she was dressing up for the two of them. It would not do at all for the world to think two crazy people had married each other, she said, seeing as her husband had yet to see the value in changing the shirts that he had bought in the seventies.

"Yes. She said she was from Nwokenta," I repeated for emphasis now, trying to pull her attention to the real-life issue that had been on my mind for three days.

"I did not know that. She never said."

"Of course she did not. How would she tell you if it never came up in conversation?"

Now Obiageli turned and looked at me. Her expression said that she did not know what bee had found its way into my head-tie.

"Well, it never came up. I am sure that in every part of this city you will find people from Nwokenta. Just like you would find people from Nnewi, Onitsha, Awka, Nanka, Udi, and so on."

"She said that her husband is from Okpatu. She said she has not been back for years."

"Oh, okay. There is nothing unusual about that."

"Hmm." There was a little silence as I pondered this, my eyes on my red-painted toenails. Was there nothing unusual about one not visiting one's ikwunne? Still, even with my ingrained sense of duty, I had only been to my mother's village a few times since she died, so perhaps Obiageli had a point.

I looked up. My friend was done plucking her eyebrows and had started putting on lipstick. She was waiting for me to say something.

"Nwannem nwanyi, something about that woman reminded me of Afam," I said after a while, finally getting to the point.

I could not put my finger on it. Maybe it was the expression, the way the tailor's eyes stared at you too long as if they were trying to read your mind, see what you were not saying. She was beautiful, the way my son was a fine man. Maybe it was the same colouring, that ebony blackness that Eugene had often commented on. The men of their family, he said, were dark-skinned, but this one, he would point to Afam proudly, this one came with the darkest hue of them all, almost a Sudanese.

"Hmm," was all Obiageli said, looking away from me and applying some eyeshadow, as if to deflect the force of my words. She pushed the lid up with the brush and held it up for a second or two to reverse the droopiness that time had wrought.

Perhaps the only resemblance between my son and that tailor was simply the mention of Nwokenta. Surely that had planted these wild ideas in my head. When the woman said she was from Nwokenta, I almost fell down from shock. Did she notice? No, I did not think so, because she carried on with the conversation and proceeded to take my fabric and do my measurements, when all I wanted was to run out of that place and never come back.

I was being ridiculous; even I knew that. But I needed to hear Obiageli say it out loud for reassurance.

Obiageli looked at me in the mirror. Then she swivelled around to look me in the face, as if the mirror did not show my true reflection.

"What are you saying? Everybody from Nwokenta suddenly looks like Afam?"

I kept silent. I did not want to sound any more foolish than I had shown myself to be. Thirty-three years was a long time to keep a secret, and here I was behaving like a novice.

"I have seen the woman. She is tall. She is dark. But if that is the only thing that is giving you palpitations, you might as well be describing half the women in Enugu. Besides, how do you think a young woman like that, who in all probability grew up here in Enugu, would have any connection with Mama Nathan?" Obiageli's lighthearted mood of only five minutes before was gone.

We looked at each other — two women over seventy, wrinkled now in face and hands, but as young in mind as we were at sixteen at Girls' High School Aba. Who had seen each other through the years and covered the grounds of a woman's life in twentieth-century Africa together. Fought through disappointments, managed the lives of wilful and yet fragile children, survived the infidelities and idiosyncrasies of husbands, the abuses of life, mistakes and failures that came in different shades. We knew each other well, better than the men in our lives did or had cared to know.

Her lips tightened into the ube shape, puckering out. I knew that expression: time for truth-speaking.

"Julie," she said and paused, gathering her energies. "If you ask me," she went on, as if she would ever wait to be asked, "I would say you have not been yourself since Eugene died. You had that sickness." My bout with depression had been more like a battle with death than an illness. "And, if you ask me, you are still recovering. I am still not happy about that prophet or seer you said came to church the other time. There are all sorts of people going about looking for others to fleece."

She was referring to a man who had come to our church the month before. He had said that long-kept secrets were about to be revealed. I had mentioned this to Obiageli and she had laughed at my seriousness. I had gone home reassured and given it no more thought. But here she was bringing it up again.

"Nwannem nwanyi, leave all this tearing of body and soul to young people," she continued now, "peering under every stone for things that are not there. You and I know that life turns and twists, but what can you do? You have to follow it gently, see where it is leading, figure it out when you get there. I do not like this imagining of things that are not." She paused. "This woman, Nwabulu, the tailor, I have known her and used her for more than six years now. She works really hard. She is discreet, too, which is why our relationship has worked. I have no idea how you can link her with Afam. That boy is your son. He has been for thirty-three years now. Thirty-three," she repeated. As if I was mad to think of him being anyone else's but mine.

"Let the young monkey not slip and fall from the tree, hmm. After all, its mother gave birth to it on a tree." Her gaze was unwavering and stern. It was obvious to her that I was losing my marbles.

"Hmm. You speak well, nwannem nwanyi. You speak well. What can one do but try to figure out life as one goes along its journey?" I asked rhetorically, borrowing her metaphor.

"Let us leave now," Obiageli said, finally ready. "We will be late and you know Nneka will not like that. This is her very first daughter to marry."

Nneka, our friend — if you used that term loosely — had five girls, all unmarried. Her third daughter had finally succeeded in finding a man. We made our way out to attend the wedding of the lucky girl whose mother would surely be the happiest woman anywhere on earth today.

That night, alone and lonely, my mind began to run into dark corners, places in which I had neither been nor shined any light for years. I tossed on the four-poster bed that Eugene had bought so long ago, thinking thoughts that were best left alone.

Something I heard on the news that evening after I returned from Nneka's daughter's wedding came back to bother me. A baby had been picked up in the new dumpster the government had built in Ogui. The interview featured men and women coming on camera to abuse the wicked woman who had done such a wicked thing. The newscaster said the baby was recovering in the hospital. What would become of that child, I wondered.

The day before, I'd seen a movie where Margaret Thatcher talked to her long-dead husband. If I'd discussed it with Eugene, I know what he would have said — that the Iron Lady had lost her mind. I would have said that their love must have been strong, undying. He would have said that that was the problem with women — they were simply too soft to handle real life.

In spite of everything, our friendship had returned in the end, when Eugene had tired of money and women. But what was life but an instrument to make sure the soul did not get too comfortable? As soon as it saw that we were becoming the proverbial old married couple, knowing each other so well that we could finish each other's sentences, and learning to like each other again after the era of puerile selfishness, the highs and lows of hormonal changes, the excitement and turbulence of child-rearing, death had knocked on our door. When we had joined the category of people he and I liked to call "the no-leave, no-transfer club," men and women who had agreed they were stuck with each other — that this was not the end of the world, that they were better off making the most of life together than haranguing each other over flaws that would never change — death snatched away Eugene.

He had died suddenly. I had been downstairs supervising the cook. Nobody could make onugbu soup like I did, Eugene often said. So I had been in the kitchen when I could have been with him and seen when he was about to fall. By the time I sent Uche, the help, up to get him for lunch, he was already gone. Almost two years later, I could still feel the stun, the hammer against my chest when I saw him on the floor of the bedroom. I still remember my surprise at how vacant he had looked. Like an empty, abandoned house — the force, the spirit, the charisma that had given life to his body gone, leaving his big, long shell behind in a grotesque, crumpled heap. And leaving me to go back to single-ness, that state I had done so much to escape.

I collected the broken pieces of myself and got ready to give him the kind of burial he would have given himself. Orimili atata, the sea which never ran dry, deserved only the best.

As I prepared for the funeral, the only snag was Onyemaechi, his first wife, who was still married to my husband. Nobody had ever brought up divorce, although the thought had come to me sometimes. She had stayed in the background, known only to a few people in Enugu. Having left us alone for many years, she now came back to claim what she said was her "right-ful" place.

"I am the first wife. He married you. I do not dispute that. But I am first. And his body and everything he has must come first to me, and his children, inulia?"

It was a bit pathetic to watch her, an old woman, with scanty hair straightened, almost fried by cheap relaxer, stand before me after thirty-some years to claim a man who had abandoned her so many years before. Her daughters must have put her up to it, tell-ing her to fight for their inheritance. It was comical, more comical than it would have been had she come all those years ago to pour hot water on me at my school. Her daughters hovered around her, too timid to give their mother the support she needed. Were these really Eugene's daughters? These dithering women, standing by their tight-skinned mother?

She had come too late. I was prepared to give her a spot in the backyard of the house in the village to receive her few well-wish-ers, a chance to throw some sand into the grave before it was closed up, but nothing more. Fortunately, Eugene had in his last years made sure that most of the property had been transferred to me and Afam. "Death," he used to say, "likes to choose its own time." How prescient he had been. Yet what had Onyemaechi done to him other than fail to bear him a son, I wondered as I signed papers put in front of me by his lawyers.

She and her daughters were now in court contesting the will, which only disposed of a small part of Eugene's considerable fortune. The rest had been transferred in Eugene's lifetime to a company in which Afam and I were the directors. But Onyemaechi and her daughters had not been left out in the cold — he had made sure that the girls and their children, his grandchildren, could have comfortable lives, living on the rent of houses in Lagos, Enugu, and Onitsha. Still, Onyemaechi told everyone she came across that I was a highway robber. Sour grapes, I thought, very sour grapes.

So when Eugene died, with all the resources I had at my disposal, it was easy to elbow Onyemaechi out of the arrangements. I ignored her antics, and when people saw where the money was coming from, they ignored her too. I told his kinsmen that Chief Eugene Obiechina, Orimili Atata I was nnukwu ozu, a big corpse. He had single-handedly built the town hall. Many had gone to school on the Obiechina scholarships he had instituted. He had taken all the titles. He was a Jerusalem Pilgrim. He was a Knight of the Church. He deserved a burial ceremony that was befitting, which was bright and clear before the face of all. They agreed with me, and told Onyemaechi to pipe down and accept a smaller role. No one was sending her away; she was their brother's wife, after all. But Eugene had to be buried properly by his only son, Afam. I smiled in triumph and set about preparing for the largest party the village had ever seen.

Afam came back from Lagos, where he had moved two years before, and, with my instructions ringing in his ears, ran around arranging for canopies, banners, program booklets, talking with the priests in Enugu and the village, and ensuring that the mortuary attendants kept the corpse clean and in a good state. We purchased goats with which Eugene's mother's people were duly informed that their daughter's son had died, even though we had spoken to everyone who needed to know on the phone or in person. We bought Ankara and made uniforms for members of the family and almost half of the village.

Obiageli helped me organize the caterers. Three cows and ten goats were slaughtered to provide meat for the guests, who came from all over the country. Afam took care of the drinks — champagne, wines, beers, soft drinks, juices. He ran errands to my favourite decorators, to the vendors of souvenirs, the sellers of meats, the announcers on radio and television.

I shamelessly asked for tributes, which filled up the program booklet. I sent Afam to the Government House to pick up one from the governor and the speaker. It was silliness, people who had barely known my husband describing his loss as "immense to the Obiechina family and the world at large," and pronouncing him an "icon" and a "legend."

The funeral was lavish, with food and drink flowing, and important people in expensive clothing. A gospel band; two large choirs; two big akwunechenyi music troupes; souvenirs for guests of umbrellas, notepads, trays, handkerchiefs, face towels with his face boldly imprinted on them. It was such extravagance, so out of touch with the pain of the occasion, but exactly as Eugene would have wanted it. It was a befitting send-forth, the best that I could do for him. Much of it was superficial, Afam argued. I agreed with our son, but it did not matter. Eugene would have loved it.

They were such different people, Eugene and Afam. And Eugene was not comfortable with difference. He had wanted a clone of himself. Yet, even as a child, Afam did not have the sort of masculinity and self-assurance that surrounded Eugene and seemed to emanate from him. Afam had many fears and discomforts — masquerades, the loud laughter of Eugene's drinking buddies, even other children sometimes. Where Eugene drew people to himself, friends swimming around him as if he were the king of the sea, paying obeisance and agreeing with every word that dropped from his mouth, Afam shrank back in shyness. Afam was tall or, more accurately, was on his way to being tall like Eugene, but it seemed that he had gone AWOL the day God gave out boldness.

What would have become of Afam if I had not picked him up and raised him as my own, as Eugene's son? I did not want to think about that.

"He must get this shyness from you," Eugene would say, though he could point to no situation in which I had displayed this weakness. "It certainly does not come from me or my people."

"It would be dull if everyone was the same," I would tell him. "Besides, he is only a child — he will outgrow it."

"I was never shy," he would state, arrogance in every word. "What use is shyness in a world where boldness gets you everything? Tell me that."

Turning to Afam, he would bellow, "Stand straight, boy. Walk tall. Your father is a rich man. Do you hear me? Nna gi bara aba."

Yet Afam had done well, was doing well. As adulthood drew near, the shyness melted away. An involuntary smile came to my face as I remembered the time that Afam, four or five years old, and I huddled in the car on the side of the Enugu highway. The rain had caught us, fast, hard, pelting our car, the skies growing gloomy and covering us with darkness in the middle of the day. So, I parked and, kept company only by the long elephant grass and tall trees that bore no fruit, we waited for the rain to stop. Afam was scared and clutched my hand. The sun would come out, I reassured him. I began telling him the story of the Osa and his mother, and their cunning in the famine that struck the land of the animals, a story my own mother had told us — me and Afam, my brother.

Only last year, Afam, my son, had written and produced a single for Nigeria's famous musical twins, based on that story. It was not my cup of tea, but it had many admirers and my chest rose with pride.

In later years, Afam and Eugene would fight about everything. What course Afam would study — Eugene thought business, maybe law; Afam thought music but compromised and went to engineering. Eugene thought he should go to America, to Harvard or MIT, when he finished his first degree; Afam said no and went to Canada, a country nobody had heard about, his father complained to me. When he was ready to come back home, Eugene wanted him to run the companies. Afam told him that he wanted to go into music and run his own production company. He had never lost his love for music and he foresaw money spouting from every note out of the new musicians' mouths, from every fast beat that made its way into the world. Globalization and the internet, he told me, were about to make Nigerian music the biggest thing since the personal computer. Many arguments broke out over this. Eugene stopped talking to him for a while, giving me messages instead to pass to Afam. Afam stuck by his ideas. The ice melted over time and the two started speaking again.

But, just before Eugene died, a battle was raging over when and whom Afam would marry. "An only son, the son of the Obiechina house," Eugene would tell him, "has responsibilities to himself, but most importantly to his family. A responsibility to marry quickly, to marry well, and to sire sons. You have the responsibility to make sure the compound, the name, the lineage does not die, do you hear?"

Afam would laugh, making his father want to go mad. "Daddy," he would say gently, "this is not the Dark Ages. This is the twenty-first century. I will marry when I find someone I can love and live with. Mummy is praying, so I am sure it will happen soon."

In this matter, I could see both sides of the argument. But I wished Afam would hurry up and find this woman he could love and live with. I was eager for grandchildren, not to carry on the Obiechina name but to hold in my arms. Thankfully, when he discovered that a young woman from Kenya was the one, his father was gone. Had he not seen all the Igbo girls around? Eugene would have roared.

My son, Afam, was of course named after my brother. When I suggested the name to Eugene, who was eager to name his first and, as it turned out, only son, he acceded immediately. Yes, of course, he said, my name will not be lost. The names of all the great Obiechina warriors will live again through this boy, the seed of my loins, he intoned with pride. Years later, he would tell the story the way he remembered it: "As soon as Julie returned from England with the baby, I called him Afamefuna, may my name and those of my ancestors live forever."

"Amii o," his listeners would chorus back if they were Igbo men of a certain age.

Should I have told Eugene? I asked myself now. While he lived, there had never been any urgency in my spirit about this, no fear. Not even after he died.

My nerves had to be firmer than they had ever been, Obiageli had warned. And how right she had been. Within the week after Obiageli sat in my 504 and told me that the baby would be returned if I did nothing, while the thoughts and doubts churned through my mind, I received the letter I had been waiting for: the letter allowing me a one-year study leave in England. When I told Obiageli, she exclaimed, "That is it!"

"That is what?"

"Do you not see it?"

"See what?"

"Take the child and travel. Come back with him, the first son of Chief Eugene ..."

"How?"

She looked at me as if I had become slow of thinking. "Take the baby with you to London!"

"Ehen."

"Do I have to explain every little thing to you?" In fact, she did: I needed her to break it down for me. "You will travel with the child and bring him back as your child."

Would it work? Obiageli was sure it would. I would have to extend my study leave after the first year, she said, to make sure the child looked a little older, otherwise my sisters-in-law might suspect.

She carried on as if I were becoming soft in the head and needed every detail worked out for me: "And while you're there, studying, you will have to look for one of those baby-care centres to help care for the baby," she said. "This is where having a rich husband comes in handy."

I balked at this — wasn't the baby too young? — but could come up with no feasible alternative. Normally, I could have sought to take a young girl to help me, but nothing about this situation was normal.

All I remembered from that time was the jumpiness that lasted until we got on British Airways to London, my heart beating faster than God appointed. Everything wracked my nerves: from obtaining a forged birth certificate for presentation at the visa office, to making sure that I fixed my travel date for when Eugene was away. There was a time when this would have been impossible, when we were inseparable, but our emotional distance favoured my plans. Tata and I arrived safely in London.

When I told Eugene by phone that I was pregnant, already four months gone, there was no skepticism on his end. Instead, he thought I should have stayed home rather than take the study leave, so his sisters could look after me. I assured him that I would be fine with the help of British doctors and nurses. I was just as quick to tell him that I wanted the news kept quiet until the baby came, since I'd lost the last one. I told him the doctors said that I needed complete bed rest throughout my stay in London, no visitors, nothing that would agitate me in any way, and that it was either that or lose the baby. He was understanding; he sent me money often and asked me to rest. He said I should write to the ministry and resign. Nothing, it seemed, would be allowed to jeopardize the well-being of the prospective heir of Eugene Obiechina. Some important business deals came his way too, preventing him from coming to London against my wishes. Someone upstairs was working to give my boy the home he deserved.

No, I had little motivation to tell Eugene the truth when he finally visited and exclaimed at how big Afam was. Nor when he proudly compared Afam with his daughters, telling me that this baby was already showing that he was going to be a tall Obiechina man.

I extended my leave and stayed in England for another year, until Eugene insisted that I return home. London was not the place to raise an Obiechina boy.

Upon my return, his sisters looked askance at Afam. "He doesn't really look like us," Adaku volunteered. Maybe she was talking about his black, shiny skin, or his lips that were delicately sculpted, unlike their larger-than-life mouths. I ignored her, pretending not to hear.

"His feet are planted more firmly on the ground than a fifteen-month-old," Chinyere, the second sister, said one day.

Eugene laughed and said, "That is my boy. Why wait when the world is waiting to be taken?"

I sneered inwardly at all of them, especially his sisters who could not live through an entire minute without thinking of their brother's money and how to spend it. Once I made the decision to take Afam as my own, I was resolute in going all the way. I told the lies that needed telling, maintained silence and made the omissions where nothing needed to be said. My sisters-in-law bit their lips and fell into line. With the birth of the long-sought son, their brother would not have it otherwise. My resolve was strong and stayed so through the ensuing years; I had done what I needed to do. Any guilt was long ago blown into the four winds. Obiageli kept our secret well, sometimes I thought even better than me. To her, Afam was my child and no one could believe differently.

And nobody — not me, not Eugene, not Afam — had suffered from it. Eugene had raised a son, and he had died proud. There was a son in the house. The obi of the Obiechinas would not close up. And love lived with us. Even though Eugene's relationship with Afam had been rocky at times, there had been love between them. As for Afam, would the motherless babies' home have been better than the love, the luxury in which he had been raised?

I had been given the opportunity to be a mother. Thank God I took it, for I never got pregnant, not even when Eugene took it into his head that we needed more children and sent me to England for those newfangled, terribly expensive technologies that came out in the eighties.

What was a mother really? True, Afam did not slip out from between my legs, like Ifeoma, Obiageli's second daughter, all wet and gooey with slime and blood. I caught that girl myself, her mother screaming enough to wake up the entire neighbourhood.

Yes, it was true that I suffered no labour pains, no recovery from a Caesarean section. But that was not all that made a mother. I held Afam when he was little. I remembered the day he went to school for the first time; I remembered the song he sang the first day at nursery. I remembered how he would always ask for me when malaria struck. Me, not anyone else. I remembered the first tune he ever hummed, the shine in his eyes when he smiled. I remembered his first letter from boarding school, the first dream he remembered on waking up.

I had known the greatest earthly love a woman can know, loving a child and being loved in return. Who could say I was not worthy? The girl in the news the other day, the girl whose baby was picked up at the dumpster in Ogui — she was worthy. I did not judge her. I wished she could have told someone, had someone she could lean on, someone who would have been happy to take that child and raise her. Perhaps that was what had happened to Afam. Perhaps Mama Nathan had picked Afam up in a dump somewhere. Yet I, who raised a child who would have had a miserable childhood, a difficult life — who could say I was not worthy to be called a mother?

When I finally slept that night, I did not dream of the child who had been abandoned in the dump, as I had feared. I dreamt of Eugene rising from his grave to point accusing fingers at me. I had no fear, but only wondered why he had left his bed so late. And then I dreamt of Nwabulu, the tall black tailor.

CHAPTER EIGHTEEN
NWABULU

I tapped my feet impatiently. I did not like to waste time when there was work to do in the shop. I should simply have told Mrs Obiechina that I would buy the fabric myself. I knew, with no sense of pride, that she would like any fabric I chose; I was good. Instead, I had — foolishly — agreed over the phone that we could go to the market together. I could have gone and come back in the time I had been waiting.

Thirty minutes later, when I saw her climb down from the Mercedes, her movements slow and cautious, I knew it had been a mistake. With a sigh, I resigned myself to not finishing the school costumes I had planned on completing that day.

When she came in she said, "I am really sorry for keeping you. I had to stop at the pharmacy to get some prescriptions and it took longer than I expected. Gbahalu, inugo."

With those apologetic words, how could I continue to nurse irritation? I smiled and said, "Nsogbu adiro, Ma. It is no problem at all. I was just wondering if everything was all right."

She suggested that we use her car, which was a good suggestion; the air conditioner in mine was broken. Besides, it would be uncomfortable for her because of her size. I waited for her to get in the back and then went to the front to sit beside the driver.

"No," she said. "Please come and sit beside me so that we can talk as we go."

"Yes, Ma." It did not matter to me where I sat, though society said big people sat in the back behind their drivers. I obeyed and we drove off.

The scents of her car, her person, all said luxury. In my next life, I mused, I would be sure to come as the child of a rich family. I smiled to myself at this thought. My husband would say, "You have to be patient; this life is not yet done." I often told him that, in my next life, I would be a man. My emphatic tone would make him laugh. "It is not easy to be a man, you know," he would reply. "It is *easier* to be a man," I would inform him. "Okay," he would say, conceding defeat, "but you have to finish this life first with me as your husband and then I can come back as your wife." I smiled again.

Mrs Obiechina looked at me, a questioning smile on her face. What was I smiling at, her own smile asked.

I said, "I like your car, Ma — it is very comfortable." "Comfortable" was not the right word, especially if you compared my old Honda with this Mercedes.

"Hmm," was her response, as if this was not important. "Will the market be very full? I sometimes get very hot there." As she said this, she fumbled in her big black bag for what turned out to be a beautiful red fan, the type that society ladies fan themselves with at weddings.

"It is always full," I said. "But I know a shortcut to the shops I want us to visit. It should not take us long."

"Do you go often?" she asked.

"No, I am often too busy to go myself these days. I usually send my girls to buy the things I need. Unless there is a special reason."

She smiled. "So I am a special reason?"

"Of course you are special, Ma," I laughed, going with the flow. "It is not every day that one's son gets married."

"That is true." She continued to smile. "And how about you? Are your children grown?"

"They are growing, Ma. My son just entered the university."

"Hmm. How many do you have?"

"Two. Son and daughter."

"Oh, two. At least that's more than one, which is what I have."

"Oh, you mean your son is your only child?"

"Yes," she said, but her smile was warm, as if she did not mind that she had just one child.

"Eyaaa," I said. She and her husband must have waited for a long time; she was not young and, in her days, women married early.

"Hmm," was her simple reply.

"We must make sure you look gorgeous that day, then."

"Careful, you don't want me to outshine the bride. She may never let me near my son again."

We both laughed. And then we talked about mothers-in-law and daughters-in-law, and I told her that I had been lucky in that regard. My husband shielded me from all interference, especially because I had only two children, which my mother-in-law was not too happy about. I did not add that my husband was not too pleased with that either — not in the beginning. She said she had not been so lucky, even though her mother-in-law had died when she married her husband. Her eight sisters-in-law had been more formidable than any mother-in-law. She had promised herself that she would not be an interfering mother-in-law, and she hoped that she could keep to that. In any case, her son and his fiancée lived in Lagos, so it was unlikely she would see them that often.

"Is it not strange," Mrs Obiechina mused, "that you have a child, you feed him, wash his buttocks, wake up with him at night, listen to his bad dreams, and wipe his tears. And then one day, the child grows up and belongs to another, and tells those dreams to another?" She paused, then answered her own question: "It is strange, but it is the cycle of life. If the child does not do this, you would be worried, and would consult pastors and wonder what was wrong with him."

I hoped one day to be at the point when I could give out my children in marriage. It would be a major achievement. I did not add that no one had given me out, and I hoped to be alive to do that for my children.

And so we chatted until we got into the hot, busy, overflowing market. We walked past other goods on the narrow roads, avoiding barrow pushers and people walking briskly in search of what they came to buy. Traders called out to us from their shops.

"Madam, come, I have the best cosmetics."

"Aunty, bring Mummy here now. I have a nice seat on which she can be comfortable."

"Aunty, Mummy is sweating o. Come in now, my fan is working."

We were slow. I matched my impatient legs to Mrs Obiechina's shorter strides until we found the cluster of shops that sold fabric. There, we focused on finding the best cloth and not being stolen blind by traders who could smell money from thousands of kilometres away. We chose the fabrics together. Mrs Obiechina was leaning towards a red lace, but I thought that a deep blue cord would be slimming and look regal on her. I also got a white lace for a blouse. Though she said she had lots of whites, I said

I would make this in the simple, elegant style that was now in vogue. In the end, she agreed with me. She smiled indulgently at my enthusiasm. I would have got better prices if she had not come with me, but I did the best I could and she settled the bill. Then she said she wanted some ukpaka. I said that I could get the oil bean cuttings for her. So she stayed in the shop with the fabrics, talking to the trader, while I dashed to the other side of the market to get some of the items she wanted — ukpaka, ogili Igbo, some okporoko, and abacha. Her thanks were effusive when I returned.

Back in the car, she asked, "Tell me, how did you become a fashion designer? Since my friend Mrs Nwajei found you, she has been spending all her money on clothes." She laughed, her tone suggesting that I was about to draw her in as I had her friend.

I noted that she did not say "tailor," which often connoted a smaller kind of dressmaker.

"It is a long story," I said simply, although I could have said that it was the only trade open to me at that time or that I loved making clothes.

"I would like to hear it one day," was all she said, her eyes lingering on my face. Mrs Obiechina had a way of making you feel that she was really interested in getting to know you, the real you, not the dressed-up one you presented to the world.

When we got back to the shop, I said goodbye to her, urging her not to get out of the car.

"Are you sure I should not come in?"

"Mba o, I have got your measurements, Ma. I will go in and start cutting immediately. You know that this can take time. I want everything to be ready for the wedding." I could see that the trip to the market had tired her. But there really was no need for her to come into the shop, and I had a lot of work to do — I had spent too much time in the market.

We waved goodbye as the Mercedes drove off.

Chidinma came by the shop one day. I was surprised to see her. She often complained that Trans-Ekulu was too far a distance to travel just to see a friend. I laughed. It was only a thirty-minute journey from Uwani on a slow-traffic day.

She came in, her buttocks jiggling in her long skirt. She was still fleshy, as she had been when we were housemaids on the same street over thirty years ago. But now she had four children to show for all that flesh, I teased. With my non-existent backside, I would have been perfect to strut about in a bikini on TV, she teased back, except that my ambitions had always been too low.

It was interesting how life wended its way to unexpected destinations. I, the would-be government secretary, was now the tailor. Chidinma, whose sole ambition in primary school had been to do the work of a tailor, instead ran a hairdressing salon. She sent some of her clients to me, though I could not always return the favour because salons were plentiful in Trans-Ekulu, and where women were willing to traverse the continent for well-made clothes, the pull was not quite as strong for hair.

I would never forget standing on our street in Independence Layout so long ago, begging her to let me go to her people. They took me in, Chidinma's people. Those people were my saviours, and I owed them my life. Over time, when I thought about it, I glossed over what it had been like to search for the house in Abakpa after Chidinma left me, how I had slept under a tree in front of another house that night, praying that no evil marauders would come upon me, that no animals would eat me. I glossed over their exclamations at my bedraggled, hungry state when I eventually located the house the next morning. Instead, I thought how Uzoamaka and her husband let me stay to take care of the baby she had just borne so that she could go back to her shop.

Their accommodations, as Chidinma had told me, were constricted and they lived within a very limited budget, Uzoamaka's husband, now of blessed memory, being a plumber who only got work from time to time. They could barely afford to feed themselves, let alone another mouth. Yet they took me in and treated me as one of their own.

It was very difficult at first — tending another baby, soothing him when he cried, wiping his bottom when his gut emptied itself. A baby who was not Ezinwa. But when I started to pretend that he was Ezinwa, it became easier, and it was not long before I began to love that boy. Obinna, Uzoamaka's first boy, now lived in Lagos and never came home to see his widowed mother.

It was from Uzoamaka, watching her while I tended the baby, that I learnt the basics of sewing and tailoring. I was surprised that I was good at it. I was even more surprised that I liked it. Sometimes I chose the styles. When Uzoamaka's husband brought back an old black-and-white television given to him by a rich man he worked for, I watched the presenters on NTA, and improvised and made suggestions. I found that I had a knack for fashion and for business.

After I had lived with Uzoamaka for seven years, she called me one day and told me that it was time to set up my own shop. By that time, we had moved from Abakpa to Uwani. And, by the nineties, my shop had grown. I had three tailors.

I never went back to school. But books remained my friends. I learnt things on my own. I broadened my reading as best I could, knowing that one day it could be useful.

When Ifechi came for my hand, I told him that Chidinma's sister and her husband were the family I had always known. Although he insisted on going to Nwokenta with his people, he respected my wishes and paid them the same homage that the parents of a woman are due when she is to be married in Igboland.

Now, decades later, Chidinma and I sat in the shop, teasing each other. That was what we had done since we were girls. We poked at each other's soft places. We shared a bond greater than mere sisterhood, a bond of shared pains and laughter. Our love was strong and would always be.

She made a joke now about one of my young seamstresses in the shop and I laughed.

"It is good to see you laughing," she said. "That last time you came to my house, you looked like a boiled rat."

She was referring to my visit weeks before when I told her that I'd run into Urenna. If I expected comfort on her soft shoulders, I came to the wrong place, she had told me in no uncertain terms: "You are worked up over that irresponsible boy? That boy that kept calling you 'the housemaid,' who kept saying, 'I don't know the housemaid'?"

"I don't think I will ever forgive him," I had said. Did he even want my forgiveness, someone inside my head had asked.

"Look at you. Do you have nothing more important to do or think about?" she'd asked. "Continue to throw a tantrum like a child. See if it helps. Someone told me that he is on marriage number three. Yes, I did not tell you," she'd continued. "What good would that piece of information do you? That his parents are tired of him?"

I had known she'd maintained some contact with Urenna's sisters, whom she'd raised, but she had never mentioned Urenna to me.

"*I cannot forgive him,*" she'd mimicked me. "*He did not ask about our son, he did not ask about his son.* Does he care? Has he cared all these years?" she'd asked rhetorically. "Please, in the name of the Virgin Mary, I ask you not to let Ifechi see you like this, eh? Do not let that good husband of yours see you like this. Not for Urenna." She sneered at the name like a rag picked up from the dustbin.

Chidinma's harshness had poured cold water on my agitation, and I'd gone home that night, my head righted. When I'd told Ifechi the next day, I had reached a measure of peace, and I'd thought he had been relieved to see that the chance meeting had not turned my world the wrong side up.

"Uloma and Ozioma kwanu?" I asked Chidinma about her girls, two beautiful if not terribly book-smart young women — genes were strong things. They were now in their twenties, and their mother could not wait for them to marry.

"Still no husband o, my sister," she said, sounding so serious.

I laughed. "You know that marriage is not everything."

"I know it is not everything," she responded dourly. "When are you leaving your own?"

I laughed. Chidinma could be so dramatic.

"How is the shop doing?" Chidinma asked, changing the subject, fumbling in her purse for something. I waited until her hand came out with some groundnuts.

"It is doing well."

"Thank God," she said.

I was not sure what God had to do with any of it, but I exercised wisdom by ignoring that. God was the one thing we could not agree on. Chidinma was a Roman Catholic and would be until she died.

"Did I tell you that I have a new customer? Mrs Obiechina. Her son is getting married in a few months, and I am making clothes for her for the traditional wedding and the church wedding. And she is rich — she did not haggle for a second when I told her the prices. Now, she is even bringing her friends to make aso-ebi for the wedding."

"That is very good. Is she inviting you to the wedding? Maybe you can take me, eh? And I know a baker o, in case they do not yet have a baker for the cake?"

I laughed at her. That was Chidinma, always looking for an opportunity to make money. She often said that she had no choice; having five children had not been the greatest decision she made in life.

It was a destination wedding, I told her. In Kenya. All the events were happening there. So, no, I would not be going, or taking her with me.

- - - - - - - - - - - - -

What I did not tell Chidinma that day — mostly because I did not know it myself — was that Mrs Obiechina and I were on our way to establishing some kind of friendship, if you could call a seventy-year-old and an almost fifty-year-old woman friends.

I had long stopped wondering what excuse Mrs Obiechina would provide for bringing her big, perfumed self to my shop in the middle of a busy day. Twice, sometimes three times a day, she dropped in — for ten, twenty minutes, sometimes an hour.

"Good afternoon, my dear," she would say, entering the shop. She would smile at me as if I brought her joy by just being there. "Kedu? How is the work going?"

"Good afternoon, Ma," I would reply. "Work is going well."

There was a time when I wondered whether she dropped in to check on her expensive fabrics and, exasperated, I would ask Ifechi why a woman would leave her clothes with a tailor if she was not confident in that tailor. He would smile at me in that infuriatingly calm way, and ask if she was taking up more than two seats. She is heavy, I would say, so maybe one and a half seats. And my husband would guffaw in laughter.

But Mrs Obiechina didn't worry about her fabrics. Indeed, she brought more, her perfume wafting in to announce her.

"I just went to Obiageli's and thought I would come in to see how you were doing," she would say with a smile. I would keep myself from saying what was on the tip of my tongue, which was that Mrs Nwajei lived all the way in Abakpa and there was a straight route from her house to Mrs Obiechina's Independence Layout address.

But more than surviving her visits, I began to look forward to them. I was not quite sure when I made this transition, or how Mrs Obiechina wore my resistance down. Perhaps it was when she began to bring fruits to tempt my willing-to-be-tempted workers. Or when I said I liked a perfume and she brought me a bottle the next time, saying she had lots of them and gave them out for birthdays and at Christmas. Or her deep, quiet interest in my work as a tailor, or fashion designer, as she called me. Or perhaps it was when she began to show interest in my children, insisting that I call them more often and listening with concentration when I spoke about them. She wished, she said, there had been mobile phones when her son, Afam, went away to boarding school.

All I know is that we became friendly. And that I began to look forward to her smile, which started with a crinkling by the side of her eyes before it came down to her mouth, and to her stories about her son's music production business. It made me realize that I had not known the friendship of an older woman, a woman who was old enough to be my mother.

Mrs Obiechina and Ifechi also took to each other and had lots to talk about when he came to the shop. Ifechi would sit and listen to her like she had the wisdom of God in a pouch some-where. Her eyes lit up when she saw him, and she said that I had made a really good choice, that I was a truly lucky woman. Would she still call me lucky if she knew my past? I wondered. Lucky people did not lose their parents early, were not sent off to work in homes where they did not receive the love that every child should; they did not get pregnant outside of marriage with the child of a boy who did not care. And, I felt a squeeze where they said the heart should be, they did not then proceed to lose the child. But I kept these thoughts to myself, in part because what she said was true. I was very lucky to have found my husband.

It was a strange world, I would find myself thinking occasionally. Who would have thought I would be friends with this woman from a different world? In the past, I could have been her housemaid, but in this time, we were friends, in a manner of speaking.

One afternoon, she told me she had just stopped in to see her doctor. "I hope all is well," I said, surprised by the genuine concern that welled up from my heart.

"Yes. He likes to monitor my blood pressure, which goes up sometimes. And my blood sugar. And my cholesterol. And my heart rate. An unending list of things, I tell you. He tells me to stop eating fried eggs and beef. As if I have more than one life to live. As if any of us are leaving here alive." She laughed, a hearty laugh, her big arms jiggling to the sound of her mirth.

She must exasperate her doctor, I thought, but I found myself laughing right along with her as she lowered herself into her favourite spot in my reception — the two-seater couch that welcomed you with the right combination of softness and firmness. I did not wonder how long she would stay this time.

CHAPTER NINETEEN
JULIE

I sat in the dining room, a dark ornate room, furnished with the beautiful brown chairs and long dinner table that should have seated many more people than the single person sitting there this night. Dinner was served at six thirty, the same time that Eugene had insisted it be served when he was alive. I had no energy to say to the cook sometimes, "I do not want to eat. I have no appetite." Today he presented a bowl of watery, bland nsala soup. My cook could cook many things, but nsala soup was not one of them.

I ate by myself. And then I watched CNN. It was a habit I'd formed with Eugene, this news-watching, and I continued even after he died. I often wondered if the people at CNN started their day by praying for evil things to happen in the world. Today, it was something about the Middle East. Wars would never end. I could not remember if that was what it said in the Bible. Or it could be that wars would increase in the end. Was this the end? When a leader and his wife sat down on golden stools, stuck in power, and let children die? Though my eyes stayed on the screen — what else was there to look at when one had lived in a house for thirty years? — my thoughts roved through the day.

Obiageli found my budding friendship with the seamstress very amusing. "He who climbs the oji tree should attempt not only to get its fruits but firewood too," she quoted one of my favourite proverbs back at me. "You will get well-made clothes out of her as well as friendship?"

I ignored her.

"Please, I still need my best friend," Obiageli went on. "Tell her that she should go back to her own secondary school and find her own best friend. Ah ah, what is this?" She laughed till tears came out of her eyes. And I joined her, so infectious was her amusement.

"Is it because she is from Nwokenta?" she asked me more seriously.

My son was curious, too. On several occasions when he called, I would say I was at my tailor's shop. "You are there again! Is everything all right, Mummy?" he asked one day.

I had long finished the last of the nsala soup when he called, talking about work. "I promise to come visit," he said eventually. "It is just that lots of projects are taking off right now and it is such a bad time to take time away from work."

"I know," I reassured him, as I knew he wanted me to. "I am fine, really. If I need anything, I will let you know," I said, knowing it would get him off my back.

"Okay then. If you promise."

"I promise."

We said our goodbyes. A sigh escaped me. Why did everybody think that becoming old meant becoming foolish, senile? Everyone, including old people like Obiageli nwannem nwanyi, thought that becoming old was synonymous with gullibility. I thought about my son as a young boy of three, wanting me to pick him up when he came out from his class at the nursery school and wrapping both of his arms, long even then, around my neck. I thought about the joy of being loved, being needed. And then I thought of this young man who was off living his life somewhere, loving but not needing the old woman I had become.

Who was this seamstress who was taking all his mother's time, I imagined my son asking himself in Lagos, London, or Frankfurt — wherever it was that his business took him. Did he wonder, I grumbled, what I, a retiree, a widow, lay reader in church, former chairwoman of many organizations — Inner Wheel Club, town meeting, churchwomen's organization, Union of Teachers, Enugu branch — did he wonder what I did all day? No. But the minute I developed a new friendship, sleep vanished from his eyes.

I sighed. It is important for a woman to have a life, I heard my mother say in my head. It is most important for a woman to have children, but she must have a life outside of her children because one day they will grow up or refuse to grow up. Either way, they will still leave you. I smiled. My mother had never really said that, never really said anything beyond the fact that a woman must have children to be called a woman. But whenever anything like a nugget of wisdom popped into my head, I attributed it by force of habit to that quiet force of nature I had called Mother.

I did wish Afam could show a little more concern than he had, but I chided myself: everyone must live their lives. His business was taking off; he had a new love in his life, soon to be his wife. He called often. Of his love, I could not be in doubt. Perhaps if I had married a little earlier, I would have had grandchildren already, like Obiageli. But even she could stay only so long in her children's homes. Her stories of being careful what you said about and to your in-laws were enough to inspire any old person to stay put in their own home. True, there was the joy of grandchildren, but you soon had the sense that you were overstaying your welcome.

Thinking of grandchildren, I wondered when my son and his fiancée would start a family. Many newfangled ideas were now becoming the norm. First, it was having fewer children. One time that meant having four, but at church I heard new couples saying they would have two, even one, no more. I had had one because I had no choice. Given a choice, I happily would have had six. Some, like my son, say they did not even mind the sex of the children. The world was full of wonders; the one constant thing, as they said, was change.

Where had the time gone? How did it happen that everyone now called me Mama, and treated me with deference but also with care, like I would break if they looked away for a second. My bad knees did not help. Afam mentioned knee-replacement surgery. I did not want surgery. My doctor said it would help to lose some weight, to stop eating everything that could be called remotely tasty. Was that living? I asked him. He told me to take walks with Eugene. The walks had not prevented the stroke that came to kill him, so I stopped walking. I could not bring myself to do it alone.

I was lonely. There was no getting around it. I ached with loneliness, it was a physical pain. The nights were the hardest after the cook and the help had gone to their houses. I sometimes called Obiageli right after I'd eaten, but I could not stay too long on the phone. It cost money and made Emma jealous. Once, I had asked the cook to watch CNN with me — Amanpour, World News. He was a man in his fifties and had been with us, with me, for more than ten years. His discomfort as he'd sat on the edge of the seat, responding in monosyllables to my questions about his sons in Lagos, had been hard to watch. His feet had kept up a *ratatata* sound on the edge of the beautiful, fading centre rug Eugene had bought in Kano the first time he'd gone back after the war. I never asked again. Afam usually sounded so tired when he called after work, I did not have the heart to keep him on the phone.

It surprised me to see that Eugene had left such a big hole, that he had mattered this much. I got what I needed. Did Eugene get what he needed? the truth monster asked. He had been selfish, the other part of me said, the one that took my side when I had tough choices and had to make a decision. But so were you, said the truth monster. It was necessary, was the reply. I got a child; he got a son. And we had become friends in the end.

For a long time, we were anything but friends — not enemies, but not passionate lovers either. Instead we were, like many of our friends, co-parents, roommates, providing the necessary picture of partnership that each needed at social events, playing the part that society had decided for each gender within the marriage. But even that fragile partnership threatened to break down when he began an affair with a newly hired employee.

Affairs had never been a problem before. They had long been part of our marriage. On his part. I lacked energy for the passion and the idea of getting into one, perhaps out of one. It was enough to get into one marriage. But Eugene, it seemed to me, would never grow out of his need for the chase and the new adulation that came with each affair. My nonchalance was hard won; I had only one son, after all, with the latent fear that Eugene would seek another elsewhere. But when I did come to this detachment, it was genuine. Until Mmaku.

When Mmaku came along, I was already principal of my school. Afam had just entered boarding school, at Eugene's insistence, and life was rolling along on even, if unexciting roads. Eugene had greyed, grown a proper pot-belly and flesh everywhere else, and looked every inch the middle-aged, successful Igbo man who knew his place in the world and made sure everyone else knew it. The symptoms of the disease — adultery or jealousy, depending on whose side you were on — were the late-night, furtive phone calls taken in other rooms. I knew that adultery was Eugene's middle name, but he had been careful not to bring it home. What was different about this one, I wondered.

When I mentioned it to Obiageli, she waved it off. She knew about his philandering ways. "He always comes back," she said by way of reassurance. "Why are you worried?"

"I am not sure. This seems more serious. Phone calls in the middle of the night. And he has slept outside many more times in the past six months than he has done throughout our marriage. He does not sleep well, as if his own bed has suddenly become itchy."

"Maybe you need to get to know who this woman is," Obiageli had suggested, her tone careful.

It did not take long for me to find out. She was an intern, doing her compulsory work year in one of Eugene's companies.

"Twenty-one, maybe twenty-two," I told Obiageli. "What do they talk about?" I raged. "Oh, you must think I am mad. Why should they talk when they have more important things to do?"

Obiageli did not laugh. She only said, "Take it easy. This will blow over like the others."

My gut instinct told me otherwise. This one, this affair, was different. I could feel Eugene's desire to run out of the house, to be anywhere but close to me. Even his socializing — Rotary meetings, village meetings, meetings of knights in the church, old boys' meetings — faded in the face of this fervour for something else.

One day, when I knew that Eugene was having a meeting with the governor, I drove to the office just to get a glimpse of the girl. Like a character in a spy novel, I walked in and asked for

Eugene. She was visibly shaken when the manager introduced me to her.

She was tall, fair-skinned. I would not call her beautiful; she wore too much makeup for a girl her age.

I stared at her. My mind, perhaps my expression too, registered the horror: she was pregnant. Anywhere from three to six months, there was no way of knowing.

Her voice was soft when she said, "Good afternoon, Ma," before making a quick excuse and escaping with files in her hands.

She was pregnant, I told Obiageli. And she was keeping the baby. And he was letting her work in the office where everyone knew that the two of them were sleeping together.

Why? I wanted to know. But I already did. And my friend did too. The last time a pregnant woman had told Eugene she was having his child, he had married her. He had married me. Will he do to me what he had done to Onyemaechi? I wanted to scream.

It was Obiageli who condensed it for me: "You cannot let that happen. You cannot let Eugene marry another wife."

"No," I said. That was all too clear. In Obiageli's bedroom we sat and hatched a plan, and then I went home.

We first found the young woman's mother and paid her a visit. She was a cleaner at the university. Did Eugene, that most superficial of men, know this — that his prospective mother-in-law was a cleaner?

The woman's discomfiture at seeing two dressed-up women crowding her tiny, two-seat living room was apparent. She kept retying her wrapper as though she wanted to keep her hands busy.

When she offered us a seat, we refused.

Obiageli left me to do the talking, and I brought out an envelope, placing it on the woman's peeling Formica table. I had come with a large sum of money; it was my salary as a principal for a year.

"Your daughter has been sleeping with my husband," I told her bluntly.

She stared at me, not showing any response.

Glad that a denial did not come out of her, I went straight to what I'd really come to say. "I will not let her in. Tell her that. I will go to any lengths, any lengths," I repeated, "to make sure of that."

When the woman found her voice, she simply said, "He wants to marry her."

Her tone was defiant, but I could see doubt in her eyes. Whether doubt about Eugene's promise or doubt that it was a good idea, I did not know, but I pounced on that slight doubt.

"My husband does this with young girls," I ventured in the most matter-of-fact tone I could muster. "You see, every man has his weakness. For some it is drink, for some cigarettes. For my husband, it is young girls. Today, it is your daughter. Tomorrow, it will be another young girl. I have borne it. I will continue to bear it. But what I will not bear is another woman in my home. I am prepared to die. And if I am prepared to die, then that young girl better be prepared too. He will not marry her."

"This is not my daughter's fault. No. It is not. He was the one who pursued her, deceived her."

"She is young," I conceded. I was prepared to forgive her if she let it go. "She does not understand men like this. Last night, he told me everything and asked me to forgive him," I said with studied nonchalance. "It is not the first time, nor is it likely to be the last time. I will forgive him. But tell your daughter she is young and she will marry a young man, not an old akatikoro."

"But she is pregnant!" the woman all but wailed.

I saw it clearly then — she was not interested in hanging on to a rich man, my great fear.

"I will take the child."

"You will? You do not want her to remove it? She wanted to remove it, but he threatened her." Victory is looming, I thought. "I warned her. I told her that I did not want the wahala of the first wife. I don't want nsogbu o." I did not trouble to correct her.

"I said I am prepared to take the child," I went on. "I have only one child. He is almost grown. I can raise another. She will hand the child to me and she will be free. In time, people will forget and she will marry. She is a beautiful girl. She can start a new life and marry a man closer to her age. But she must not see him again."

"What does she tell him?"

"Nothing. I will tell him myself. She must not see him again."

Eugene came in at eleven thirty that night. I had sat up waiting for him in the sitting room downstairs, something I had not done since our early years of marriage. He looked worn, older than I had ever seen him. The girl, or, I suspected, her mother had given him some unpalatable news. There was no time to pity him. He had brought this on himself and on me.

"Nno, welcome," I said.

Startled to see me, he quickly got himself together. "Julie, are you still awake? You need not have waited up."

"I did," I said simply. "Please sit down." My tone brooked no argument. He obeyed.

"I know you have been seeing that girl."

"What girl?"

I almost laughed. Even the most sensible men become like children when their hands are caught in the cookie jar.

"You know what girl. Please do not raise your voice. You do not want to wake up the servants."

"I don't know what you are talking about."

"You do. Her name is Mmaku. Let us not be childish here. She may be a child. But I am not. I know she is pregnant."

"Yes, she is," he said after a pause. "And I will marry her." He looked at me, determination written on his face.

"No, you won't," I responded with a calm I did not feel. "What do you have to offer a young girl who will seek young blood the minute she tires of you? Let us be serious here, Eugene. She is not in your league. You cannot present her anywhere."

"She is pregnant with my child."

"I know," I reminded him. "That is not a problem."

"I will not leave my child." He emphasized every word. I heard the ring of certainty in it.

"I have said there is no problem. We will raise her child. I will raise her child as an Obiechina should be raised. We will forget that this unfortunate incident ever happened."

And that was that. I saw the tension leave his face and relief take over. I wanted to sneer in derision. There was a little more talk, of course, but that was merely taking care of the details — how the girl would be looked after in the meantime, how the baby would be brought into the family.

But it was not to be that easy. Eugene left me the next morning. He went to her and, as he had done with me, he took palm wine to her village, where they accepted him. I thought I would die of shame and humiliation.

Afterwards, Eugene came home occasionally to my coldness, to strut around the house and remind me that it was still his and he could live anywhere he wanted. With me, with Onyemaechi, with Mmaku. In the past, no one expected a rich man like him to marry only one or even two wives. One son was not enough. One would think I would be happy for him, he told me. Sometimes I shouted back at him; other times I looked upon him with pity and drove him mad with my condescension. I hung on for five months of madness and sorrow, plotting for my son's inheritance. Five months that felt like a lifetime.

But one day this too came to an end.

Mmaku and her little girl died in labour. I was shocked. For a while, Eugene was inconsolable. But he survived. And so did our marriage.

Our marriage persisted beyond his attempt to disgrace me, beyond his consistent fickleness. I reminded him often that I was the mother of his only son. I put his brief madness behind us so thoroughly that I had trouble remembering exactly what Mmaku looked like, or how blazingly consuming my anger and fear had been. Forgiveness, I found, was easier on the mind, the soul, the spirit, even the body, than bitterness. I wished I had had that knowledge when my brother died all those years ago. Forgiveness for myself for failing him, forgiveness for him for being what he was.

Even with the imperfections of our marriage, when Eugene died, I thought I wanted to die. I went through days of haze. The doctor said I was depressed. Was that not something that afflicted white people and soft people suffered from? I wanted to know. God knew, my skin was brown, even browner with age. As for strength, the daughter of Headmaster and his wife, herself a principal, dared not admit to weakness of any kind. Did my own mother, the strongest person I had known, not go through this same thing when my brother died?

When I came out of the haze, I became ever more aware of my mortality. But I could not embrace this awareness. I did not worship at the altar of immortality, of heaven. I was aware that life mattered. I wanted to live. Now more than ever. I was lonely, but I did not want to die. Now, grief came and went, leaving in its wake the uncertainty of when and how it would return.

Sometimes it was with tears and sadness, other times its companion was anger and bitterness.

As I sat thinking about my grief, my mind travelled to Nwabulu. There was something about her presence, her attitude to life, her stamina, that drew one to her. I did not think of her as a daughter, but I had never had such a young friend either. Her heavy, uncultured accent — which belied her beautiful clothes — even her rough bargaining at the market when we went to buy fabrics for the wedding told me that life could not have been easy for her. "You have no idea what suffering is," I heard her tell her daughter over the phone once when she complained of too much work at school, so much work that even their teachers pitied them. "Those people who are pitying you will not get you through school." Nwabulu took life by the horns; she looked at life and said: "Anyone who runs from a sheep will run from a lion." And she looked determined to stare lions in the face. She woke up every day, got to work early, worked as hard as and harder than her tailors. She treated her workers with firmness yet kindness. In short, she was alive. Something about that was catching.

I might invite her to the house, I thought now. Maybe on a Sunday. We could have lunch, and when Afam called, as he usually did after lunch, I would give her the phone to say hello to him. That should give him enough to think about. The more I thought about it, the more I found myself nodding in agreement with myself. It would be something to look forward to.

CHAPTER TWENTY
NWABULU

When I woke up this morning, I did not go through my usual routine. I instead headed to the garage that we had converted into my workroom. Today was the deadline for Mrs Obiechina's clothes. They should have been ready yesterday, but I was not enamoured with the sleeves on two of the blouses. I brought them home with me, and woke up with a clear and precise vision of what they should look like. So I came in and quickly undid the sleeves and got on the sewing machine. I needed to give her the best that I could. The wedding was seven weeks away. Just yesterday, my husband had laughed at me and wondered aloud whether I had ever devoted this much attention to anyone's clothes besides my children's.

"You are not even going to this wedding," he pointed out.

"She asked me if I would come." I could see that he was surprised by this. I answered before he could form the question: "Of course, I'm not going. I can't afford it, and I would not let her pay for it. What would I be going as anyway? Friend of the bridegroom's mother?" I laughed and he joined me.

"If I had a mother," I said afterwards, "I would make sure she looked lovely for her son's wedding."

My husband had stared at me thoughtfully. I would have liked to see a picture of what was passing through his head.

Now, he came into the workroom where I was sewing the sleeves. "You are up early," I said.

He bent and kissed my cheeks and then rubbed them with his slightly rough hands. A warmth spread through me. I wanted to pull him to me but it was not the time. His afro, wet from his shower and still worn the way it was in 1980 when I was a housemaid and he a young boy living the vital life of an okolobia, left drops on my face.

"Yes, you are not the only one who enjoys the early morning quiet," he said, his voice teasing.

I smiled in response. I often joked that since our daughter Onyinye left the house for boarding school, it had become too quiet. I threatened to have another child just to fill the place with noise. But we both knew that road had been closed years ago. I found having children too hard.

Having babies reminded me of Ezinwa, and for the first year or two — three years with Chukwuemeka — I could not let them out of my sight. My fear was unreasonable; Ifechi pointed this out carefully, kindly, and then not so gently. But I could not let go of my fear, or of my son. I could not even use the bathroom without taking him with me. I also could not let anyone else care for my children, and so, for six years, I could not work. I sewed at night when the children slept so I could stay awake to watch them. Clothes were never finished on time, and I lost customers. Our marriage struggled. Though, because of Ifechi's giving nature, we found a way to live peacefully, if not very happily.

After Onyinye, I told Ifechi that we could have no more children, but he was determined to have more. He came from a large family, one of the many differences between us. He wanted five, he said. But on this matter of more children, I would not, could not, budge. I could not tie five children to my waist, and that was what I wanted to do with my children, hold them close.

I went to the doctor, had a coil put in, and went home, with a tight, defiant countenance, to face my husband.

Nothing would make me change my mind, but I could see his point: he loved children, and was the warmest father anyone knew. But I could not imagine going through the process of pregnancy again and keeping unrelenting watch, with beating heart and clammy hands, over another child. It was the only serious issue we had had in twenty-one years of marriage; it threatened to break us apart where nothing else had or could. But my husband came round. When it was time for Chukwuemeka to go to secondary school, I did not want to send him to a boarding school. Ifechi insisted. I remembered our quarrel over having more children, the unhappiness of living with the weariness of never sleeping at night while I kept watch over the children.

"Let us try it for a year," Ifechi said. My son loved it, and stayed on for five more years. I did not think I would survive it, but I did. When the time came for Onyinye to go, it was still difficult, but I knew that this time I could do it. I remember being surprised, even hurt, that my children could live without me, indeed wanted to live apart from me sometimes. But I packed my feelings into the bag in which I put things that baffled me about the world and went on.

"Are you happy with the blouses now?" my husband asked me, leaning over to look.

"Yes, they are much better."

"You are a genius. I am sure she will love them and come back for more," he said, in his characteristic admiring mode. He was forever using superlatives to describe me to his family, his business partners, everyone he came across. Ask my wife, he would say when someone brought him a family dispute. My wife says this, he would say to someone else whose children were causing him heartache. He asked my opinion in business, and had taken my advice when I said that he might do better if he focused on the computer business he had been nursing, if he retired from the civil service. To my shock, he took me seriously, and thank God, he and I had not had much reason to regret it.

My fairy tale had come true with Ifechi. It was not the glossy, prince-saves-the-princess-and-live-happily-ever-after fairy tale like the ones in Ikenna's book. It was a warts-and-all, real-life romance.

"Are you going to deliver the clothes yourself?" he asked.

I delivered to some of my customers, the older ones, the richer ones, the ones who requested it, the ones who needed the clothes to arrive at an event or a party. I usually sent someone, but sometimes I delivered them myself. Seeing as it was Mrs Obiechina, my friend, I certainly was going to deliver them myself to her house and check the fit for any adjustments. I had called already and made arrangements.

"Yes, this evening, on my way home."

"Okay, I am off to work. Ezigbo m, have a great day. I will see you this evening." We hugged and held each other. I put my head on his shoulders, though he was shorter than me. God, if there was any such being, had rewarded my pains very richly indeed.

I left the shop at half past four and drove to Mrs Obiechina's house. The part of town where I had spent my first years as a housemaid in Enugu had changed — more houses, more flower beds, more tarred roads. I wondered if my school was still there, if Daddy and Mummy would recognize me, driving my own car.

I wondered where Daddy and Mummy were now. Chidinma said that she heard that Ikenna now lived abroad in the USA. His father lived by himself in Lagos, where he had been transferred years before, while Mummy lived alone in Enugu. Perhaps she had given up on cleaning and mopping, and dealing with his tantrums, I thought. Good for her. I wondered if I would ever see Ikenna again. Life, I mused.

I found Mrs Obiechina's street. It was lined with imposing houses, although some had peeling paint and overgrown gardens, evidence that the family had fallen on hard times or that children had moved to Lagos or London and had little use for a house in Enugu. When I found her number, I tooted my horn and waited. A man, perhaps in his fifties, opened the gates. Did he have a family? I wondered. Was he able to feed them on his gateman's salary? I drove in towards a large, arresting house, slightly dated in style, surrounded by the sort of flowers you saw only on the television. A small gazebo stood in the corner, inviting you to "Don't Worry, Be Happy," like the old song said. Whoever had built this place had wanted all and sundry to know that there was money.

I parked close to the gate and walked up the path to the entrance with the bags of clothes. A woman — she looked like a cook or help of some sort in her uniform — opened the door. When I told her I'd brought some clothes for Mrs Obiechina, she smiled: I was expected. She led me into a sitting room where she gestured for me to sit while she went to get Madam. Around me, everything spelt luxury — the flowery smell of the room freshener, the wooden console and mirror by the door, the Arabic-looking furniture. But what I was most interested in were the pictures on the mantel. I stood up to get a closer look. A man, who must have been her husband, herself, much younger than she was now, a young boy. What was familiar about him? I pondered as I moved nearer to pick up the picture. But, before I could do so, Mrs Obiechina came into the room.

"Good afternoon, my dear." Her voice was as soft as always, and yet you could hear that mettle of steel somewhere.

She held out her arms for a hug. I embraced her and she clung to me for a second.

She was dressed more casually than she had been when I last saw her — a big blouse over blue jeans. She was a trendy old woman, I thought, letting my inward smile reach my face.

"Good afternoon, Ma," I said respectfully.

"So happy to see you in my house, at last." A gentle reminder that I had declined all her attempts to bring me this way.

"What do I offer you?" she asked, pressing a bell on the wall. Would it not be nice to have help at the touch of a bell? Perhaps I would install one at home for my girls. I imagined Ifechi laughing at my silliness.

"Nothing, Ma."

"Ah, ah," she complained. "You cannot come to my house and not eat anything. If you do, I will stop eating okpa at your shop," she threatened mockingly.

I broke into laughter. Mrs Obiechina had discovered my favourite okpa seller, Mama Chibike, who made the best okpa in the whole of Enugu — properly red with good palm oil, soft without being mushy, with salt and pepper in just the right combination. Mrs Obiechina said it reminded her of the okpa her own mother had made.

"I think my stomach is upset," I explained in a placating voice. "I have not been able to eat all day. Not even Mama Chibike's okpa." It was not a good thing not to eat something in a house you were visiting for the first time.

"I told Mr Akanu," she said, pointing at the short, roundish man who had come in apparent answer to the bell, "to make you some hot, fresh fish pepper soup. Maybe we will put it in a flask for her to take home," she said, half talking to me, half talking to the cook.

"Okay, Madam," he said and left.

We sat down in the sitting room. Beautiful, I thought. An imposing painting of a tall man stood in one corner. That must be her husband; he wore his wealth like his isi-agu and red cap, as his due. His mouth was a little too wide for his face, I thought. His eyes looked straight at me and I turned mine elsewhere. They fell on another picture of the boy. He was posing with his parents, outside. Was it a matriculation, or a convocation? Again, that sense of familiarity. Where had I seen the tall young man before?

Mrs Obiechina followed my eyes and smiled. "Ah, you are looking at my son, Afam. That was when he graduated from the University of Nigeria. Many years ago now. Did I tell you he was the best student in his class? He studied engineering before he switched to music. His father was livid." She said this casually; the memories were obviously not painful. Then she launched into several stories about him. The light in her eyes made her look younger, and it was easy to tell that he was her joy. I knew what that felt like.

I was persuaded to eat the pepper soup. It was spicy, hot, and delicious. Afterwards, because I wanted to get back to the shop and do some work before it was time to go home, I asked if she would look at the clothes I brought.

"Come this way," she said to me, leading me into a bedroom.

She took them out. She noticed right away that I'd changed the sleeves on the blouses. "They are different from the ones you sketched," she noted.

"Yes. I changed them. I think these will look better, less heavy, current but not too trendy."

She nodded and, picking a set, went into the adjoining bathroom. When she came out, I nodded approvingly. The style, a mermaid skirt with a few gathers on the bottom, fit her big body well; the simple blouse sleeves covered the thicker part of her arms and slimmed down her body considerably. She looked stylish but not overdone.

She studied herself in the mirror. "This is lovely," she said. "Obiageli did say you are the best seamstress in Enugu." She turned around several times, admiring herself.

The other two outfits elicited a similar reaction and I felt proud when I saw the glow on her face.

"I cannot wait to wear them," she said. "Thank you so much." She called out for the woman who had let me in and asked her to bring her bag. She asked if I would accept a cheque and I said yes. She made it out in meticulous, flowing cursive and clear spaces, the writing of a teacher. I took it and looked at it. She had added some extra money.

"Thanks very much," she said. "My last tailor still has the clothes I gave her seven months ago."

"You are welcome, Ma," I said. It had been a good day.

"You are going back to Trans-Ekulu?" she asked when I eventually told her I needed to get back to the shop. "I was going to visit Obiageli after you left, but my driver is not back yet." Mrs Obiechina frowned at her watch, a slim gold thing that sank into the folds of her wrist. "He says he is in a traffic jam, something about an accident." She sounded put out. "Perhaps you could drop me at Abakpa, at Obiageli's place?"

"That would be no problem, Ma," I said, wondering what she would think of my car. It was nice enough, but not a Mercedes 4MATIC.

She was grateful for the lift and reached into her bag for her phone to tell her driver to meet her at Obiageli's house. Then she got up with difficulty to go and get dressed. I hoped she could get help for her knees, I thought.

Outside, I pushed my passenger seat back so she could sit more comfortably. She smiled her thanks when she had settled in. I got in and drove out. In my side mirror, I saw a black car pull out from the side of the other compound behind us while Mrs Obiechina was complaining about her driver.

"It's as if he thinks he can do anything and get away with it," she said. "When you give him the car for an errand that should not take ten minutes, he stays away for hours. He was Eugene's driver, and Eugene would not have stood for any nonsense." She stopped, then continued, "Ehn, every man, high or low, thinks he is bigger than a woman just because he has a penis between his legs."

I thought of the man who had greeted me respectfully on those occasions when I'd walked Mrs Obiechina to her car. He looked like someone with a family and responsibilities. I hoped he would not be careless and lose a job he must desperately need.

"I am sure he will be back soon," I murmured.

I decided against going through Otigba Junction, where the accident had happened. I took a road that helped us cut out Bisalla Road. It was a quiet street that I'd taken several times before.

It turned out to be the wrong decision. Afterwards, I could not explain the speed at which the two cars, an SUV and a sedan, both black, cut us off; one looked like the car that had pulled out behind us when I left Mrs Obiechina's house. I could not explain how they brandished their guns in the daylight and bundled two women — one, the tallest woman on her street, the other, possibly the largest woman on her street — into an SUV. I could not explain how the sight of guns and the stern faces of young men could make your vocal cords forget their function. I half expected my long frame to be squeezed into a trunk, like I had heard in stories, but it was into the car that they'd pushed us. One, sitting beside me, deftly and quickly blindfolded and gagged me. I assumed that they were doing the same to Mrs Obiechina. I could hear her struggling. She was a fighter, but you did not fight a man armed with a gun with your bare hands. That was foolishness.

The whole thing took only a few minutes. It was like television: a part of you was watching it in bemusement, but the other part of you knew it was real, and was getting acquainted with the kind of fear it had never known before. I only remember thinking, my children, Ifechi.

CHAPTER TWENTY-ONE
JULIE

I of course had heard of people being kidnapped — the east was becoming a treasure trove for people who sought to abduct others for money. A man on the next street had been kidnapped. We all said that he was crude and ostentatious, flaunting his money with his convoys of SUVs to match, his mobile policemen, his loud parties that went on into the night. It had taken weeks for him to be released. Although he had lots of money, his wife had access to nothing, and was one of those women whose husbands insisted they could not work. That story reassured me now. It had taken weeks, yet the kidnappers had kept the man alive and eventually let him go. I tried not to think about another man who had been tied up and left in the boot of a car. He was found by his people, hours later, dead.

Before Eugene died, we were given a list of precautions to take during a seminar in the women's group at church: vet domestic staff; where possible, do your hair or your child's hair at home; do not discuss financial transactions in public; avoid quiet roads; look around to see if your car is being followed. In short, I remembered thinking then, use your common sense. Eugene's men's group had talked about prostate cancer, the risks, screening, PSAs, and treatment options. He had asked me later if I thought we should pay for police protection, have policemen drive everywhere with us. I said no. One never had any privacy; adding policemen to our retinue was just giving away money unnecessarily. What that would do, I told Eugene, was draw attention to ourselves, and should that not be avoided when you did not want to be kidnapped? He agreed with me, even though he liked to show off.

Childish as it sounded, I never thought it could happen to me, and in Enugu, where I had lived most of my adult years. Bad luck must seek others, not us.

It was clear that the kidnappers had targeted me. I had heard one of them ask in the car if they were sure they had the right woman. And the other replied that he was sure it was me. The first one insisted it was not my car. Was I Mrs Obiechina, they wanted to know. I could have lied, but they would have to know who I was to get the ransom. I said yes, hearing the *ka-ching* of coins, the Obiechina Industries money, drop in their heads. I was a good catch, even I admitted it. I hoped the demands were reasonable and that we could get out soon. How much would such young men want anyway, and what would they do with it — buy cars? I wanted to ask them.

They removed our blindfolds the next morning but not the ropes with which they had tied our hands. Our mouths were free. We were lucky to be old women, the kidnappers said.

For days they kept us in an airless small room painted a sickly yellow. They had taken our phones, our bags, everything we had on us. They had asked for numbers. The head of the gang told us to comply. No harm would come to us, he promised. Our prayer should only be, he said, that our people loved us enough to meet their demands quickly, and we would be out of there soon, even the next day. Otherwise things might get very difficult. He sounded soft, but he'd hit me with his gun when I'd struggled in the car, bruising my shoulder. Though he did not shout nor speak menacingly the way they did in those Nollywood movies, his boys obeyed him without question.

I hoped they would get their money, and soon. I hoped we would be some of those who'd lived to tell the story and dance in thanksgiving in church. In the meantime, I thought, we needed to pass the time, take our minds off our troubles somehow.

"So, tell me more about yourself," I said to Nwabulu. "How did you become a fashion designer? Here we are, with plenty of time on our hands."

She seemed reluctant at first. "You tell me yours," she said, "and I will tell you mine."

It took me a few seconds to think about where to start. And then I plunged in, starting with my brother Afam, then circling back to my father and my mother. Sharing my story with Nwabulu made my life seem interesting, fresh again. I was honest about my early life, omitting little of importance.

Her perceptions, which she inserted from time to time, jolted me.

"Was that not too heavy a burden to place on a child?" she interjected when I spoke about my father's desire for me to look after my brother, her forehead wrinkling in a frown.

It sounded unbelievable, but I had never thought about it like that. Even though I don't believe that it was. But I knew that the seed had been planted and I would worry about it later. If we ever got out of this room alive.

I carried my honesty over into my marriage to Eugene. I told her how we met and the circumstances under which I'd married him. These days I saw single mothers, single women who had not married yet and who might never marry. It was still not a choice many would make; it was still difficult to live like that. Society had not changed that much, but it had changed some from my time.

"But what about Onyemaechi? Did you not wonder how she would feel? How her children would feel?"

There was no judgment in her face, only curiosity. I tried my best to answer her.

Onyemaechi, I told her, stood no chance at all with Eugene once our son came along.

My honesty could not extend to how I got Afam. So I tactfully took a break. It was night; they would soon be bringing our supper of water and unsliced white bread pulled from the loaf, just as they had pulled us out of our lives.

We would rest, and Nwabulu would tell me her story tomorrow.

CHAPTER TWENTY-TWO
NWABULU

Auntie Julie's story was engrossing, so very different from what I had imagined it would be. She was warm, warmer than when I first saw her in my shop with her Chanel sunglasses, the beautiful long bubu, and the delicious fragrance preceding her gentle voice. In our confinement, we had gone from Mrs Obiechina to Auntie Julie, at her request, and I was no more just her tailor but her daughter.

She made a movement now. I looked up from my feet, still painful from where they were tied, though more loosely now. She was waiting for me to begin.

Where to start telling one's story? I gave it some thought and started with my name. "My father named me Nwabulu because he said I was gain — his profit, his benefit — even though my mother had died bringing me into the world."

"Nwabulu," Auntie Julie said, "Nwabulu, it is a beautiful name. A child is gain. That is true. A child is truly gain, a joy, and advancement in the world."

I thought so myself, too. I told her how I wished I knew my mother, how this feeling had grown stronger with each child that I bore; I told her about my father's death, about my stepmother, about being sent out to Lagos to work.

"A housemaid," Auntie Julie said. I heard the note of surprise, of something that sounded like admiration. It had been many years since I'd given much thought to my early years, and it was interesting to bring that young girl to life again. Perhaps I would see the grand design of which Ifechi spoke: that God was working his purpose out and moved in mysterious ways.

When I told her about getting pregnant, she shook her head. "Poor girl — and did they send you home?" The gentleness of her inquiry made me see even more clearly how time changes everything. No woman of her age would have said the same to me at that time; I could not have said the same to myself.

I told her that they did. I told her about my stepmother's designs to marry me off to any old man who would take me off her hands. Her eyes of pity followed my face. As I was about to speak about Mama Nathan, we heard voices and the padlock open. The boss — the name Auntie Julie and I had given the young man who was in charge — came in.

"Your people are tempting me," he said, brandishing a gun and waving it around like a toy. "Your people are tempting me," he repeated. "They are trying to tempt me to do what I had not planned to do. And believe me, neither you nor them will like what I do if they push me o.

"You," he said, pointing the gun at me, "your husband thinks he is haggling over meat in the market. Is that all you are to him? Meat in the market? He is talking kobo kobo to me when I am speaking of real money." He pointed the gun at Auntie Julie. "As for you?" he said insolently. "As for you, your friend, Madam Obiageli, or whatever you call her, is tempting me o."

He pulled out a BlackBerry and dialled a number, putting the phone on speaker. We heard Mrs Nwajei: "Hello," she said, her voice sounding tremulous, not the happy, high voice I was used to hearing.

The boss poked Auntie Julie.

"Hello," Auntie Julie said.

"Julie, are you okay?" We could all hear her anxiety.

"I am fine, Obiageli, nwannem nwanyi," she said in a low voice.

"Tell her you will soon not be so fine," the boss urged, kicking her leg.

"Did they hurt you?" Mrs Nwajei asked, out of breath.

"Tell her we need the money soon otherwise ..."

"They need the money soon, Obiageli. Can you raise it? Have you spoken to Afam?"

"I am doing my best," I heard Mrs Nwajei say. "Afam is coming here tomorrow. He will bring the money. If he does not, Emma says we will." Emma, her husband. The miser. Would he bring money to get Auntie Julie out of this place?

"Are you okay? Are they letting you have your medication? Do you have food, water —"

The boss aimed another hard kick at Auntie Julie, causing her to yelp loudly, before ending the call.

"She thinks we are running a hotel here, abi? Pray your son brings our money o. Otherwise wahala go dey."

The boss swivelled round, leaving as suddenly as he had come. Auntie Julie was massaging her thigh where he had so callously kicked her. I scooted over on my bottom to massage her leg and wipe her tears.

- - - - - - - - - - - -

We sat in silence for a while, our thoughts on the boss's demands. Would Ifechi be able to raise the money? We each ran a business, but money did not flow like water in our house. Certainly, there was no room in our budget for kidnap ransoms.

The next day, after a few hours' sleep, Auntie Julie asked me to continue my story.

"Tell me," she said, "I want to hear what happened, did you marry an old man?"

I did not marry an old man, I told her. A woman whose son had died had come to inspect me and then went to talk to Mama Nkemdilim.

As I began to talk about Mama Nathan, how I had been forced to marry her dead son, I saw Auntie Julie blanch. I saw her cringe.

"Did you say the woman's name was Mama Nathan?"

"Yes. I never knew her real name. In those days, everyone was Mama somebody or other."

There was silence. Then: "And you are from Nwokenta?"

"Yes, Ma."

"I do not feel well," she said, and I saw something like fear enter her face. Her forehead became clammy with sweat, her face wrinkled in pain.

I shouted for our abductors, who stood guard outside our door, coming in from time to time to take us to relieve ourselves. I shouted for what seemed a long time before one of them appeared.

"Please get her some water. She is not feeling very well."

He took one look at Auntie Julie and left. I did not hear the click of the padlock. He came back almost immediately with the water, knelt down and gave her some.

She took a couple of gulps quickly.

"Easy," I said. "Easy."

Gone was the freshness that she carried around like a cloak, the freshness that I imagined was the result of money and comfort. Makeup no longer concealed her wrinkles, and her sunken cheeks gave her a pinched look, as though the Rapture had taken place and she was the only one left behind.

— — — — — — — — — — — —

"Tell me the rest of the story," she pleaded later that evening, after a long period of silence. Her spirit had come back, but she still looked older, tired.

I told her how I had Ezinwa and about his birth, which had seemed more painful than any human could bear. I spoke about how Mama Nathan had become possessive of my little boy. And how, one day, she had stolen Ezinwa and vanished to God knows where.

"Stop!" she ordered, raising a trembling hand as if to restrain me physically.

Was it being cooped up here for days, with only bread and water for nourishment that was making her look sick? Or worry for her child, who would now have to abandon his wedding plans to deal with this situation? Did these thugs realize how bad this was for her hypertension?

"Hey," I shouted, trying to get the attention of the guards again.

"No," Auntie Julie said. "Don't call them. Finish your story."

"No, Ma. You do not look well. Do you think you should lie down?"

"No," she said. Her breath came heavy and audible. "No. I will be fine. I will be fine. Just go on with the story, please. What happened after Mama Nathan took the baby? Where did she go?"

"To Enugu, but I did not know this until years after. She died, and she was brought home and buried. She did not come with the baby, and nobody knows if my child died, or if he might be alive somewhere even now."

Our ordeal was exhausting me, sharpening the pain I carry with me always. Tears slid down my face, clouding my vision. I did not wipe them off.

Auntie Julie stared at me but said nothing. We were silent for a little while. Then, without prompting, I went on with my story.

I told her about Chidinma. How her sister took me in. How I started my tailoring shop. I skipped over the men whom I had shared my life with during that time — the one who went with me to the village and, having heard there that I had had a son out of wedlock and facing the obstructions my stepmother invented, decided I was not worth the trouble. Or the married army major whom I had dated, to the dismay and outspoken disapproval of Uzoamaka, who had by then taken on the role of mother.

I spent many years searching for Ezinwa. When I said this, I saw an expression I could not decipher pass across Aunt Julie's face. Did she not believe me, I wondered. I carried on. The search turned up nothing. Nobody seemed to know where Mama Nathan went when she left the village; her clansmen either claimed ignorance, or didn't make any special effort to help me. It seemed that I was not destined to have a family. Uzoamaka's family became mine. Even after I made more money, I lived with them in Uwani, where I took over the rent. Until I met Ifechi.

It was a good marriage, I said. He loved me, and often said how in awe he was of my resilience. A ghost of a smile passed across Auntie Julie's face.

I told Auntie Julie that I planned to develop a clothing line, make shoes and bags with local materials like Ankara. I planned to exhibit at a fashion show in Lagos next year. My daughter had suggested it. It was usually young people who did these things, but who was to say that I could not do as well as them? Life was not over; it was only just beginning. Or so I thought until the kidnapping.

CHAPTER TWENTY-THREE
JULIE

Nwabulu's voice stopped. The rest of her story had come from a long distance away, blurred in comparison to the earlier part. For some reason, I thought about the announcements on NTA in the eighties, the ones about missing children. A child would look into the camera, forlorn, silent tears coursing down its cheeks. The announcer would say, "This child was found wandering along Zik Avenue this afternoon by a good Samaritan who brought him to our station. He is about four years old. He does not know his address. He was unable to state his father and mother's names."

Afam would ask me, his eyes big and solemn, "What if he does not have a father or a mother?"

"Don't be silly," I always replied, smiling for reassurance. "Of course he has a mother and father. Everyone has a mother and father. Just like you do. Now repeat your name and address to me."

"Afam Obiechina," he would say.

"Your address," I would prompt.

"Number 5, First Avenue, Independence Layout, Enugu."

"Your father's name?"

"Chief Eugene Obiechina."

"And your mother's name?"

"Mrs Julie Obiechina," he would answer.

Mrs Julie Obiechina, I thought now. I was his mother. I raised him. Taught him his address, taught him his alphabets. Potty trained him, kissed him goodnight. Steadied him when he tried to lose himself in teenage years. Was planning to help raise the grandchildren he would give me. Me, not any other woman.

But I looked over at the woman who sat across from me, her back leaning against the wall, her face pensive, streaked with the now dried tears she had cried for the boy she had called Ezinwa. Against my will, pictures flooded my mind, of the young woman she must have been, of Mama Nathan snatching the boy and escaping to Obiageli's house, of the despair Nwabulu must have felt travelling on that bus to Enugu and through the years. I shut my eyes and heart. I did not want to feel anything. But I saw the tears, and heard the quiet pain. And I knew that it was time. Time to tell the truth.

Liars, my father had often told us, were always found out. I had been found out. But it was not Nwabulu whom I had lied to — it was Eugene. Did it matter? a voice asked me. It was time to tell the truth, regardless. What were the odds that our paths, Nwabulu's and mine, would cross in this life? That we would be caught in this situation together? The universe had spoken. I would obey. And take the consequences.

I opened my mouth and began to speak.

CHAPTER TWENTY-FOUR
NWABULU

It sounded too fantastic to be true, otherworldly. I rubbed my eyes to make sure I was not dreaming. No, there she was and her lips were still moving. I stared at her, seeing not the polished woman who had walked into my shop a mere three months ago, but a child thief, a haggard, old-looking woman, whose wide mouth was spouting truths that flogged my ears. I wanted to know the sort of woman who took another's child and kept him for years. How could she carry out such an act, steal a child, and live for years undetected? How was that possible?

Tears escaped me, quiet sobs too. I wished I could cry the way I did as a child, loud and hard, to relieve the pressure in my chest, a volcano on the verge of eruption.

"You are a thief!" I shouted at one point.

"I did not know that he had any family who might have been willing to care for him," she said quietly.

"But did you look? Or were you looking to deceive a man who was married to another? Did he even know he was deceived? That my son was not his?"

She was silent.

"I know that this is hard for you but —" she began.

"No, you don't. Nor do you care," I interrupted. How could she care? Did she know how many tears I had shed over the years? That I still had nightmares that left vivid, horrific images in my mind, that I wondered if my son was a beggar, an armed robber? No, she could not care. Not enough.

"We gave him the best. He went to the best schools. He is a Canadian citizen now; he has access to the world."

Demonic emotions ran through me: I wanted to pull out her hair, slap her, punch her, kick her like that insolent young kidnapper had done. But I could not get up from where I sat. Instead, I screamed, snarled like a dog.

A guard came in.

What was going on, he wanted to know. Both of us were silent. He warned us not to make any more noise, otherwise we would not like the consequences.

I wanted to get up and walk and throw my hands about, but here I was shackled, imprisoned with the woman who had stolen my child. The young man in the photographs in her house had looked so familiar because he looked like me, like my son Chukwuemeka, like my mother.

— — — — — — — — — —

I could not bear to look at her. When I did, her pleading eyes never left my face, forcing me to look elsewhere. Why should I be made to feel like I had done wrong, when she was the one who was guilty? Was she any different from these young hooligans who had kidnapped women old enough to be their mother or even grandmother? Had she not taken the child without any concern for the mother?

That night, my anger did not let me sleep at all. It consumed me, ravaged my soul.

On the second night, Julie woke me up. I had been thrashing around in my nightmare, searching for my son. My body shook uncontrollably. She whispered, "I am sorry, Nwabulu. Gbahalu." She said this over and over, until I lay still. "Gbahalu," she repeated, "gbahalu."

As I lay there, a feeling of calm came over me, a feeling of peace. For, in spite of everything, I had found my son at last — Ezinwa. My worst fears, that he might be hungry, living in poverty, or worse, dead, had not come true. Instead, this woman had raised my son. He was probably a big success, thanks to her and her husband. What could I have given him at that time? Who was to say that if Mama Nathan had not died, I would have laid my eyes on him again? Or that if Obiageli had returned him to Mama Nathan's family, they would have let me have him?

After a while, I sat up and took a deep breath. And, as if we had been having a regular conversation, I asked, "What is he like?"

She smiled a tremulous smile. "He is like you to look at. Tall, very dark skinned. His voice is deep, though. He is industrious, like Eugene, but his father would have had a fit to think that all the money he spent on a Canadian education was not for work at Microsoft, or to run an engineering conglomerate. But he is doing well as a music producer," she said proudly.

"His father," she said.

I thought of Urenna, who did not know that he had a child, who did not care. And, for a second, I was glad that Ezinwa had had a father who cared about him.

"He met the Kenyan girl he is about to marry in Canada. Lovely girl. His father would have thrown a fit about that too. And what would he have done if he knew that she was keeping her name? I wonder. Afam says if their children are all girls, he will not mind. Eugene would have hit the roof. He would have disowned him." She burst out laughing, as if this were the funniest thing in the world, the way young people turned the world upside down.

It was clear that she liked to talk about Afam, and she had plenty of stories. At some points, I was jealous; at others, I simply soaked it in, seeing him through her eyes. The picture she painted was of a perfect, unblemished, industrious, kind young man.

I tried not to get ahead of myself imagining our first meeting, Ezinwa's meeting with his siblings, but I couldn't help it. I knew Ifechi would be happy for me, he who had wiped many tears and soothed me after many nightmares. He was the only one who had any inkling how this must feel. Eventually, I fell asleep.

-- -- -- -- -- -- -- --

When I awoke, I looked over at Auntie Julie, who was lying on her side, her face to the wall. The callousness of these kidnappers made me angry. How could they keep an old woman in this state? They too were making choices like Mama Nathan had made, like Auntie Julie, hurting others because they could not have what they needed. I moved over to touch her, using my hands to propel myself.

She was unnaturally quiet. "Auntie Julie! Julie, Mrs Obiechina!" I shouted, but there was no response. I reached for her hand. It felt heavy in mine as I searched for a pulse, the way I had seen them do on television. I found nothing.

"Guard! Hey!" I screamed.

"We need to get to a hospital, quick," I begged when one of the kidnappers came in.

The young man looked frightened, fumbling in his pocket for a phone. He spoke into it, telling someone, the boss most likely, what was happening. He kept nodding up and down like a lizard while he received his orders. At one point, a quick smile touched his face. He nodded again.

The other guard came in. "Wetin dey happen?" he asked.

The first one quickly told him. Then he said, "The boss said the money has come in. He has picked it up. We will meet him at that place."

"Wetin we go do with these ones now?"

"The boss say make we carry them go put for the junction."

Chineke, they were going to take us somewhere and leave us, leave Auntie Julie, on the road.

"She needs to go to the hospital o — tell your boss you must take us to the hospital," I pleaded, but the first guard ignored me, went out and returned with a blindfold. Soon darkness descended.

"Please don't cover her eyes." For some reason, I thought this might make Auntie Julie worse, even though I could not tell if she was dead already.

If they heard my plea, they gave no indication. Instead, they tied my mouth the same way they did when they first kidnapped us seven days before.

"She dey smell," I heard one say. I heard grunts, sounds of heaving. They were carrying her out.

"Kai, wetin dis woman dey chop sef. Ah ah," I heard one of them complain.

After what seemed like a long time, they came for me. I was forced into what felt like a small car. We must have been travelling for thirty, maybe forty minutes along a bumpy road when we came to a stop. The kidnappers heaved and grunted, and I heard what must have been Auntie Julie coming to rest on the ground like a heavy bag. They pulled me out of the car and untied my mouth, then my eyes. It took a little time for my eyes to adjust to the glare of the sun-drenched day. By that time, their car was already too far away for me to register any more than its colour.

I found Auntie Julie on the ground, lying very still. Please, God, I thought, don't let her be dead.

I touched her, held up her hands, and finally found what it was those doctors on television look for, a telltale vein pulsing up and down faintly. My vocal cords and hands and feet found their strength, and I flung myself into the middle of what looked like a deserted road.

But God was at home that day. A car came along, and inside was my beloved Ifechi. The kidnappers had told him where to find us after he had paid the ransom. We both sobbed and I pointed to where Julie lay.

"Hurry!" I cried, "I think she's had a stroke."

It is difficult to get a human being into a car, I acknowledged afterwards, thinking of all the awkwardness I had seen in Nollywood movies. An overweight woman like Julie was even more hard work. I was weak and my hands hurt, but at last we managed to heave her into Ifechi's car. I got in beside him and we sped to the hospital.

I heard myself praying out loud, something I had not done in many years. Julie had to live, I prayed. How would Afam marry without her there? Who would tell Afam that I was his mother? Would he believe me? Would he think me mad? Would he ever be able to love me? Would he say he did not want to be the housemaid's son? These questions rose in my heart.

But it was not only my desire for my son that pushed me to pray. Julie had to live. Our week of captivity together, our meals of bread and water, our laughter, and our stories had created a bond between us that seemed like seventy years, not seven days. I knew what her laughter sounded like, I knew the movement of her cheeks when she chewed her food. I knew that she snored when she slept; I knew the determination in her eyes and the gentleness of her spirit. I knew that she suffered some incontinence — how could a woman who had not birthed a child suffer incontinence, she had asked me, only yesterday. That was one of the mysteries of life, I told her. Her laughter was hearty and long, heartier and longer than my joke.

No, it was not only Ezinwa that made me pray she would live. It was Julie herself. We had shared a bond not easily broken, two women doing their best in their world.

ACKNOWLEDGEMENTS

It has been my dream to write a novel since I was a child. I thank the Lord Jesus, the giver of all good gifts, who makes my dreams come true.

This book is dedicated to my parents: Prof. (Chief) Obidinma Onyemelukwe and Dr Rebecca Onyemelukwe. I will always be grateful for their support, love, faith, and encouragement throughout my life, for being my first champions. I thank them for being living examples of tenacity and grit, their gift of stories, and what part of their gift of storytelling I received. I love you both. Always.

I thank my husband, Fred Onuobia, for his love, support, encouragement, unwavering faith in me and my abilities, and dreaming big dreams for me. I love you. Thanks also to my loving and amazing children, God's gifts to me — Kelechi, Oluchi, and Udochi — for bringing joy, love, meaning, and inspiration to my life. I can't wait to read your books.

I am grateful to my sister Akaoma for her love, friendship, encouragement, and tenacity: you inspire me; to my sister Ijendu, my brother Soke, and my sister Tochi, thank you for all the love and support.

Many thanks to the many who supported me in different ways as I worked on this book: to Jane Craig for her love and support through the years; Ikhide Ikheloa for incisive, honest reviews of this and earlier manuscripts and, more importantly, for his friendship; Ukamaka Osigwe for her love and friendship through the years and for calling me that early morning to ask when I would get to work on the book; to Chinelo Oraghalum Ezenwa for her love and friendship over many years; to Anwuli Ojogwu for reviewing the manuscript, linking me with important resources and hand-holding through this process; to Florida Uzoaru for reviewing early drafts of the book and sharing her thoughts on it; and to Ike Anya for support during this process. I am full of appreciation for each one of you. "Thank you" doesn't seem enough.

Thank you to Scott Fraser, publisher at Dundurn Press, for your enthusiasm for this book and bringing it home to Canada. Many thanks to my editor, Dr Jenefer Shute, for your nitpicking and working to keep the spirit of the book even as you helped me polish it.

ABOUT THE AUTHOR

CHELUCHI ONYEMELUKWE-ONUOBIA is a lawyer, academic, and writer. She holds a doctorate in law from Dalhousie University and works in the areas of health, gender, and violence against women and children. Cheluchi divides her time between Lagos and Halifax.